Editors – Tracey Haggert and Christine Lomas

Cover design – Jenny Groat

Cover photo – Glenn Lomas

ISBN – 978-0-9732674-0-2 (e-book)

ISBN-978-0-9732674-1-9(paperback)

The Challenge

His life was one cheap bottle of booze to the next. Once upon a time he was loved, had a family and a name. Now he was just a face. People called him a bum and avoided him like the plague.

He did not know when his life took the turn it did. When he left his parents' home years ago, he had dreams and goals. Now, instead of dreams he had demons. Every night he would intoxicate his body with whatever was available so he would not dream.

But there was no escaping the creator of dreams. No matter what this shell of a man put into his body, the creator would still find ways of bringing up past images of a life lost. Old faces which once smiled at him, but to see him now, the faces would cry. Life had lost him in the shuffle. He lost his own life in the midst. Now he just existed, not living for a reason, just for his next drink.

The creator of dreams was not going to visit him tonight. The mix of chemicals and other toxins he put into his body would block the creator's message. It would be a mixture of cheap booze and the high off aerosol cans. Tonight he'll lie by the side of the street, which had been his home for too many years. It was usually peaceful on the street. The odd time he got into a fight over a sip of cheap wine, or sometimes he would get beat-up for no reason. Tonight it was quiet.

People would walk by paying no attention to the little man huddled in the corner with newspaper insulating his clothes, urine and vomit stains on his pants. It had been years since the man stopped caring about his appearance, and stopped caring in general.

Tonight he was going to keep to himself. He always did. Why start something when you have a very good chance of having a knife plunged into your chest over a belt of liquor. Tonight like every night a slab of concrete would be called his bed.

Tonight was different as he saw someone who caught his eye. It was late, just before midnight. The only people who ever ventured on his street at that time were drug dealers, gangbangers, hookers with their pimps or people looking for cheap service. But the person the man saw tonight did not fit the description of any of those souls.

At a distance it looked like a woman. Long dark hair, maybe five and a half feet tall at most, but it was not the walk of a woman. Too rigid. Too intense. The small stranger had strong looking shoulders, which could not be mistaken for a woman's.

He could not make the face out very well. The lack of light on his street and the amount of chemicals in his body meant he could only see a blur headed his way. It was definitely a man.

The street occupant squinted, trying to get a look at the strange little man, but the man was moving too fast. He was not running, not necessarily, but he was travelling much too fast for a walk. The figure was no longer walking rigid, but appeared to be stalking as if he was part cat.

The wino lost control of his bladder when he saw the man's eyes. It was still difficult to see the eyes clearly, but regardless of his drunken state, he could see intensity and hate in those eyes.

The stranger's eyes were a deep black and were focused on the wino. He knew the man was going to attack him, maybe knife him, steal his shoes or rape him. It would not be the first time.

The wino had barely time to gasp when he felt the pain in his throat. He attempted to raise his arms in hopes of fending off the attacker, but he did not get a chance.

All at once he felt a massive head rush followed by intense pain in his chest. When he died he did not see his life pass before his eyes. If he had he would have only seen disappointment and waste.

By the time his arms, fell to his side, the attacker was gone.

After pressing the snooze button for a second time Frank Ryerson finally got up. His wife Jill, rolled over pulled up the covers, and curled into a little ball. He envied her for the extra hour of sleep she got.

He climbed into the shower, eyes slightly squinting and let the hot water slowly wake him up. He let the water massage his neck while he rolled his head, shoulder to shoulder trying to get the morning kinks out of it.

He stood still letting the water soak his head, wondering about his work, wondering if it had lost its allure. He was so excited when he became a detective, eager to be the best on the department. He still felt that way, he wanted to be the best, but the job wore on him.

The older detectives warned him about it. The job was a beast, and as much as you would try to separate your personal life from your work, it had a way of finding a way in. Sometimes it would enter through dreams, and sometimes a rare case would come along that would be like a pesky itch that couldn't be reached. Hard to understand, sure—but something veteran detectives understand all too well.

Frank tried to secure his personal life the best he could. He didn't have a lot of friends outside of work, only one really—Thomas. They had grown up together and would in years time share a working relationship.

They had met in high school in their junior year. Both of them would be considered loners, and neither went out of their way to be friendly with the other. Both of them had a thirst for knowledge and took their school work seriously. They would see each other frequently in the school library, both flipping through books trying to get homework done before they got home.

One day they left at the same time, and headed together in the same direction. During the course of their 20 minute walk they discovered they had only lived two blocks away from each other. Both had lived in the same subdivision for most of their lives, and neither had seen each other, except in school.

In 20 minutes they found a kinship very familiar with best friends. They hit it off from the very start, sharing similar interests, and curiosity in their differences. Neither put on a show to impress the other, and after a couple of weeks, it was like they had known each other for years.

Thomas was brilliant. School seemed to come so easily to him, something which Frank envied, but Thomas also worked really hard at it. He would spend hours doing homework and reviewing work sometimes sacrificing his personal life. He was goal driven and it came as no surprise that years later, Thomas would end up as the city's youngest Pathologist.

There were times when they would walk to a party together, and would just walk right past the house, so they could continue their discussion. They would end up at a park and just sit on the bleachers or swings and look up at the night sky talking about everything from the meaning of life to girls.

Frank's life changed when he was 17. His father whom he looked up to, his idol since early childhood died. Frank was sitting up at the kitchen table doing homework while his mother was finishing cooking dinner. His dad was upstairs writing a letter to a friend when they heard a crash.

Frank immediately sprinted up the stairs. The noise came from the office, and dread crept all over him. If his dad would have dropped something he would have cursed out loud or yelled down things were okay. When he burst into the room his dad was on the floor next to his chair. He immediately shook him and pleaded with him to get up.

When his mother made it into the room seconds behind him, he yelled at her to call 911. There was nothing anyone could have done. They later found out it was a brain aneurism which took his life. His father had died even before he hit the ground. Even if he had the aneurism in a hospital room, with a full medical team and equipment, he still would have died.

He loved his father and wished he could have told him that. His father knew that he was loved, but that didn't take the sting of never being able to tell him.

The night before his funeral he wandered over to Thomas's house and just sat in the beanbag chair located in the corner of his room. Thomas lay on his bed and just waited. He wanted Frank to be the one to talk and let things out.

Frank was always quiet with his emotions, girls were emotional, and he was too tough. But he was hurting, and Thomas was his best friend. Despite trying to hold it in, risking embarrassment and shame, he cried. He let it all out. They spent the night talking about his dad and eventually into lighter subjects. The tears turned into smiles, and a weight was taken off his shoulders. He didn't think he could have cried in front of any other person, not even his mother, and he would have never have done that in front of his father while he was alive.

The service was difficult, but Frank thought he got most of the tears out the night before. His mother was still taking it really hard so he took it upon himself to greet the visitors and strike up conversations with people who were acquaintances or strangers. For the entire time Thomas stood next to him, being his emotional rock and friend.

It really hit home at the burial when he saw the casket get lowered into the ground. He couldn't help but think of things his father would never see him accomplish. He would never go to Frank's wedding or hold his grandchildren. He started to get mad at his father, but he took a deep breath and tried to focus himself. His father didn't choose to die, he didn't want to leave his wife and son behind. He didn't abuse his body, and was healthy for his age. He should have lived another 30 or 40 years but everyone dies. His number came up just way too early.

When the service was over Frank shook a couple of hands and hugs to some aunts and uncles. Thomas walked up to him and both gave each other a meek smile than gave each other a hug, and that was when Thomas could not hold it in any longer.

He cried on his friends should, letting the tears flow. He cried for Frank's loss and his pain. He loved him like a brother and Frank's pain was his. He just held him tight while he cried into his shoulder. Thomas knew he should be the strong one, he should be there for Frank, not the one in need of comfort.

On Frank's end he was surprised by the tears. He held Thomas tight and loved him even more. From the first news of his father's death, his best friend was there for him. He didn't even need to say anything, just having him around was all he wanted. He didn't want to be alone, and he never was.

When Thomas let go, he tried to compose himself and gave a little apology. He walked over to Mrs. Ryerson and gave her a hug but was able to keep his composure. As Frank looked on, he knew he would kill or die for Thomas.

In time, they went to university, their schools were separated by a five hour drive, but that didn't stop them from seeing each other every couple of weeks. Frank used to work at a crappy pub off campus on Saturdays as a bouncer. It wasn't much of a job, but the pay was decent enough to keep him coming back.

It was at the crappy pub where he had met Jill. Jill—such an unattractive name if he was honest with himself. He wished she would go by the name Jillian. It was a much sexier name. He tried calling her Jillian a couple of times, but she wouldn't allow it. It was bad enough he had a dull name in Frank. But, together, Frank and Jill—well, it sounded like a boring, unattractive couple.

He even thought of Thomas. Heaven forbid you tried to call him Tom or even Tommy. Thomas was an uptight sounding name, but he wouldn't answer to another.

When he met Jill, never Jillian, his life changed forever. They had met in a coffee shop, where they spotted each other holding the same novel in their hands. They shared a table, talked about the author and eventually themselves.

They agreed to meet again, and soon the two became a serious couple. Neither had planned for it, and Frank promised himself he would focus on school before any sort of relationship, but like John Lennon said, life is what happens to you while you're busy making other plans.

Thomas met up a few times with them, and he really liked Jill, but started to miss a lot of the weekend get-together's. Frank called him up, asking if there was something wrong. "Frank, we've been friends for years and we will be friends for the rest of our lives. But I can't put that stupid smile on your face, like that girl can." Frank was glad they were talking on the phone, because he was sure he had a stupid blush, spreading across his face. "She's a great girl, a keeper. And I'm happy for you… and for me too. Listen man, not having to see your ugly face every other weekend has given me a chance to catch up on my work load. We'll plan a boys night every once in a while, but you spend some time with her, and brainwash her into thinking you're a good guy. Okay?"

The courtship lasted for two years until the day Thomas stood as his best man. Jill and he wanted a family and started trying right away. After a year, Jill finally got pregnant, but the ultimate happiness turned into the ultimate sadness when they lost the baby after three months. They tried again and they encountered two more miscarriages, each more devastating than the last.

They decided to stop actively trying, telling themselves, if it happens it happens. But nothing ever happened again. It was the one hole in their marriage, and neither knew what to do with that hole, or how to fill it in. After 18 years of marriage, Frank believed that they would never have a family, and though she never admitted it, he believed Jill felt the same way.

Frank stepped out of the shower, and looked at the steamed over mirror. He didn't clear the glass, because he didn't want to see the reflection in the mirror. He took a deep breath, and prepared to get ready before he ventured downstairs to start another day.

3

Carl Lethgate barely sat down at his desk when his phone rang and he was notified of the homicide. He slowly nodded his head while listening and said they would be there as soon as they could. Ryerson was only a couple of minutes away and they would meet in the parking lot.

Before he got up, he needed to collect his thoughts. He opened up a folder on his desk unrelated to the case, and pretended to read it. This case was on the verge of getting really messy and he felt totally helpless. He felt a heaviness in the pit of his stomach, and he knew it wasn't from a bad cup of coffee.

When Ryerson pulled in, Lethgate flagged him down and got into the passenger seat. Lethgate quickly filled his partner in with the information he had. Ryerson, upon hearing it gave a sigh, and tapped on the steering wheel with his fingers while starring ahead. "Ok, let's go," he said as they pulled out of the lot.

Usually when they were in a car, the detectives would refer to it as their fortress of solitude. They wouldn't talk about work-related items, but instead talk about news, sports, music or family, anything to give them temporary peace to disconnect from work. There were moments when they couldn't avoid talking about work, and this was one of those times.

"What do you think the chances are this one is going to be just like the others?" Ryerson asked.

"I have a bad feeling about it. I think we're going to be looking at the exact same thing."

Waiting at the red light, crawling through morning rush hour, Ryerson had the same bad feeling. "If the public gets a sniff of this..."

Lethgate understood. They hadn't yet officially labeled it as a serial homicide, but it was looking more and more like one. With the details of the murder unfolding, the press would have a field day and they would be inundated with media requests. Nothing gets national attention better than reports of a serial killer. Neither wanted that, but they felt as though they were speeding towards a brick wall with no brakes.

"Let's just work the scene. Who knows, we might catch a break," said Lethgate.

"You think so," Ryerson asked skeptically.

Lethgate could still feel the dark pit in his stomach, "No."

"What's your take about the bites?" Ryerson asked.

On each victim there was a single bite to the neck. There were no other wounds on any of the bodies, just the throat wound. The one thing no one could get their head around was the blood loss. The previous bodies had extreme blood loss, enough blood that they believed the bodies were drained and dumped. There was no giant puddles of blood around the body to suggest it taking place at the crime scene, but there was no proof of any dumping. They held onto the dumping angle, but with deep skepticism.

The discomfort they both shared was made over a lame joke by Lethgate at the scene of the first murder. He tucked his thumbs into his belt and with a bad cowboy impersonation said, "I think we have a vampire on our hands here." Of course there was no such thing as vampires, both detectives knew that. There was a chance it was some mentally disturbed man with a vampire fascination. When the media catches wind of these killings it will be a merge of media frenzy, public interest, public outrage, public fear, political pressure and personal pressure all equalled one thing—a shit show.

Both Ryerson and Lethgate avoided mentioning the word vampire.

The crime scene took place in an old alleyway, the sort of location you would see in an old crime movie. It was secluded, dirty and stank of urine. The detectives talked to the first officer on scene and made their way into the alley where the body was. They didn't have to worry about accidently stepping on any evidence, they had been given an all clear. Forensics was on scene and were cleaning up their equipment. They glanced over at the detectives and nodded that it was okay to check out the scene.

They walked over to the body and hovered over it, looking for something that may have been missed. Lethgate stepped back from the scene and looked up and down the alley, looked up at the buildings, and around them, then went back to the body, remaining quiet the entire time. Ryerson made a few notes and ran his hand through his hair.

"Do you see anything," Ryerson asked hopefully.

"Nothing. Maybe we'll get lucky with a tip or a one of the business's picked something up on a security camera."

"This guy is still fairly fresh. Do you think he could have been dumped?" asked Ryerson.

Lethgate stood up and looked around again just in case he missed something. "It's always a possibility, but..."

"But you doubt it."

"Yeah." Lethgate slowly shook his head in confusion. "Look at this guy, he almost looks like a mummy. I don't need to wait on an autopsy to be told he is missing a massive amount of blood. Look around, no blood, just a couple of drips by his neck. If they were draining it from him, there's no sign of struggle. Of course, the way this guy smells, I bet his toxicology report will show that he was drunk— you can't help but notice the stink of booze on this guy. But drunk enough to be drained of most of your blood and not wake up from it? I dunno."

They spent another hour walking around the scene. The body was taken with only minimal interest from passerby's on the street. This was a rough neighbourhood, and nothing good ever happened in a seedy alley in this part of town. The lack of attention was a good thing but how long would that last.

"Hopefully we'll know more in the next couple of days," Ryerson said optimistically.

The case started two months ago when they found a homeless man dead. Nothing news worth about that. Homeless people are murdered in countless numbers each year but nobody notices, except the morgues. The majority of people don't care or want to hear about homeless people. If you close your eyes, maybe it will go away.

But the murder was far from typical. The body was discovered underneath a bridge close to the river. The man had a large chunk of his throat missing.

There was speculation at the scene that the man was drunk, fell in and drowned and was washed back up on shore. It was probably some animal that took a chunk out, post mortem.

The only problem with that theory was the previous autopsy. It revealed the body had been dead for a few hours. It may have been enough time for his clothes to dry, but his stomach and lungs were void of any water from the river. The report also stated the death was caused from extreme blood loss, likely from the bite wound. The bite wound was also determined to be human, not animal.

An animal attack expert was consulted on the possibility of it being an animal bite. The expert said it didn't look like a typical animal attack. The bite mark didn't match up nor did the attack – there was only one bite. Usually an animal would gnaw or take several bites. There would also be tearing as the animal would pull and struggle with the body.

The autopsy also indicated no signs of drugs or alcohol in the body, which would have meant the man should have been able to struggle to fight off the animal. There was always the possibility he could have been attacked in his sleep, but for him to be killed before he woke up was unlikely.

A forensic dentist was called in to confirm that it was a human bite. The doctor was however, puzzled by the bite because she said it would have taken a very powerful jaw to be able to accomplish this in one smooth motion. Further examination of the wound showed traces of human saliva.

To add to the confusion, the autopsy report also stated the body was virtually drained of blood. There was a small amount of blood left in the heart and vital organs, but nearly 90 per cent of his blood was missing. Only a few drops of the victim's blood were found beside his body and there were no needle marks to indicate the blood had been drained.

While Lethgate and Ryerson tried to wrap their head around the case, two weeks later another murder occurred. Another homeless man, located in a dumpster with three-quarters of his blood missing and a bite mark on the left side of his neck.

The only difference in this case, besides location, was the bite was on the left side and the previous victim had been bitten on the right side of the neck. Neither detective doubted the murders was done by the same person.

No hairs or fingerprints were located at the scene and DNA sample recovered around the bite came back negative on the DNA database. Neither detective expected to find much of anything from this scene too.

4

While in the car Ryerson turned to Lethgate, "So do we call him the vampire killer? Dracula Jr?"

"That's not even funny Frank. If word starts to spread about this, we're going to be in a media storm."

Ryerson looked out the passenger window as they made their way through city traffic again. All the massive buildings around them with swarms of cars on the road and people on the sidewalks, made it easy to feel small and insignificant. "Where the hell is the blood going? It's one thing to bite a guy, maybe the killer has some cannibalism in him like Jeffrey Dahmer, but there's a large, rapid blood lost."

"So you're thinking Dracula Jr?"

"No I'm thinking who's going to play me in the TV movie they're going to make on this case."

"Oh good. It's about time we got famous. Who do you have in mind," Lethgate said smiling. He turned the car off of the busy street and worked his way into a downtrodden neighbourhood. They had plenty of calls there through the years so they knew the shortcuts.

"I don't know about me, but for you I see a young Sidney Poitier."

Lethgate let out a genuine laugh, it was a nice tension breaker. "Not a young Denzel Washington?"

"Nah, Sidney all the way."

Both were interrupted from their future fame when they saw what appeared to be a husband and wife having a heated argument in front of their house. Well, the husband was heated, and the wife stood with her head slightly lowered. The man was waving his hands around and suddenly pushed his wife down to the ground.

"Better call it in," Lethgate said.

"No, no. Turn around we can take it."

"Frank it's a black and white's job. My pay scale is murderers, not domestic abusers."

"Come on, just like the old days," he undid his seat belt and with his finger twirled it around so Lethgate would turn around.

"Man, you can't be serious," he moaned, but still pulled into a driveway and turned the car around.

As they pulled in front of the house, Ryerson said, "You take the woman and I'll handle the tough guy."

"We should really call this..." but Ryerson hopped out of the car before the sentence could be finished.

The house was a simple two-story with red brick. The white trim around the windows was cracked and flaking off, and the wood seemed to be rotting and in dire need of replacing. There was a small garden in front, but they could see it wasn't cared for. The only thing that seemed to be spreading was weeds in the garden bed.

When the couple looked over, Ryerson flashed his badge and identified himself. They both started speaking at the same time. Ryerson put his hand up and the husband and wife were silent. He noticed marks on the wife's face. If he had to guess, they were a day or two old.

"Miss, you go with my partner here, Detective Lethgate, and Sir you come with me. We'll hear both sides of the story and we will sort things out in a smooth and civilized manner. Do both of you understand?"

They both nodded.

"Good. Sir, follow me this way and tell me what this is all about."

Lethgate and the woman walked up to the old porch, which was long over-due for painting and some new lumber, while Ryerson stayed with the man in the front yard.

Ryerson walked toward the big elm tree in the front yard. The tree looked so strong, free and powerful, yet it was in one of the shittiest neighbourhoods. The street was run down, with rusted cars sitting in cracked oil stained driveways. The lawns had yellow, depressed looking grass, which seemed to reflect the mood of its owners.

He took a quick look at the man. The guy had an old stained shirt that had enough fabric to cover his belly button, but not enough to cover the fat, hairy stomach that hung over his belt. The man's face was not shaved, and there were yellow stains on the corners of his mouth.

"What is your name Sir? Frank asked with a feeling of nostalgia.

"Shannon Chambers, Sir. My wallet's inside the house. Do you want me to get it?

"No Mr. Chambers, I don't need that at the moment. Why don't you tell me what happened."

"Please, call me Shannon."

Getting on a first name basis. Being very polite and respectful. Fatman had done this before. "Ok, Shannon. Tell me what happened. How did she get the bruises on her face?"

"Well Sir," started the fatman. "Amber, that's my wife. Well, anyway, Amber was yelling down the stairs about something, you know how that is. "He grinned to the detective to further build a bond and understanding between the two men. "Well, I couldn't hear her over the TV, well, anyways, all I hear next was a crash. She fell and then she started crying and screaming and..."

"Cut the shit Shannon. We saw you push her down, which by law means I should slap the handcuffs on you and take you down to the station for domestic violence. Did you hit her too?"

Shannon Chambers looked as if he was hit himself. A stunned look appeared on his face, due to the force of the question. He scratched his enormous belly, which seemed to turn on his voice again.

"No, of course not, I..."

"Listen Shannon. I don't want to be here all god-damned day. Okay? We drove past and saw you put your hands on her. Did you also beat her up before we pulled up?"

"No! I..." He was shifting his hefty weight from one foot to the other.

"You know what really pisses me off Shannon? It's when people lie to me. Tell me the truth."

"I swear."

"Listen you fat piece of shit." Ryerson stepped forward with his voice in a low but very threatening tone. He was angry with the lies and didn't have the patience for domestic abuse cases any more. He should have let Carl take the man, because he had unlimited patience and obviously Frank didn't have any at the moment. Shannon stepped back because he was convinced the cop was going to hit him, then throw him in jail. "I hate it when people lie to me. You be honest with me, I'll be honest with you. Know what I mean?"

Shannon had no idea what this crazy man in front of him meant, but he agreed because he was scared not to.

"I see a drip of blood on your shirt Shannon." He quickly raised his hand to stop the fatman from speaking. "Don't feed me any shit about shaving, damn it, look at yourself man. I bet a razor hasn't touched that ugly face in days. I don't see any blood on your hands, but what I do see is some impressively clean hands at the end of some pretty dirty arms. Plus you wife, Amber is it? I saw old bruises but I bet there are some fresh ones ready to bloom. She doesn't have any swelling on her face from what I can see, but I bet if we looked inside her mouth we could probably see some fresh looking cuts. Hell, I bet her lip is growing in front of my partner as we speak."

Shannon did a choppy exhale which sounded as if tears were soon to follow. His head was down and his eyes were studying the tops of his shoes as if he might find an answer by staring at them.

"Did you hit her?" Ryerson repeated.

Shannon was about to lie, but the detective took a step towards him as he asked the question, waiting for a lie so he could hit him. He took a deep breath and a barely audible "yes" escaped his lips.

"That's better. Doesn't it feel good to tell the truth?" Ryerson wished all his confessions came this quick and easy, but he knew the type of man he was dealing with. The fatman was just a bully—he could deal it out, but when it was given back to him, he cowered. "If it was up to your wife to charge you or not, would she?"

"I don't under..."

"Would she press charges or would she be too afraid of what you'd do to her if she did? Be honest with me. I'm in no fucking mood."

"N,n,n,no, I don't think she would."

"No thinking Shannon. I want a solid yes or no answer. Would she press charges if we asked her?

"No."

"Then let's not have this happen again." Ryerson started to walk away from the man. As Shannon stood there stunned, unsure of what was going on.

"Umm, s,sir? Umm, what is going to happen?"

"My partner and I are leaving," Ryerson said abruptly.

"Are you taking me to jail?" asked Shannon.

"Do you want to go to jail?"

"No."

"Okay then, there is your answer. There is something I want you to know Shannon. When I get back to the station I am going to have a little red flag placed beside this address and your name. And just to let you know, information gets to me pretty quickly." Ryerson stepped in as close as Shannon's belly would allow. "If I hear that you have beaten your wife, I will personally step on your throat. Don't play with me and don't test me. If I hear a single peep or rumour, I'll be all over you! Understand fatman?"

Shannon Chambers was stunned and scared. He swallowed, blinked a couple of times and scratched the outside of his thigh.

"Y,y,yes sir."

"Good. Have a nice day Mr. Chambers."

The fatman was left standing beside the elm wondering if what had happed was real. He was waiting for the cop to come back to him with handcuffs, but the man just walked over to his partner, pulled him aside, and after a couple of minutes they walked over and got inside the blue Ford. The black cop who was talking to his wife looked angry and glared at the fatman, but eventually got behind the wheel and pulled away.

"What the hell was all that for?" asked Letgate. His hands were gripped tightly around the steering wheel trying to control his anger. "You so badly wanted to take the call, which wasn't ours to take. We needed to let a patrol and the courts handle it. You wanted it so bad, and you just let the guy walk away."

"If we would have just called this in, they would have locked him up for a couple of hours and he would have beaten the shit out of her when he got out. You know as well as I do, she would have begged us to let him go. She won't be the one calling the cops, it will be a neighbour sick of all the noise coming from their house."

Ryerson looked out the window as they drove back to the station. He didn't pay attention to the people on the streets or the buildings which lined the street. He rode in the car in a haze. He looked but he did not see. The only thing he saw was the story unfolding in his head while he explained his actions.

"She wouldn't have pressed charges or filed a restraining order," he reiterated. "If we had hauled fatman in, he would have returned home with a vengeance and you know it. We could've offered her safety and shelter but she wasn't going to take it. You saw her eyes, she would have said no. What we ended up doing was cooling him down and saving her from a beating. She wouldn't have let us help her."

It didn't matter. Mr. Chambers should have been immediately arrested for domestic abuse when they witnessed it. He would have been charged regardless of his wife's opinion. But there was no convincing Ryerson. They had been partners for eight years and Lethgate knew he was a great man to have beside him if things got hairy, but sometimes he just didn't know Frank at all. Ryerson knew the law better than most, but he also has a dangerous laid back approach to some cases. The laid back part had nothing to do with the paper work they were always up to their elbows in, but more so with his people skills, as if other people's problems were an inconvenience to him.

Lethgate knew the woman would want her husband taken away or file a restraining order. She was frightened it would anger him and that it was her fault, but the son-of-a-bitch should have been cuffed and placed in a cage for the night. There was always a chance she could have got a restraining order and asked for help. She at least deserved the opportunity to ask, but Frank, a representative of the law who was supposed to help such people as herself, did not give her a chance to receive help.

He was also angry with himself for not standing up to Frank, but the strange thing was, he was slightly afraid of Ryerson. He didn't fear the man himself, or that Ryerson was going to do something to him. There was something hidden, much like an onion with different layers. He loved Frank, he trusted him with his life and Frank trusted him, but some of his layers were dark. He couldn't put his finger on it, but it frightened him.

He had never been more ashamed of himself or his partner.

"Let's get back to the station and see if we have any news," Ryerson finally said.

"Yeah, But don't get your hopes up."

5

When they returned to the station they went over the links in the case. All three murders had similar bite marks to the throat, bleeding the victim to death. There was hardly any blood at the scene and little blood remaining in the corpses.

The victims were all homeless, and attracted little attention. The victims' locations though, differed. The first body was at the river, with plenty of dense foliage around. The second body was located in a dumpster. It was determined the body was killed nearby and was disposed of and hidden in the dumpster. Yet, the latest body was located at the edge of an alley with some small businesses located nearby, plus, the location was visible to motorists and pedestrians. This is what the detectives focused on.

"Someone must have seen something," said Lethgate.

He took off his jacket, rolled up his sleeves and got a cup of coffee. This case was starting to worry him. There was something wrong about the latest victim. The killer had been so careful up to this point, why would he get sloppy and risk the chance of being seen.

Lethgate knew some serial killers got bored after a time. They sometimes do it for the thrill of the chase. Yet, in this case, the chase had barely started. Most get bored after a couple of years and a handful of victims. The killer was making a slight change in his methods and this put him on edge.

The coffee room was located off the hub of the building and had a few tables with mismatched chairs. Lethgate rarely sat in the room, he would rather take his drink back to his desk. It wasn't the squeaky chairs and the uneven tables that bothered him but the smell and the feel. The room stank of stale coffee from pots long forgotten and the room felt very heavy. Working in a police station was very stressful, being exposed daily to the worst of human nature, and this was the room people would escape to, to wind down or find their second wind in another cup of coffee. Sometimes the stress and frustration a person felt would be left in the room, sort of like a cosmic fingerprint. Some places Lethgate could get vibes from, sometimes good, sometimes bad, and this was one of those areas. He poured some cream and went back to his desk.

"He does it in an area where he could be seen. All we need is to find one driver, or one person walking down the street to give us a lead, then we can finally start getting somewhere." Lethgate sat down with his hot drink, careful not to spill any on him.

"I've sent some guys over to question some of the store owners in the area," said Ryerson. "Maybe one stayed late and saw or heard something, or maybe they might have known Stray Woody."

Stray Woody was a term most of the cops on the force called a deceased homeless person. Stray, like a stray dog and woody because they are stiffs. It seemed cruel and heartless, but if you refer to the person as a murdered human being, it can dig into your soul and tear you apart. It was a morbid release to the men and women on the force.

Ryerson sat at the edge of his desk and positioned himself in front of Lethgate.

"I've also made sure that the owners get asked if they have any video cameras facing the street. If we're lucky we might be able to spot the guy and get some sort of profile on him. It's a long shot but it can't hurt."

Ryerson went back to his desk and ran his hand through his hair. It was times like this he felt useless. On most cases there was a lead. There were fingerprints, hair, clothes fabric, and a motive. Something. His frustration was mounting and he was on the verge of snapping. He felt the build-up of past pain and worries on his shoulders. The tear ducts behind his eyes started to burn but he forced himself to shake the feeling.

He leaned back in his uncomfortable, reclining wooden chair—an ancient relic he refused to give up, and let out a deep breath. He took a solid breath through his nose and slowly released it through his mouth. Relaxation was key to surviving in this job, and Ryerson made sure he stayed relaxed.

There was more than enough tension in his line of work to send more than one man over the edge. He did not plan on becoming another statistic. He ate properly, got plenty of sleep and exercise.

But panic attacks are made in the mind. The brain sends messages to the body to bring forth the panic. He hated the idea of having a weak mind. Of not being able to control his own thoughts, bringing on a physical reaction. It made him feel less of a man, and it made him feel out of control and powerless.

He started to relax when they got the call. They would go see Thomas tomorrow.

◊

They drove to the morgue and pulled around the back. They checked in and made their way to Thomas' office. The building was very clean and very white. Sort of like a hospital but the smell of cleaners and disinfectants was much stronger. And, unlike a hospital, there was not much on the wall to make the place look inviting. It was very sterile and very business-like.

Thomas was the cities youngest head Pathologist, greeted them with the autopsy reports opened on his desk. He had a great working relationship with the police department, and being best friends with Frank surely help with that.

Thomas is the lead Pathologist in most of the murder autopsies. He was very precise, and a perfectionist almost to a flaw. He was terrific in a courtroom: able to relax and educate a jury with information most people would find too sickening to talk about.

Thomas got up from his chair when he saw them. He gave a big smile. "You're still working with this guy?" he said to Lethgate while Ryerson smirked. "You must be a glutton for punishment."

"Yep I drew the short straw at the station."

"You won the lotto of life my friend," Ryerson said smiling to his partner. He walked over to Thomas and gave him a friendly little punch on the arm.

"Hey buddy. Did we get something new or just the same old stuff?" Ryerson asked expecting another roadblock in the case as both detectives took a chair in front of Thomas' desk.

"If you consider hair and fingerprints, same old stuff, yeah."

"What!" Lethgate unintentionally yelled.

"You heard me, fellas. We have all sorts of fingerprints on the victim's neck and on his forehead."

"Forehead?" Ryerson asked. "Must have been holding the guy's head still."

"I don't think so," said Thomas. The stocky man in the slightly tinted glasses got closer to the detectives and explained what was bothering him.

"The bite mark was on the left side of the victim's neck but the fingerprints on the forehead are vertical—straight up and down. It seems very awkward. All signs indicate the killer came up on the victim's right side. If the killer went straight for the neck, odds are he grabbed the chin first or grabbed the guy's hair. If the killer did hold down the victim, his hand should have been going across the victim's head, not up and down. Here let me show you.

He walked over to Lethgate and told him to lean back in his chair. He stood on the right side of Lethgate.

"Alright, let's assume Carl here is the victim and I'm the killer. Lean back more Carl. Okay. Let's pretend he is lying on the ground, and I'm coming up after him. Just like all the other cases, the killer did not hit his victims, because there are no bruises indicating any signs of a fight or a fall. Death came by loss of blood, from the victim's jugular vein, from an apparent bite.

"It appears to me the killer must have kneeled down beside the victim and must have turned his head like this," Thomas reached for Lethgate's neck and turned it so his chin was touching his right shoulder.

"Anyway, as you can see here my right hand is across Carl's neck and my left hand is going across his hairline, holding the victim's head in place. Well, if you point your thumb down a bit, it will go over his forehead and leave a thumbprint.

"But the thumb is facing down if I do that," he continued. "The prints on the victim have them going up. It is impossible for the killer to have done it otherwise. We know the killer was on the right side. He couldn't have killed on the other side because he would have been too close to the alley wall. My guys at the scene said there was no indication of the body being moved," he said to the detectives making sure he kept eye contact with them making sure both of them understood.

"Impossible?" Lethgate asked with Thomas's hands still holding his head to the side.

"No, it is not impossible, but pretty unconventional. This guy is quick. Somehow he kills his victims in an amazing amount of speed, and the way I showed you with Carl was the quickest and easiest way for him to have done it."

"You said it was unconventional, but not impossible to kill him that way?" asked Ryerson.

"Not impossible but very uncomfortable. Plus the print is fairly light. I mean, if he attacked the guy, the killer would have wanted to hold him solid so there was no chance of a struggle."

"But there were no struggle marks on the first two victims," added Lethgate.

"None that we could see. It appears to me, and this is nothing scientific, but it appears as if the killer just placed his thumb on the guy's forehead to make sure we got a clean fingerprint."

The detectives sat in silence trying to digest the information. This wasn't making any sense. The other killings were so clean and near perfect. Why was he suddenly sloppy?

"What can you tell us about the hair sample?"

"Long black hair, no recent drug use."

"What else?" asked Lethgate.

"The homeless guy was sucked dry... don't we all want to be sucked dry." Ryerson and Lethgate rolled their eyes. "I know, keep my day job right?"

"He had hardly any blood in his body but what remained of it was scary. The guy had full-blown AIDS, Hepatitis, and there were huge amounts of alcohol and aerosol. The man was getting high from aerosol cans.

"You guys joked before about vampires," said Thomas. "Well, if we never catch the guy, he'll die of AIDS."

"Thanks, Thomas."

Thomas handed the remainder of the report over to Ryerson. He learned over the years of experience, detectives didn't want medical jargon, just the basic meat and potatoes. Besides a full medical report he would include a simple summary. The medical mumbo-jumbo was intended for the court rooms.

"Well, it looks like we finally have something to go on," said Lethgate.

"But how can he kill a person by biting him? There is hardly any blood around the scene, we joke about drinking blood, but..."

"Hey, man, we live in a sick world. We have guys who go out and kill for sexual pleasure, for a fun time and for no reason at all. Some like to eat their victims and some like to drink blood. It is sick, but it is also a reality."

"But there has been no sign of a struggle. And the amount of blood. No human could ingest that much. And the speed. I got a bad feeling about this."

"A day at a time, bro, a day a time. Let's look at what we have and wait to see if anyone saw anything. Maybe we'll find another lead."

6

Leads in a murder case are usually only warm for the first 48 hours. Each day, that passes in a murder case generally means the trail starts to cool and the murderer has a better chance of getting away. If the detectives have no leads after the first week and have nothing to go on, they have to depend on witnesses coming out and shedding a new light on the case.

This case was shaping up just like any other case until they received some information from one of the officers questioning business owners around the murder scene, it then turned the case into a bizarre contest of catch-me-if-you-can.

The phone rang at Ryerson's desk while they were examining some of the murder photos taken at the scene.

"Detective Ryerson."

"Yeah, hi. Frank this is Mark Dekins at the *Tribune*. How are things going?"

Ryerson was Dekins' source at the station. The force's public relations officer was not good at feeding the press information. Dekins who was the crime beat reporter for the *Tribune*, would usually call the P.R. officer to get a quote, and use some of Ryerson's information for filler. Ryerson trusted him. He never leaked any off the record information, and he never used his name. Plus, Ryerson figured someday Dekins would be of use if he ever needed a favour within the media and if the information was hot, Dekins paid well.

"What's up, Mark?"

"I know you're busy, so I won't take up too much of your time, but how much do you know about the murders regarding the homeless guys?"

"Oh, shit!" Ryerson thought. The media has started to get wind of the murders and soon the strange details would start a media frenzy. In a city of 4 million people there were lots of murders that the public did not care about. Namely, homeless or hooker murders. In the past, the department had dealt with serial murders regarding prostitutes and the paper would bury it as a small brief on page 35 or something. But with victims being bit in the neck, this potential monster of a story would get front page headlines from now until the trial... if they ever caught him.

"Yeah, I know about the murders, I'm investigating them." Ryerson was keeping a laid back tone.

"Hey! Good stuff. So, do you have much? Are they related?"

"The latest one is not like the others. The first two *may* be related but we're not sure," Ryerson lied.

"How did this one die?"

"Throat lacerations," Ryerson was making sure he sounded nonchalant and brief.

"Does the victim have a name?"

"John Doe."

"Great. Umm, any leads?"

"Nah. It's probably some other bum or junkie that killed him for some change."

"Hmmm, this will make an exciting exclusive. Thanks Frank, talk to ya again."

"Yeah, no problem, Mark. I'll keep you informed if we come across anything new." He lied again.

"Alright, thanks."

As Ryerson breathed a sigh of relief, Officer Davies came up to his desk.

"Sirs, I think I got something regarding the murder in the alley last night."

Both Lethgate and Ryerson bolted up straight in their seats. They looked at each other with strange looks. The two previous murders had absolutely no clues or leads. This one, by the same killer, had hair and fingerprints, and now something else.

"What do you have Aaron?"

"Well, you know the pawnshop on Wentworth, half a block east of the scene?"

"Yeah" Lethgate said.

"I asked the owner..." he opened up his notes and searched for the name. "Duffy. Steven Duffy." Both detectives knew the store well. The pawn shop had a shady history of dealing with stolen property from known thieves. This was not the first time Mr. Duffy had to deal with a police officer. "Well, I asked him if he happened to be in the store last night around 2 a.m., the time of the murders and of course he was at home."

"What do you have, Aaron?" asked Ryerson on the verge of yelling anxiously.

"Let's go to the viewing room," Aaron Davies said. He led the detectives to the viewing room, which had an old wooden table with countless initials and words scratched on its surface. He closed the door behind Ryerson and Lethgate.

"I took Det. Ryerson's advice and asked if he had a video camera set up facing the street, and of course he did so he could film the front display.

"I got this video tape off of Mr. Duffy."

"Who the hell still uses video tapes?" Muttered Ryerson.

Davies put the video inside a VCR that probably hadn't been used in years and pressed play. The quality of the tape was very poor. It was a combination of a cheap camera and a video tape that had been recorded over numerous times. But it was still better than nothing. If only the owner would have invested in a better security camera. Everything was now digital, quality imaging, and all stored on a hard drive.

The image on the TV screen was black and white with lots of lines going across the screen. The front of the store was well lit, which made viewing easier, but it was impossible to make out cars or anything across the street.

The two detectives and the officer watched the time framed video of the street. There was nothing outside and Ryerson and Lethgate were straining their eyes to catch a peek of any figure passing the window. The next frame of video showed a man standing in front of the video appearing to be looking at the camera. Lethgate's heart jumped. The man was very short, almost looked like a young teenager, but he could tell by the face that this was no teen. He squinted to try to see the man more clearly but the video quality was poor. The video jumped again, with the man still standing in front of the window. He appeared to be a short man, light skinned, but hard to tell from the black and white video, wearing a long coat. The man did nothing but stood in front of the window and stare at the camera.

Occasionally parts of the video showed a car driving along the street, but the man still stared. For minutes the video just showed the one man standing at the window until finally it showed him slowly walking away.

"Mr. Duffy installed a cheap video camera to monitor the front of the store. It's practically an antique and the thing barely works. Now what the camera does is film for 10 seconds every 30 seconds."

The detectives now were just staring at Officer Davies, waiting for him to continue. Davies seemed to enjoy the drama and was basking in it.

"Not much good even if there was a robbery, because 20 seconds would be cut out. But the weird thing is the amount of time the man stood in front of the window. It may be nothing, but, if the video runs for 10 seconds, every 30 seconds, then the man stood in front of the window for ten minutes on the video. Meaning he nearly stood there for half-an-hour. It's like what they do in horror movies when they just stand there for a long time not moving."

The detectives tried to do the math in their heads but kept on thinking about the video.

"The camera is fairly cheap and was programmed to display the time in the bottom left hand corner, at the top of the hour. When we see the man walk away, it is recorded at 2 a.m. near the time of the murder, and, he is headed west, the direction of the alley." Davies said playing junior detective.

There was a long pause before one of the detectives could reply.

"Did any other cameras show anything? How about the store across from the pawnshop do they have a camera?" asked Ryerson.

"Sorry. Only the pawnshop store had a camera facing towards the street. We have looked at other videos but either the camera faces the cash only or the camera is too old to pick up a clear image of what's going on outside."

"Just leave the tape with us Aaron. Thanks." Lethgate added.

"It's him, that's the killer," Ryerson said after the room cleared.

"Why would he stand there for so long? What is he doing?"

Ryerson shrugged, "I don't know."

7

Lethgate and Ryerson watched and re-watched the video. The videotape in the pawnshop was not the best quality but they had a solid identification. The man was short possibly five-foot six and from the facial features they could make out, he appeared to be native Indian. Being a native Indian should reduce their search considerably, and both finally had hope in closing this file.

They had to get a photo made from the tape and distribute it among the officers. At the moment, no picture would be released to the public or media. The less known about the case the better.

"Do you think we should deal with a psychologist on this one?" asked Lethgate.

"Well, I don't know of too many other experts in this field. Maybe we should get a profile on him." The police departments often dealt with psychologists in some murder cases, especially serial murders, to get an idea of what patterns the killer may follow, and get a better idea as to what they are thinking. They sent a synopsis of the crime and much of the case file to a psychologist the department had dealt with in the past.

"Okay. Well, at least we have something now. We should set up surveillance starting tonight. We'll cover a couple of areas each night. One set up in the alleys and one around the train yard. This guy has a taste for bums so we will start there," Lethgate said not meaning the pun.

An officer approached the two. "Call on line two. It is for either one of you." The officer walked away.

Ryerson picked up the phone.

◊

"Detective Ryerson."

"Hello detective, my name is Alex Frey. I guess I am what you can call a vampire expert and I think I can help you out."

Ryerson was shaken by what the man had said. His stomach did a flip when the word vampire was mentioned. "Mr. Frey, there is no such things as vampires."

"Well someone is killing some homeless people and it's not just random murders. I read in the paper today about the latest victim. There wasn't much information, but I can guarantee you this is not the first place this has happened. But he is being sloppy for some reason, and I have no understanding as to why. In my line of work you have to really search the newspapers for information. The powers that be don't let the information leak out. So don't worry about the media detective. Regardless of how big this case gets, the media will not be peppering headlines about vampires. There are certain people with a lot of power who will keep this hush, hush.

"I am calling to offer you some help. You have no idea what you are dealing with and, you don't have a clue in how much danger you are in. I am risking my own life in calling you, but there is something very wrong happening, and this is only going to get worse. We can get together and I can take a look at the evidence and maybe I can see something that you don't."

Ryerson rolled his eyes. A nut wanted to get off looking at crime scene photos and wanting to be a junior Sherlock Holmes. In the past they have had citizens demanding to see crime scene photos because they said they had rights. What they had was a sick fascination with death. "Mr. Frey there is no such thing as vampires. I'm sorry I can't help you."

There was a pause on the line.

"Mr. Frey?"

"If there are no such things as vampires why haven't you hung up yet? I can help you detective. I'll give you my number and if you think that maybe a vampire is involved in this case, give me a call."

Against his better judgement Ryerson took down the number and hung up.

"What was all that about?" Lethgate asked.

Something was ringing in the back of Ryerson's mind. In most cases he would just let it go as a crank call. But his mind kept on flipping back to the conversation. This guy was talking vampires – how the hell could he come to that conclusion by reading some short articles in the paper? An alarm was ringing in his mind and he never ignored it.

"We need to do a background check on an Alex Frey."

The Vampire stood by the window and looked out at the city. There was a time he could remember the clean waters and fresh air. Now it was all just sick water and sick air.

He watched the entire thing happen and there was nothing he could do to stop it. Over the years, he had watched a civilization slowly destroy the planet. He was raised to honour the planet. To respect and be thankful for everything she provided. Now everyone took everything for granted. Man killed for sport and polluted and destroyed the environment for money. He lowered his head in shame.

Vengeance would be his.

Dazinski and Patrick walked slowly by the crime scene. The yellow barrier tape was starting to be taken down. Both had seen many crime scenes. Although they were not police officers, their jurisdiction was limitless.

They looked at the top of the buildings taking in every angle. It was not important that the scene was being taken down. They had full files on all the killings, including pictures and autopsy reports. The police did not know they had the information, and they wouldn't know. Nobody but a handful of people knew where they were and why they were there.

"He's getting bolder again," said Patrick. He was a plain looking soul. The kind of man that would not get a second look, just what he and the organization wanted. He was five foot ten, 190 pounds, thinning brown hair, a not a noticeable mark on him. He kept himself clean-shaven all the time. Any facial growth bothered him. Growth was a sign of being undisciplined. Patrick knew about discipline. He went straight into the military after he left high school.

His past seemed like another life – he was resurrected into the life he knew now. A life where all the curtains of mystery were revealed. He just stared off in the distance remembering a life, long ago.

◊

Patrick parked at the far end of the strip mall taking in his surroundings. He knew he was at the right location, he just didn't understand.

Two weeks earlier Patrick was happily living the army life. Early in his military career his Sargent spotted something special in him, and recommended him for special training. He took to the training like a duck to water. He was a sponge absorbing information on weapons, hand to hand fighting, tracking, the ability to blend in with his environment.

He had numerous physical and mental tests. He was never told any of the results, but no news was good news in his book. Patrick was on the shooting range when his instructor told him to report to his office. A sharp, "yes sir," and he headed in the direction of the office but he noticed his instructor was not following. He paused for a short moment and continued on his way. An order was an order and he followed them well.

When he entered the office, a man was sitting behind the desk wearing a suit and tie. Definitely not army. Not willing to show his decisiveness he walked up to the desk and stared straight ahead waiting for further instructions.

"Sit down soldier," said the man. "You can relax, I want to talk to you."

"Yes sir."

"I have been following you for a few months now. I've seen your reviews from your superior officers, your medical records, your scores on the firing range." His hand drifting to a file in front of him on the desk. "You're a decent shot—against a red bulls eye, do you think you can shoot a man that easily?"

"Sir?"

The suit waved him off. "All in time." He stood up and walked to the front of the desk and sat on the corner of it. Patrick didn't like the closeness of the man. "I'm here to offer you a job. As you can probably tell I am not army. I'm not from any department of the armed forces. You could say I am from the government but that isn't all together true. They wouldn't even admit to my existence, yet..." he waved his hands around him in a showing manner. "Yet here I am talking to you with classified information at my disposal."

He stood up from his seat on the corner of the desk and returned to his chair. "It is my job to look for recruits. I can't tell you here what the position I am offering you is all about. All I can tell you is that you will never have a boring day. You will continue with your training but under our supervision. Life as you know it will never be the same."

"I don't understand."

"Nor do I expect you to soldier. I am here to offer you an exciting life the army will never be able to match. I am here to offer you a new world with plenty of danger and excitement. Any rush the army can provide you is nothing to what we can." Patrick still had no idea who 'we' was.

"I am here looking for men. Not some grunt pussy that follows orders and can march in a straight line and can hit a target from 300 metres. I am looking for a man who is willing to have his life turned upside down, who can see the world and discover the truths of that world."

The suit was looking at Patrick right in the eyes—barely making any movement, studying him all the time. "I am asking you to take a leap of faith and discover what you are made of."

Back in the parking lot he was questioning his leap of faith. He scanned the stores. A dollar store, convenience store, shoe store, a deli and beside the deli the building he was looking for, RGC Logistics. He looked down at his watch; he was a few minutes early. Scanning the parking lot and the few people that were walking about, everything appeared normal. And that was what worried him.

When he entered RGC Logistics a woman sat at a desk working behind a computer. She didn't glance his way when she told him to sit down. There were six chairs in the plain white room with a couple of paintings of old buildings and a sunset, lining the walls. He took in the surroundings quickly and noticed something strange about the wall behind the secretary. It seemed to come out a few feet too far. He was sure there was a space behind the wall with someone in it, probably watching him very closely.

He heard the sound of the door and another man walked in. The secretary gave him the same greeting as he sat in the chair across from Patrick. Definitely military he thought. The man sat with excellent posture and body fat had never seen his frame before. Neither man said a word nor make eye contact.

A door leading into the inner part of the building opened and a meek appearing man stood in the doorway. He looked at the two men and motioned for them to enter. What Patrick and the other man entered was a simple room converted into a classroom. To one side were four one-piece student desks while the front of the room had a cart with a projector with a laptop sitting on top, plugged in on the side. There was no black boards or projection screens in the room. A closed door was on the far wall.

"Sit please gentlemen," the small man said gesturing to the student desks. "My name is Mr. Friday. I will be changing your lives and teaching the history and necessary tools you will need to survive. I expect your full attention. I don't want any questions or comments when I am talking, you will have a chance to ask questions when I am done."

None of what Mr. Friday said made any sense to Patrick and he was sure the man beside him was equally confused but he didn't show it. There was something very cold and dangerous about this small man, he just couldn't put his finger on it.

"You two are about to be told one of the greatest secrets the world has ever known. A lot of money, time and lives have been sacrificed to keep this a secret. You two will be given the job of making sure this secret is never revealed." The man gave his version of a dramatic pause. "The existence of vampires."

Patrick wanted the man to repeat himself but he knew he heard the man all too clearly. He tried to keep a poker face, but the man beside him was unable to.

"Is something funny Mr. Hayward? Did I say something to amuse you? You better wipe that smile off your face before I take it off for you."

Once again Patrick felt it hard to repress a stunned look. The man beside him—Mr. Hayward, had about 5 inches and at least 60 pounds on Mr. Friday. But the look on Mr. Friday's face told Patrick the man was serious. He dared a glance beside him and could see that Mr. Hayward had seen that same look.

"Vampires have been in existence throughout history. Our job is to make sure they don't get too powerful because if they did, our world would never be the same."

He turned to the laptop and hit a key. The projector came to life showing an image on the white wall behind Mr. Friday. It was a picture of a dead man. There was blood on his face and his eyes were open with a lifeless stare. There was no questioning he was dead. What brought a gasp to Patrick, with which he could not repress, was the man's mouth. It had been cut open along both sides of his cheeks showing the sharpest, scariest looking teeth he had ever seen. It was something which should have been inside a wild animal's mouth, not a human.

"This gentlemen," Mr. Friday said pointing to the image on the wall, "is a vampire."

For the next 6 hours Mr. Friday told the two men the history of the Organization and the existence of vampires. They had a 15 minutes lunch where they were given a couple of sandwiches, which looked like it may have come from the local deli, and a choice of coffee, tea or water.

Patrick didn't have much of an appetite but forced himself to eat and washed it down with a bottle of water. They later had a five minute washroom break before they continued on for another hour before finally ending for the day.

"I please ask when you two gentlemen leave that you do not talk about what you have learned, to each other. And I don't think I have to stress to not tell anybody else. Ever."

Mr. Friday gave them a smile, "I will see you tomorrow at 7 am... or o-seven-hundred hours for you military boys."

The following day was much more of the same. Relearning history with vampires in it. "You will encounter many vampires' gentlemen. Many will be docile and will help you, mainly out of fear. But others will want to tear out your throats. I recommend to you that you take extreme prejudice with all vampires and assume they want to tear out your throat. This belief may one day save your life."

"Umm... excuse me Mr. Friday?" a voice beside Patrick quietly said. The voice startled him because it was the first time in two days either man had spoken.

Mr. Friday turned hard towards Mr. Hayward. There was no disguising the anger in his eyes. "I told you no questions or comments until I am done. We have a week's more to cover before I can say I am done with this part of your training."

"Ah, yeah. Sorry about that." Mr. Hayward slowly raised his hand towards his head and run it through his short cut hair. "I just don't think this is for me. I want to serve my country and all, but ahh," he said shaking his head. "I just don't think this is for me."

Mr. Friday slowly shook his head as if he understood what the young man was saying. Then in a heartbeat he reached into his jacket and pulled out a gun shooting Mr. Hayward in the head. The noise was almost deafening. Patrick flinched but quickly sat straight up in his chair. Beside him, Mr. Hayward's head was all the way back with brain on the wall behind him. Even with the ringing in his ears Patrick could still hear the blood pouring out of the back of the man's head onto the floor below.

With a calm demeanour Mr. Friday slowly put the gun back into the holster inside his jacket and looked at Patrick. "Do you have anything you want to say Mr. Patrick?" he asked.

"No sir," Patrick calmly tried to say and quietly shifted his desk a few inches away from the still draining Mr. Hayward.

Mr. Friday gave Patrick a half hour lunch break and when he returned there was no sign of Mr. Hayward. The wall and floor was cleaned of blood and brains, yet he could not smell any trace of a chemical cleaner. As the class continued, Patrick could hear in his mind the dripping of blood on the floor.

"Unlike many intelligence agency's we will not give you a detailed background on any of the missions you are on. If you are following a vampire, we will give you names of known friends and family, job and residences, but that is all."

"If you are tracking with an order to eliminate you don't need to know about their past. The only thing you should be concentrating on is locating and eliminating the target. That is all."

Patrick attended RGC Logistics for 8 days of classes. On the final day Mr. Friday stood in front of Patrick with his hands folded down in front of him. "Any questions?" he asked with a slight smirk on his face.

"I'm sure I have a million questions, but I just want to know what's next?"

Mr. Friday slowly shook his head in the affirmative. "After this you will have about six to eight months of—well let's just call it our version of boot camp. It will be a combination of physical work and classroom work. We will strengthen your mind and body."

"But," Patrick's stomach lurched at the sound of 'but'. "First you have a test. Follow me."

Patrick followed Mr. Friday to the door that lead deeper into the building. Inside the room was shelving loaded with boxes with skids lined up on one side of the wall. It gave the appearance of a typical stock room. Mr. Friday moved towards a fire pull station on the wall and placed his thumb on the red plate. A section the shelving moved slightly up and rolled soundlessly to the side.

Behind was an elevator door which both men got on. It was hard to judge how fast the elevator was travelling, but Patrick figured if it was a typical elevator, it lowered 20 feet before the doors opened.

The room was white, 20 feet by 20 feet. On each wall was a door. Mr. Friday moved towards the door directly ahead of them. He stopped at the door and turned to face Patrick. He reached into his coat and pulled out his gun, handing it to Patrick.

"You will be needing this," he said with no expression on his face.

When the door opened Patrick was shocked by what he saw. It was a much larger room than the one he came from. Sitting on the right side of the room, tied in a chair was an attractive blonde woman who looked at the men with genuine fear in her eyes. Her eyes were bloodshot from crying and tears were streaming out of them.

Patrick didn't see the little girl at first. She was a little blonde girl who stood at the far end of the room. She had a leg iron attached to her. It was obvious to Patrick the two were related. Mother and daughter he expected. He looked at Mr. Friday with a bewildered look.

"Mr. Patrick," he said as he nodded towards the tied up woman on the wooden chair. "This is a vampire. She is very dangerous and a killer." He moved his gaze from the woman to the little girl. "She is also a vampire."

He looked at Patrick waiting for eye contact. When it was met, "I want you to kill the girl."

An immediate cry of anger and fear came from the woman. She shook herself in the chair, the ropes holding her down, and the chair squeaking under her in protest. She met Patrick's eyes and then looked at the gun. "Please! Please don't hurt my baby!" she managed in between sobs.

Mr. Friday's expression did not change with the pleas. "This is your first test. This is not a range target Mr. Patrick. Do you have what it takes to be with us?

"They may look like us," a slow scowl appeared on his face, "but they are not human, they are vampires!"

The woman screamed again. "You bastards don't hurt my baby! Don't you hurt my baby!" Her words got muffled in her tears and turned into screams. Patrick looked at the end of the room to where the little girl was curled in a little ball with her hands covering her ears. He could see her lips mouthing the word 'mommy'.

Patrick looked back down at his gun. He looked again at Mr. Friday.

"As you may have learned from Mr. Hayward, we don't have a lot of people back out of this job. Your job is to find, and if necessary kill vampires." Again with another gesture of his hands if he was a want to be circus ringmaster, "here are your vampires, now kill the girl."

Patrick understood clearly. Mr. Friday didn't play games. He would be killed as quickly as Mr. Hayward was killed. He walked out into the middle of the room between the mother and the daughter. He took a deep breath and tried to block out the screams. It was impossible. The shrilling scream from the mother and the chair repeatedly squeaking under her was making his ears hurt and his stomach nauseous.

He looked over at the little girl and somehow still managed to hear a click come from her end of the room. The little girl heard the click too as she looked down at the shackle around her right ankle. It had opened up. The lock must have been released by remote control. The little girl unsure of what to do, didn't do anything at first.

She looked at her mother a long time than back at the shackle. She slowly shook her leg and when the clamp fell free from her ankle she jerked away from it, as if it were a snake. The little girl took a deep breath of her own and stood up, her back flat against the wall. She looked at Mr. Friday, to Patrick than to her mother. Fear froze her in place.

"Let her go god damn you!" screamed the mother. In an instant Patrick spun with the gun raised in his hand and shot the mother. The bullet tore a hole in her throat and her eyes opened wide in disbelief. Her head wobbled on her shoulders and she tried to focus her eyes on her daughter but darkness was the only thing she saw.

Patrick was shaken. Not that he had killed the woman, but because he had missed his shot. He wanted to shoot her square in the chest, not the throat. He felt his hand tremble slightly. He was trained to shoot for the biggest target on the body, and to not always rely on a head shot. The odds went down considerably when aiming for a smaller target. Plus, a head can move, the centre of the body, not so easily.

He quickly recomposed himself and faced the girl. It was her life or his, and he wasn't going to die today. He raised his gun trying to cover the slight tremor that was starting again in his hand. He aimed for the little girl's chest, took a deep breath and hoped the bullet would find its mark. Mr. Friday and the Organization wouldn't tolerate a bad shot. He pulled the trigger... CLICK.

It took a moment for Patrick to realize the gun was empty. Mr. Friday had only given him one bullet for the gun. He also didn't hear at first the scream coming from the little girl. "Mommy no! Mommy!" Instead of the little girl falling to her knees she sprinted at Patrick, with a malevolent look on her face.

Patrick stood still watching the girl run at him. He noticed her lips were curled back and sharp teeth were exposed. In one action he stepped towards her and swung his gun hand down hard. There was a sickening crunch as the butt of the pistol crashed into the young girls head. Patrick realized why the gun was empty. He was supposed to be attacked by the mother, not the girl. He looked down at her, she laid unconscious at his feet when he pulled her up and using both hands, wrapped them around her head and as quick as he could snapped her neck.

She partially fell to the floor, only being held up by a fist full of hair. He dragged the girl over to Mr. Friday and dropped the dead girl at his feet. Mr. Friday looked at the girl than back at Patrick.

"I told you to kill the girl. Not the mother."

"Girls dead." Patrick said matter-of-factly.

"I didn't give you permission to kill the mother."

Patrick, feeling numb inside took a step towards Mr. Friday not caring if the man had another gun tucked inside his jacket. "For the past eight days you have gone over how evil and dangerous vampires can be. Then you put me in-between a mother and her daughter.

"Not to forget that under extreme distress vampires can display extraordinary strength." Patrick locked eyes with Mr. Friday who met his gaze. "I would consider ordering the death of her daughter gave that woman extreme distress." Nodding to the dead vampire slouched in the chair.

"Besides that the woman had partially loosened the ropes around the wrist to the point that there was a little slack around her wrists. Not to mention the rickety, squeaky chair you put her in. If she wasn't able to pull free from the ropes, that chair could have broken if she became more violent."

Mr. Friday stood his ground and let Patrick talk. "I eliminated the greater threat first. It was the logical thing to do, and if I faced the same situation I would do it again. Remember, you chose me because I wasn't some mindless, grunt pussy." Patrick thought about how he missed the shot and the small tremor in his hand. He hoped Mr. Friday never noticed.

Mr. Friday looked at the dead woman and down at the dead child. "You will have a couple of days to get any affairs straightened out that you need. A car will come by your residence on Saturday morning. We will contact you beforehand with a time. You will not be able to see family or friends for at least 4 months before you will be granted some leave. Communication with them may be difficult so let them know—you wouldn't want them to worry.

"Of course I don't need to tell you any conversations about what you are really doing to anybody will result in your death and theirs."

"Yes sir." Patrick knew any danger he faced from Mr. Friday was no longer there.

"Good luck with your training Mr. Patrick," Mr. Friday said as he turned and walked out the room. Patrick stood briefly in the room with the two corpses. "Thank you sir," he said in the empty room. He stepped over the dead girl's body and left the room.

◊

When Patrick started studying vampires in great detail and learned their ways he was envious of their power. He envied their longer life, the increased strength—the power in killing a man for survival. To kill another man, for his blood, was something Patrick found magical.

But with this envy also brought hatred. He hated the fact these people had this power and he didn't. The only way he felt powerful was knowing he was trained to kill them when it was ordered.

During his four years on the job he was assigned to eliminate three vampires. Two of the vampires had web sites trying to stir up action. The sites were quickly shut down and the vampires were eliminated shortly after. The last made the mistake of attacking someone in a busy nightclub. The vampire tried to run but was tracked down after 2 days and a bullet was placed in his brain. He loved his job, but his partner was another story. In his mind, his partner Dazinski was a slob.

He shaved every other day, sometimes letting it go three days before any grooming took place. His clothes were sometimes wrinkled with his shirttail sticking out. In Patrick's mind Dazinski was weak. The two had been partnered for the last 6 months. Dazinski had been with this division for fourteen years and as far as he knew, never killed a vampire. Dazinski was a so-called communicator; he talked to them. He always said they are human, but with only an extra gene or two. "You can always catch more flies with honey then you can with vinegar," was his policy.

What an asshole. If Dazinski ever put his life in risk, Patrick would kill him. He did not need a partner. He did not want a partner.

"Let's come back later when everything is down," Dazinski said as he walked back to the car.

Patrick watched him with detestation. But his partner was right, they would come back later and look around.

10

"Here is the scoop on Alex Frey," said Lethgate. "Alex Frey, born June 7, 1964 in Montreal and moved overseas when he was three. His family lived in Austria for a number of years until his parents died in a car crash. Both parents were from wealthy families and were well off.

"No criminal record, no history of mental illness. He is not employed but with rich parents, I'm sure he inherited a nice little nest egg. He lives here in the city, 125 Harrington Street."

"Is that all we have?"

"For now. He has been a quiet well behaved boy, no record or complaints. Maybe he is just some nut."

"Where'd you get all the information on him? Do we have a file on him?"

"Mostly google," said Carl with a grin.

"Maybe he has been tipped off by someone on the department, too," said Ryerson. "When Dekins wrote the piece on the latest murders, it was buried in the back of the paper just a few paragraphs long. There was no indication of vampires."

"Well not too many guys know too much about the case and we have never said vampire outloud. Maybe we should leak some false info on the case and see if it reaches Frey. If it does, then we know it is a leak."

"I don't know what worries me more. Knowing there is a leak, or finding out there is no leak at all."

◊

The Vampire looked into the window. The woman was making herself a sandwich at the kitchen counter. She was middle aged, about 20 pounds overweight, with a cherub face. The woman may have been plain looking but there was nothing plain about what she did.

Cathy Ferguson, was one of the top designers in the city and was making a national name for herself. There had been rumors she would soon be having fashion shows in London, possibly Milan. She lived in a gorgeous two-floor house with a beautifully landscaped backyard. Cathy always wanted to live by the water, but instead of buying a house on the coast she decided to bring the water to her house. The backyard was raised about eight feet in the back to accommodate a small waterfall that filled a lily pool. The pool was lush with flowing plants that trickled down towards the house. She did not want the water to end in her backyard, so she managed to create an opening in the side of her house where the water would be pumped into her upstairs bedroom. The water flowed into a beautiful Roman fountain. The fountain was surrounded by an enclosed solid marble floor with a one millimeter gap between the floor and the marble wall.

The water would cascade down the wall into the living room below creating a quiet, flowing wall. The renovations cost her a mint so she had no choice but to keep on working hard. She needed the shows in London and Milan, and she needed them to be a hit. Her expenses were slowly overtaking her earnings. But that did not matter to her. She was living life the way she always wanted too. She was living on the edge, pushing herself, forcing herself to achieve. In a man's world she would do things her way. Growing up she had always wanted to be remembered, for people to know her name and to recognize her face, and she was well on her way.

The Vampire did not know her face. He knew she had money because of the house and the security system it had. But security systems didn't worry him. The system was now disarmed, he made sure of it. Regardless of it being on or off, he would not stay around.

He went to the back door and smoothly picked the lock. Living for as many years as he had, he learned to and try almost everything out of boredom.

Cathy was ready to cut her turkey on rye when she felt the draft. Confused, she looked behind her. She didn't leave any windows open, regardless of how hot it was, she would rather turn on the air conditioning. Her mouth dropped when she saw the back kitchen door open. She was not more than ten feet away and she didn't hear a thing. She knew she had locked the door. It was locked because she always went into the backyard through the sliding glass doors in the living room. She picked up the knife she was using to make her sandwich. It was a normal kitchen knife. She wished she had a long cutting knife or at least a steak knife. But the feeling of having some sort of weapon in her hands made her feel slightly better.

She went to the door and peeked out. All was dark and quiet. The motion sensor was one of the best money could buy, and the backyard was covered in darkness. But how had the door opened?

She felt a cold chill on the back of her neck and turned to see the man. She thought she was going to die on the spot because of the shock. He was not there a second ago, and it seemed as though he appeared out of thin air. The man was not looking at her, turning his back to her as if he were looking around the kitchen seemingly admiring the room.

"W-what..."

He spun around and took her down before she could finish he question, and almost before she could finish her breath. The Vampire drained her of most of her blood and left her to die. He looked down at the body and once again looked around the kitchen. He lowered his head and left the house.

11

The murder of Cathy Ferguson hit the local paper's front page and made numerous papers across the country. The stories talked about the young designer's rise to fame, and how she was murdered in her home, but it did not talk about the details of the death.

Ryerson was puzzled as to why the press wasn't jumping all over a vampire-like killer. Any good reporter should be able to put together A+B+C = serial killer. Every investigation had information leaked to the press no matter how much they tried to stop it. Alex Frey popped into his mind. Frey had told him that certain powers that be would cover up the information. So far it seemed to be true.

"Do you think we should pay him a visit," Lethgate asked almost reading Ryerson's mind.

"Yeah. Yeah, I think we should."

◊

Dazinski watched the police action from down the street. He and Patrick were tipped off about the murder and were on scene before the first 911 vehicles arrived. They were not in the house, they had no need to enter, knowing what was in there. Neither man would admit it but the case had turned dangerous. They had a vampire on a killing spree and now it was spreading to the kinds of people the press took an interest in. If it would have continued killing homeless people they could have easily kept it quiet.

The Organization had been keeping an eye on this vampire for years, tracking him across the continent. He was a killing machine, spreading terror wherever he went. The Organization managed to keep the killings out of the news and hold back the terror that would have erupted. The vampire had been on their kill list for a long time. But when they would close in, the Indian would disappear again.

Many hunters had been assigned to track down and kill the vampire, this time it was Dazinski and Patrick who were given the job. Inexperienced with this vampire, both had separately done their job flawlessly in previous hunts. Years ago Dazinski was in Denmark tracking a vampire that killed the mayor of a big city. Dazinski made sure he took care of the media first, sending conflicting reports, so the owners of the papers would suddenly tell their editors to scale down coverage. The resources they had behind them were immense. They knew how to keep a secret and how to keep people's noses out of their business.

Dazinski had been a hunter for nearly 15 years. He had been hunting vampires when his slick partner was fumbling to undo a bra in the backseat of his daddy's car. Dazinski knew Patrick did not like him. He didn't care. Patrick was a clean cut, by the book, army boy. He knew Patrick was a tough son of a bitch, or else he wouldn't be there. Dazinski would tolerate the disgusted looks regarding his appearance and the way Patrick would talk down to him, but in the back of his mind, if he was pushed too far he would rip out army boy's throat before he knew what hit him.

He was not an army man. He hated authority when he was a young man, and still had distaste for it today. When he was growing up he had seen the inside of a jail many times. Dazinski had a liking for Jack Daniels and would spend weekends drinking his way to Nirvana. He would get into bar fights, and when the cops came he would get into a fight with them.

He was on his way to a life behind bars until one night in a bar by the coast everything changed. It was a dump of a bar, with shady patrons and an even shadier owner. It was a Tuesday night, a few ugly men sitting around with a couple of ugly women trying to make a dollar or two.

Dazinski was at the end of the bar enjoying his JD not paying attention to the crowd. Two men walked into the bar and immediately did not fit in. First of all they looked like they had shaved in the past two days, and they did not have any cuts on their face. This was the type of bar where peanuts cost money and the fights were complementary.

The two sat a few stools away and ordered a drink from the bartender. He returned with two drinks for the men, keeping his head and eyes low. Eye contact usually meant confrontation.

The men did not bother Dazinski, he had Jack as his company. But the men caught his attention when they started talking.

"What a shit hole," one of the men whispered.

"All of them are trash," said the other.

Neither man had said it loudly: they were just talking between themselves. They had no intention of starting anything. But Dazinski did hear. And, Dazinski lived to hear little things like that—he didn't need much prodding when it came to fighting.

The one man put the beer glass up to his mouth when the bar stool smashed into the back of his head. His head whipped forward down onto the bar where the glass shattered against his mouth.

The man standing next to the victim stepped back and looked shocked. He looked at Dazinski and looked down at his friend. There was a gurgling sound coming from the man. He slowly lifted his head and there was a pool of blood on the bar. Dazinski was partly relieved because he was worried for a minute that he had killed the man. He wanted to fight and hurt people, but he didn't want to kill anybody. He fought for sport.

The bloodied man slowly lifted his face towards Dazinski. His eyes were unfocused but finally focused on Dazinski' eyes. Dazinski looked down at the man's mouth and his bottom lip was in two pieces hanging around his chin. His mouth was split back to nearly his ears. There was a huge amount of blood pouring from his mouth and nose but Dazinski could not help but see the teeth in the man's mouth. They looked like small razors, and the man without his lips, gave what appeared to be a small grin, sending a cold chill down Dazinski's back.

The man mumbled something to Dazinski. He may have sworn or said he was dead, it was hard to tell when there are no lips around the man's mouth to read.

One of the customers from down the bar came running in looking for a piece of the action as well. In this place it was always the more the merrier. The other man just arrived when the bloodied man's friend turned lightening quick, grabbed the man's neck and in one motion broke his neck and ripped out most of his throat.

Dazinski stepped back a step but still kept eye contact with the bloodied man. If Dazinski was drunk before he wasn't now. But Dazinski did not back down. He never believed in hit and run. He started it, he may not finish it, but he would not back down.

"Yo deb," the bloodied man said. Translation: 'you're dead.'

Dazinski just shrugged and looked at the bloodied man's friend. He too seemed to have a mouth full of sharp teeth.

The bloodied man took a step forward and walked into a quick palm strike right below his nose. The man's eyes teared over and Dazinski struck with a kick to the balls. When the man doubled over Dazinski reached over to the bar and grabbed a beer bottle bringing it down on the man's head.

Dazinski had no training in marital arts, he just fought a lot and he was good at it. When he fought he felt invincible. He may not always win, but he felt peace. He felt fluid when he moved, he reacted with his hands and feet before his brain would think. His speed and strength were extraordinary.

The bloodied man's friend was again stunned seeing his friend put down. He lunged at Dazinski with incredible speed. Dazinski saw the man coming up and brought his arm up quick. His attacker had forgotten about the broken bottleneck in his hand. His hand went straight up to the man's throat. The man's eyes bugged out when he figured out what had happened. Dazinski, knowing he was fighting for his life, twisted the bottle neck driving it deeper into the man's throat. He didn't want to kill, but he knew if he didn't he was dead.

As the man slouched in his arms Dazinski was tackled from the side being driven through one of the tables. The bloodied man had regained his composure and was flailing at Dazinski. The blows were like little jackhammers raining down on him. Dazinski swung at the man who was only about a foot away from him. He bent his arm knowing his fist would not have much momentum behind it and his elbow cracked off the man's jaw. Feeling the man's body weight shift Dazinski rolled over on top of the man and started swing haymakers. The man grabbed Dazinski by the shoulders and pulled him down to him. The bloodied man bit deep into Dazinski' shoulder. He felt a wave a dizziness and felt as if he was going to faint. In a panic he tried to get up but the man's grip was too strong and he felt his blood being literally sucked out of him.

He reached for the man's eyes and stuck his fingers deep in them gouging deeper and deeper. The man stopped biting when he began screaming. When Dazinski was released from the grip he leaned his weight forward continuing to dig into the man's head with his fingers.

When authorities showed up Dazinski was passed out with his fingers deep inside the dead man's eye sockets.

Dazinski woke up in his hospital room. There were no paintings on the wall, no flowers, no windows. Just his bed and an IV stand. He looked down and noticed he was handcuffed to the bed rails. He did not care, he felt like death warmed over. His shoulder was aching and he still felt light headed. He must have lost a lot of blood, he could barely lift his head to look around the room.

As his head dropped back down into the pillow he heard the door open. He could not see the person because he did not have the strength to lift his head again. Two men walked towards him. Both were in black suits, hair slicked back and they looked dead serious. Goddamned cops never seemed to smile.

"You'll have to talk to my lawyer, I have nothing to say."

"We are not police officers," said the first man. "The police will not be involved. We're in charge now."

"Oh, I'm sorry. You can fuck off, then talk to my lawyer."

"We are surprised you are still alive," said the second man. Neither man moved, they both stood like statues with their hands down by their sides looking down at Dazinski. "Most people do not live after encountering a vampire.

"What the fuck are you talking about?" Dazinski had a head rush. He had to talk lower.

"Vampires, Mr. Dazinski," Said the first man. "You picked a fight with not one vampire but two."

"Vampires are in most cases very passive. They generally don't attack. But when someone tries to drive a bar stool through their skull they have a tendency to get mad." There was not even a trace of a smile on the second man's face.

"But for a man to kill one vampire let alone two is astounding," said the first. "You may not believe it but I think you should. A few more seconds with him latched on you and you would have been dead. You're a very lucky man."

"What the fuck do you want from me? Am I under arrest?"

"You are not under arrest," said the second. "Like I said, the police are not involved in this. There will be no public record of what happened at that bar. We have an offer for you."

"We want you to join our organization," said the first. "You're a natural fighter. We can fine-tune your skills. We will clothe and feed you, give you a future."

"Future doing what?" His head was starting to pound and his shoulder was aching.

"Hunting vampires." The second man locked on to Dazinski' eyes. "You will be an asset. But you will have to clean up. No more drinking. The life you knew is now gone. It will be a new life for you."

"What if I say no?"

"You die," said the first matter-of-factly. "Our organization likes to keep vampires a secret. You are a dangerous man to us right now. If you say no you die.

If you say yes and try to get away you will die. If you ever tip another bottle of beer or booze to your lips again you will die. We want you with a clean mind and body."

Dazinski studied the men. They were not going to wait long for an answer and he could see they were dead serious. He could feel they were serious. He always trusted his gut feeling, and his gut feeling was telling him to say yes before they smothered him with a pillow or snapped his neck. He was in no condition to defend himself.

So it was in a plain white room where Dazinski said 'yes' to becoming a hunter. He later learned of the Organization. They had money from various governments but no one in these governments knew of them. They did not exist on any budget report. Only a handful knew of the Organization but its power was limitless. They had connections everywhere. They could buy any politician, judge or cop. And they could easily kill any politician, judge or cop.

In a short period of time they trained Dazinski to become an even more dangerous man. They trained him with weights and instructors but they also trained him with books. The Organization did not want stupid hunters. Knowledge was power. Dazinski trained vigorously at both. Because he knew if he didn't he would wind up dead. He didn't learn much about the Organization, but what he didn't know didn't hurt him. He now had a purpose and a feeling of true power. The power of his mind and the power to control his anger.

When he looked over at Patrick he knew the little shit would not understand if he told him. The Organization's power seemed unlimited, but Dazinski would still snap Patrick's neck if he got in his way. He could cover it up from the Organization. If not, he would do what he always did—he would face it like a man.

12

Standing in the knee high grass, the horizon seemed to go on forever. The colours of the sky turned from a light yellow to every colour imaginable. When the eye focused on one colour a new one would appear on its edge.

He slowly ran his hand along the tops of the grass and the Vampire turned his back to the sunset and headed back to the village.

He had joined the small tribe a few months earlier. They were a breakaway group from a much larger tribe. There were about 50 or 60 men and women with nearly 20 children under their care.

They welcomed the Vampire and took his arrival as a sign from the gods. The white man was moving into their lands and fear was high among the people. There were rumours of killing and slavery of tribes in the east. Their lands taken away and the white man's numbers seemed to grow like rats.

For years the people of the plains saw the white man travel across their land, both leery, yet curious of each other's existence. But now there were whispers of blood shed from horse backed men with powerful weapons killing for just the sake of killing.

But now the gods had sent the Vampire to stand against the white man. To drive them back to the shores and drowned them into the seas.

The Vampire had never seen a white man before. He had made his way from the wilderness of the north. Over the years he migrated along the coast, his own tribe long dead. He accepted invitations from where he was welcome and would stay for a few years before moving on.

An itch would start in his mind when he was in one place for too long and would eventually leave, unsure of his next destination.

This new tribe told him of the 'white devil' and their weapons. The Vampire couldn't understand the power of such weapons and why they were able to defeat so many tribes so easily. The small tribe didn't have any of the white man's weapons to fight back with, but they had heart and passion of their forefathers.

The Vampire didn't like their idea that the gods had sent him to rid of the white devil. He wouldn't say anything when the subject was brought up, and would spend a lot of his time away from the others. He was thinking of leaving one night soon, to find another tribe.

He lay in the tall grass for a long time reflecting on his life trying to remember some of the faces from his past. Some of the names remained but the faces had faded like a distant dream. That was his curse—outliving family and friends, losing them in person, than losing them in his mind, always feeling alone. He glanced up and saw the appearance of the first night stars, and started to make his way back.

By the time he got back to the tribe, all was quiet. A lone fire burned, guiding him, welcoming him. The idea of a warm fire made him hug himself in anticipation of the warmth. He sat down on one of the logs when a shadow to the left of him gave him a start.

"Sorry, didn't mean to startle you," said Aiyana. She was a plain looking young woman in the village. Behind her back, the villagers would refer to her as ugly, saying her eyes were too close together, her cheek bones too pronounced and too large of forehead. The Vampire didn't think she was ugly, but she certainly didn't have traditional beauty most men sought.

Embarrassed the Vampire shook his head. "No, my fault. I was so focused on the fire I never saw you there."

Aiyana smiled sheepishly. At times she felt invisible, at least by the men in her tribe.

"Why are you still up? It looks like everyone else has gone to sleep."

Aiyana looked into the flames, slowly chewing her bottom lip. "Sometimes I feel more comfortable on my own."

"Would you like me to leave?" The Vampire asked with no resentment. He knew how she felt.

"No, please. Stay."

They shared the silence, taking turns watching the stars then watching the hypnotic dance of the fire. Aiyana cleared her throat, which suddenly sounded way too loud. She looked over at the man and asked a question that was gnawing at her mind.

"What is it like to be a vampire?"

"How do you know I'm a vampire?"

Confused she replied, "Everyone says you are." She never once considered they were wrong.

"But did you know that I was one?"

"No. You look normal like anyone else." She looked at him closer, seeing the shadows move across his features. "Actually," she said looking closely at him, "Your face looks... smoother. Almost younger than when you arrived."

The Vampire smiled. "Everyone looks different by the light of a fire," he laughed to himself. "It's that or the fresh open air. But who told you I was a vampire?"

She was puzzled with his questioning. "It was Mapiya, she told us. You are a vampire right?"

"Yes, I'm a vampire. Just curious how she knew that." Aiyana only shrugged.

She picked up a small twig and tossed it into the fire. She shifted her weight on the log and curled her toes into the cool dirt. She looked over at the Vampire not sure if she should ask him. She let out a deep breath, once again the sound seemed too loud for the silence. She went ahead and asked, "What are you going to do about the white man?"

The Vampire didn't look her way, just continued to watch the fire. "Nothing."

"What! Why? Do you know what they are doing to our people?"

The Vampire didn't respond. He just watched the dancing ambers changing from red and black under the fire.

Aiyana looked down into her hands. "I met a woman who was taken from her tribe by the white man. She lived with them for five seasons before she barely escaped with her life. She was out for a walk when the men took her. They tied her up and raped her for days. She thought they were going to kill her when they travelled to a small village and she was sold. She became a slave to another white man. She was forced to clean and look after him. She said although the man never hit her, he continued with the raping."

Her gaze turned up to the stars while the Vampire sat silently looking into the fire.

"She said she met another of our kind living nearby. She was told stories of raiding parties of white devils attacking our people. Killing most, keeping the women to rape and any young men for slaves.

"The white man breeds like mice. They keep coming and coming. They have brought sickness to our people and have slaughtered thousands upon thousands. There is no way we can fight them off. There is no way to fight their numbers and feed ourselves at the same time."

Aiyana looked at the Vampire who was still looking down. "We need your help."

Finally the Vampire looked up and the woman was scared by the look in his eyes. The hairs on her arm and back of her neck stood on end.

"You have described nothing I haven't seen from our own people. I have seen slaves. I have seen women held against their will. I have seen peaceful tribes wiped out and peaceful tribes turn savage.

"There is no difference between us and the white man. He may have stronger weapons, but the anger and the violence in this heart—well; I have seen generations of that in our own people."

Aiyana was hoping for a passionate defense of her people, but inside the Vampire was only defeat. "Our people will die," she whispered in desperation.

"Eventually," he emphasized, "We all die."

He rose from the fire to find sleep he knew that would not come.

◊

A couple of weeks went by and the Vampire did a good job avoiding Aiyana. Her words had more of an effect on him then he'd like to admit. It was true he had seen horrible things done by his people. The white man was an invader—they were unknown and that made him nervous.

He went for a long walk enjoying the open skies and the relaxing wind. It was after a short time when he realized he was being followed. Aiyana. He stopped and yelled out and told her to come out and stop hiding.

With an embarrassed look she rose from the tall grass and made her way to him. He didn't say anything just stood, looking at her.

"I'm sorry for following you," she wanted to look away but she forced herself to keep eye contact. "And I'm sorry if I upset you when we were talking by the fire." She finally lowered her eyes. "I'm just scared. A lot of us are."

The Vampire didn't say anything; he just turned and started walking. Aiyana thought he was more upset than she thought.

"Are you coming? You followed me this far." She smiled and jogged to catch up to the Vampire.

As they walked they shared stories of their past, putting distance between them and the village. Aiyana was totally fascinated by the Vampire and was embarrassed when it was her time to share her past. But the Vampire seemed delighted in old stories of her grandparents. The young woman was a gifted story teller—a cherished role in many tribes. The Vampire could almost envision her elders with their lovable and sometime embarrassing ways.

Her voice was hypnotic. It raised and lowered with a talented ease, and she paused at the right moments, keeping suspense or enhancing the humor of her tale. He had a warm smile on his face, staring down at his feet while he walked, keeping all his attention to her voice. It took a number of steps when he realized she had stopped walking and talking. He looked over and saw her staring to the horizon. He could see the fear in her eyes.

The Vampire followed her gaze and saw the dark clouds. They were an angry black and they seemed to be coming alive.

"We should turn back," the Vampire suggested.

Aiyana joined him and held onto his arm tightly not allowing him to move. "Wait," was all she said.

A stronger wind blasted across the plains bringing a light rain. "We're going to get soaked standing here. What are you..." but the Vampire was shushed quiet and Aiyana had intense focus as she watched the sky around her.

"We wait. Find out where the winds will go. We can't go running off blindly." The Vampire had no idea what she was referring to, and then he saw the clouds circling. He had never seen such a thing in his countless years.

Hail started to slice down on them and the strengthening winds rocked him back on his heels. He wanted to run, but he trusted his instincts and the young girl even more. He stayed with Aiyana.

She grabbed him by the arm and started to direct him towards the circling clouds. "What are you doing?" he demanded, but she ignored her fears and adjusted her course slightly to the left. She picked up speed and he quickly followed. It seemed the wind started to pick up speed too.

The clouds started to descend from the sky and met the earth with a terrifying roar and unbelievable winds.

"Down!" Aiyana demanded.

They both flung themselves to the ground. The Vampire raised his head and saw the dark swirling winds spinning out of control. In all his years, he had never been this scared. The winds sounded like a wild animal and the dirt and long grass lashed around, stinging his face.

Aiyana pushed his head down. She shouted something to him but it was impossible to tell what. The ground under him shook and he grabbed fistfuls of grass as if the roots would be enough to anchor him to the ground.

The concept of time disappeared. He felt like he was holding on for minutes, when in reality it was a matter of seconds. He risked raising his head and through squinted eyes he saw the wind storm moving away from him. All of a sudden the swirling black storm turned sharply and headed in the direction the Vampire wanted to run.

He glanced at Aiyana and saw she was also tracking the storm. He surely would have been dead if it had not been for her leading him closer to the storm instead of away from it. The storm tore its way across the horizon before it just slowed and faded away back into the sky.

Both of them lay in the wet grass, looking up into the clearing sky trying to gather their composure. He turned his head and looked at Aiyana, "What was that!"

"A lover's reunion."

"What?" he asked confused.

"It is believed long ago, long before our people walked these lands, that the sky and the earth were madly in love. The gods jealous of their love separated the two, forcing them to see each other, but never being able to touch. It is said that even the gods could not hold back their love and occasionally the sky and the ground meet and make passionate love before separating again."

"Love making?" the Vampire chuckled. "Someone's going to pull a muscle making love like that."

Aiyana started to laugh and could not hide her blush. The Vampire studied her face. Many in the village called her ugly, but even with her hair matted from the rain, he never noticed what a beautiful smile she had. And her eyes accentuated her smile.

Without any thought to his actions he leaned in and kissed her. Her laugh ended with a startled gasp, and she nearly pulled away but hesitantly, she returned the kiss. He put his arms around her waist and pulled her closer. The kiss got deeper and their bodies pressed against each other. She couldn't hold in a gasp when she felt his excitement.

She quickly pulled away, never having felt that from a man before. In fact, this was her first real kiss. She sat up and tried to compose herself. "I'm sorry," the Vampire said, unsure of what else to say.

"No, no. It's just that... I just have never kissed or been with, well, a man." She said sheepishly.

She stood and slowly straightened out her dress and tried to clean up her hair that was wet, with dirt and grass in it. "I understand," said the Vampire. "You have a beautiful smile."

"No I don't. I know I'm ugly. Mean children and mean adults have told me that all my life."

"They're wrong," he said taking hold of her hand, making sure she couldn't pull it away from him. "You're a smart, charming woman. Vampires are well known for their good taste in women."

She looked up again at him with her wonderful smile and a blush starting in her cheeks again. "How did you know to run towards the storm, instead of away from it?" He decided he would attempt closeness with her at another time. He didn't want to rush it any further.

"I've always been good at reading storms. My grandfather was really good at it. He could tell at a single glance of the sky or by the feel of a breeze. Villagers would always joke, if you saw my grandfather running away from a cloud, run as fast as you could after him."

She smiled at the memory of him. "He could have seen the storm a mile away. I didn't notice until it was almost on top of us."

Not letting go of her hand he said, "I think you did terrific. You saved my life. I'm glad that I didn't get caught in the middle of their love making."

She smiled and looked deeply into the Vampire's eyes. She turned to the direction of the village, neither letting go of each other's hand.

Over the next few weeks the tribe was full of gossip. The Vampire and the ugly girl seemed to be in love. They could tell by the closeness when they sat beside each other. The way they would look at each other and quickly look away. And soon it became evident when they stopped hiding their feelings and started to hold hands and share kisses.

The women were sure the two were not intimate yet. They went their separate ways when they went to sleep, unless they snuck to see each other in the middle of the night and separated by morning. But of course they could have been making love during the time they would go for their walks.

The women in the tribe admitted Aiyana was looking better. She had her hair tied back instead of it just hanging loosely and out of control. There seemed to be colour in her face and a sparkle in her eyes. She was still ugly, they agreed, but not as much. They couldn't understand what the Vampire saw in her.

The tribe was up and about on what surely was going to be another hot day. The heat had been strong for the past number of days and it had been much too long without rain. The Vampire knew they needed a good storm to help break the heat and provide some relief to the land, he just hoped the sky and the earth would stay apart or take their love making elsewhere. He never wanted to experience that again.

He saw Aiyana and could not help but smile. He heard the tribe whispering and the hidden looks they received. It didn't matter. They were both happy, and in love. It was a feeling he had not experienced in a long time. Sure there were women in between, but that was only for sex, just for the release.

"We could go to the river again," she offered as an answer to the heat.

The village was located within a two minute walk to a river. The part of the river she was referring to was about 30 minutes up stream. There was a beautiful old tree beside the river bank and after swimming and playing in the water, they would lie under the tree and watch the clouds drift by above them and get lost in each other's touch.

"That sounds great," the Vampire replied with a smile. He put his hand on her shoulder ignoring all the eyes suddenly watching them. "Maybe after we can just keep walking and see what life has in store for us." It was not a question.

She looked up at him and smiled. "Let's just take it a day at a time, okay?" She leaned in and kissed him on the lips. She ran a hand down the side of his face. She swore he had a couple of wrinkles there when she first saw him, but his skin was smooth and beautiful. She heard a small gasp from some of the female elders,probably reaction to their open affections, but she also heard something she didn't expect—a scream.

The Vampire couldn't find the source of the scream and he looked around for something that may have been wrong. He couldn't see anything and he looked back at Aiyana. She was silently mouthing something. Her eyes wide with fear, her mouth moving again, this time he was able to hear her warning. "White devils."

He turned around and saw about 50 white faced riders on horseback racing towards them on the other side of the river.

The riders rode across the river, the water splashing all around them in a misty aura, clutching their guns and clubs. They yipped and yelled as they bore down on the village. The Vampire felt the ground shake under his feet from the stampeding horses, yet he still looked up in the sky looking for a storm remembering the ground shaking from the sky and earth meeting.

He was frozen in place even when the guns started. He only moved when he saw a club come crashing down on a skull of a man in front of him. He started running away, looking around for Aiyana, she was nowhere to be seen. Screams from his people were mixed in from the yips and laughter of the white devils.

Out of the corner of his eye he saw a gigantic figure which was a charging horse. He slowed, but the horse still made contact with the Vampire sending him hard to the ground, the breath knocked out of him. He heard laughter and turned to see a white man standing over an old woman. She was hurt, blood running from the corners of her mouth. The man pulled out a knife from his belt and pulled the woman's hair back hard. He slid the knife across the front of her head from ear to ear.

She let out a desperate cry but all the Vampire could hear was the tearing, wet sound of her scalp being torn off her head. The white devil stood and hooked the scalp into his waist—he would receive a health bounty for every scalp he returned with.

The Vampire let out a cry and vomited to his side. He closed his eyes and prayed for the image of the old woman to leave his head, but the sight and sound of her was burned in his mind. He saw the man walking towards him with evil intentions in his eyes.

The Vampire tried to crawl away but the man's knee came down hard into his spine knocking out the breath he just gathered. The man grabbed a handful of hair and yanked back hard, only the sound of the knife cutting into his flesh remained.

But the fear left his body. He didn't notice the vomit taste in his mouth or the wet from his urine on his clothes. Like an out of body experience, he felt the man on his back being bucked off. The Vampire moved with speed and intensity he had never experienced before, pounced on the man. He wasn't even aware of the white devil underneath him until he tasted the blood from his torn out throat.

He felt rage and he felt power. He could feel himself running, but unsure of his intentions. He leapt through the air and pulled a rider down from his mount. Again the Vampire tore into the man, and bolted towards another rider.

The laughing and yipping from the riders suddenly quieted. One of the lead riders looked around and saw at least 10 of his fellow riders dead on the ground. He turned in his saddle ignoring the running and screaming Indians, but to see one man. He was an Indian, but he was covered in blood. His clothing was a dark red, but it was the blood around the man's mouth that drew his attention.

The Indian was clutching a club he had picked up off the ground and was headed his way. One of the men in the raiding party lunged at the Indian, but he disappeared in a mist of blood followed by a sickening crack. The speed of the club connecting with the man's skull was ungodly. The man was dead before he hit the earth, a giant hole now on the side of his head.

He grabbed the reins of his horse, ready to bolt but before he could react the Indian ran with the speed of a wild animal and tackled him off the horse. He had no time to react when he felt his hair pulled back and part of his throat being torn out. He would not be cashing in the four scalps in his waist band.

The Vampire looked around and saw the attackers fleeing back across the river. They still had strong numbers and only needed to attack him in mass, but fear had gripped them and he doubted they would ever return.

As the feeling of power began to ebb he noticed it was just not the attackers who looked at him with fear. The few villagers that were around him looked with fear, even though they knew what he was, and that he was a friend.

As he walked around the village he saw death and despair all around him. Many were crying loudly trying to come to grips with what happened and holding dead loved ones.

The Vampire looked to his left and saw a mother crying over her baby. Its little chest caved in the result of a horse hoof crushing it.

He closed his eyes tight, knowing the image of the dead baby will return, likely in his nightmares. In a panic he remembered Aiyana. He had not seen her since before the attack, which now seemed like years ago. In a panic he started to run looking down at the corpses, praying she had run away from the village and was still hiding.

He felt tears streaming down his face. It was only minutes ago he felt a strength and a power he had never experienced before, but now he felt weak and helpless. It was through his tears where he saw a familiar face. It was Mapiya, the woman who first recognized him as a vampire. She was cradling a loved one in her arms. When Mapiya saw the Vampire, she didn't have a look of fear on her face when she saw the blood covering his face and clothes. Instead she had a look of sadness, and sorrow. The person she was holding was covered in blood. He had no idea who it was, but was able to tell it was a woman and she had been brutishly scalped.

He started to walk away, trying to come to grips with the slaughter around him when he stopped. He looked back at Mapiya and towards the woman in her arms. Bile and fear rose in his stomach—he held it down but could not hold back the tears. The woman covered in blood was Aiyana.

The Vampire dropped to his knees and his hands hesitated before her. There was so much blood, he didn't want to touch her afraid he would touch a wound and bring her further pain. He let out a loud sob and rocked back and forth crying. He couldn't tell if she was dead or not, even if she was alive it would be only a matter of days before her skull became infected and she'd die from fever.

He stared at her unsure of how to help her when a pair of bright white eyes opened behind the blood mask she was wearing. Her eyes locked onto his.

Her bottom lip was quivering; he leaned in closer to hear what she had to say. She grabbed his hands and squeezed hard. Her eyes frightened the Vampire, than she spoke, "Kill them!" she said, her voice barely under a scream. "Kill each and every one of those white devils! Kill them, bring them pain. I told you! I warned you! Kill the white devils."

Her eyes rolled back into her head and she slumped back dead into Mapiya's arms. Mapiya screamed into the sky and started to sob, stroking Aiyana's arm.

She couldn't be dead. She had only passed out, the Vampire tried to convince himself. There was so much blood, but he looked down and noticed a large puddle of blood on the ground. As he stepped to his side he saw a small black hole in the beaded buffalo skin dress she wore, with blood slowly trickling out.

The Vampire just wanted to drop by her side and die beside her. He felt dead inside not knowing if he wanted to go on. But another big sob and warbled scream from Mapiya woke him from his trance. He had to back away. Each step was torture, becoming further and further away from the woman he loved, but he had to leave now or he never would.

The Vampire looked down at his hands, covered in blood from Aiyana's hands. He brought his fingers up to his face and smeared her blood under his eyes mixing with the blood already splattered there.

He rose and started to leave the village. He left the blood, and the cries of help behind him. He would now travel to the east and fulfil Aiyana's final words. "Kill the white devils." He walked out of the village leaving the woman who first discovered him being a vampire holding the body of the woman who taught him how to love again, and who he wanted to love every day of his life.

13

Lethgate and Ryerson pulled up to Frey's apartment building. Both were familiar with the building. It was a low-income apartment, and the police had been called to it for many different reasons. The front lobby had chipped tile flooring with 20-year-old wallpaper barely holding onto its colours.

For someone who came from wealthy parents Mr. Frey picked a dumpy apartment building to live in. Maybe he liked the race track too much, and blew his inheritance on trying to nail a trifecta.

Ryerson and Lethgate chose to take the stairs. The elevators in these old buildings were not the most reliable and neither felt like being trapped. The stair well was damp and dank with the smell of old urine. There was paint that was flaking off the walls in huge patches and holes scattered along it made by feet, fists and probably a couple of skulls. Fortunately, Frey lived on the third floor so they did not have to endure the smell for very long.

The corridor to the third floor was lined with holes in the walls made by angry people. The light flickered above their head giving a strange strobe effect. It felt as if the walls were slanted slightly and the hall seemed to be moving because of the light. Ryerson closed his eyes feeling nauseous. A few feet past the flickering light the hall regained its stability again.

They stopped in front of room 321 and knocked. They heard shuffling inside the room followed by a quick cough and a clearing of a throat. Opening the door was a tall, lanky man. He stood around six foot five, with long, dark curly hair and slightly bad posture. Frey was dressed in a pair of old well-worn track pants, which had rips in both knees and a faded plain blue t-shirt.

"Detectives?"

"Yes," said Ryerson. "This is detective Lethgate and I am detective Ryerson. Nice to match the voice with a face, Mr. Frey."

"Please call me Alex. Come on in."

The one bedroom apartment was not what Lethgate expected. He expected a dark apartment with candles shaped as skulls, with crucifixes on every wall, garlic hanging in door frames and a large pentagram on the living room floor. But it appeared to be a typical one-bedroom apartment. The desk in the corner had a few books stacked on it with notes neatly piled beside them. The furniture consisted of an old leather couch and love seat, both well worn.

The room was painted an off white with a yellow and blue border along the top of the walls. There was an empty vase in the middle of the table, with two coffee table books on either side. Alex kept his apartment spotless, the only area which seemed used was the computer table.

"Would either of you like a drink?"

"No I don't think so," said Ryerson. "We would like you to look at some of the pictures from the scenes."

Alex looked back and forth from Ryerson to Lethgate. His right eye was partly squinted studying the two detectives.

"Okay." He said not looking away from them.

Lethgate passed a manila envelope over to Alex.

He slowly started to loosen the string from the back of the envelope. "Please sit down, gentlemen."

"No thanks," said Ryerson.

Alex pulled the pictures out while still looking at the men. He looked down at the pictures in his hands. The first showed a man lying in a weeded area covered in blood with parts of his throat and face torn away. Alex looked at the pictures quickly flipping through them. He neatly organized the pictures and placed them back into the envelope and did up the string on the back. He handed the envelope back to Lethgate.

Lethgate slowly reached out and took the pictures back. Frey was in such a hurry to help them on the phone, now he sped through the pictures and seemed slightly off in behaviour.

"I'm afraid I can't help you gentlemen. I think this might be out of my expertise."

"Did you want to study the pictures a little longer?" asked Lethgate.

"No I don't think that is necessary. I'm sorry gentlemen."

Alex started to walk to the door and opened it, waiting.

Ryerson and Lethgate looked at one another and started walking towards the door.

"Sorry to waste your time Mr. Frey," said Ryerson.

"I'm sorry, too."

Ryerson gave him a little look and walked out into the hall. Alex slowly shut the door behind the detectives. Ryerson looked down the hall towards the flickering lights. There was something wrong with Frey. He was glad to get out of the apartment. He didn't like the way Alex looked at him. It was no loss though, he couldn't imagine the reaction if word got out a couple of detectives were using the services of a self-proclaimed vampire expert. They were better off without him.

Ryerson and Lethgate walked down the psychedelic hall back to their car.

14

When Carl arrived home he went downstairs into his sanctuary. His wife was already in bed and it was now his time. His basement was his pride and joy. He enjoyed showing it off to friends, but he enjoyed it more when he was alone.

Carl had finished the basement over the years and had taken a lot of time fine tuning it. He loved wood. He had hardwood floors with wooden walls and ceiling. The price of the material did not matter to him. He bought a bit at a time and did what he could. It took three years to finish doing the floors and walls. When he made it to detective he bought a pool table. It was a gift to himself. He also made a bar which he kept in the corner and installed a mini fridge and sink, and made sure there was room under the bar for a keg. Draft beer always tasted better.

The rest of the house was Dawn's. She did whatever she liked, and had excellent taste. His room was the basement. She let him have a place to get away and left him to decorate it to his taste, as long as she got to do the rest of the house. Tonight he was sipping on a bottle of Pinot Noir from Del-Gatto Estates.

He was standing around his pool table just hitting balls, trying to pocket shots at tough angles, going for more difficult shots passing over easy ones. He shot any ball mindlessly shooting and thinking.

Growing up, Carl wished it could have been easier. He was better off than a lot of other children, with both his parents having good paying jobs, but being the only black child in a white suburban community came with its own problems. Children can be cruel and he got into many fights when he was young.

He had heard the word "nigger" plenty of times from the children in his neighbourhood and he fought nearly every one of them because of it. He would go up to his room lay on his bed and cry. He just wanted to be like the other kids, he didn't want to fight anymore, but he didn't want to be weak.

It was finally his dad who sat down with him after coming home with another bloody lip.

"Why do you keep fighting?" his father asked with a calm voice.

"They call me 'nigger baby'," Carl said with a tear running down his face.

"Son," his father put an arm around the boy. "You can't fight everyone that calls you a name. I know some names hurt, but some day you are going to be a man. And the true measure of a man is not being strong or being able to beat someone up, it's his character. If you can go through this world and ignore the names ignorant people call you, you take the power out of those words by ignoring them. There may be times when you will have to fight, just make sure it's worth fighting for."

His father was his hero. It was Carl's proudest day when his father witnessed him being sworn in as a police officer. His father was in a wheelchair, hooked up to numerous IVs. Cancer was eating away inside him, and he told everyone he would be at the ceremony even if he had to crawl there.

It was a sad sight, seeing a man who appeared to be a giant when Carl was a child, now looking weak and withered. After the ceremony Carl gave his dad a kiss on the cheek and placed his uniform hat on his father's head. His father's face brightened and for the first time in ages, he looked like the man he knew. But the cancer was throughout his body and only a week later he died.

Everyday Carl tried to lead his life like his father would have wanted him to. As he shot the balls around the pool table he knew his father would have been proud of him. He was honest and true to the people around him, and more importantly true to himself.

As he racked the balls up, his mind drifted back to the case. It was impossible not to, this was not an ordinary case. It was amazing to him how he could be pulled into believing a myth like vampires. When the first couple of deaths happened, he and Ryerson were stumped. How could there be so much blood loss without the ground being saturated in it? And the bodies had not been moved. They were not there for a long period of time because of the stage of rigor mortis they were in.

Carl was a sensible man. Sitting in his basement he found it unbelievable they actually went to visit a so-called vampire expert. The talk about vampires came out as a joke but grew. And now it seemed their investigation was being led by it. How could two professional detectives seriously consider a vampire out in the city killing people? There was an answer there, Carl just couldn't see it.

He was also disturbed by Alex Frey. He was so anxious on the phone to help them but in person he could not usher them out quick enough. Years of following his gut instincts told him Frey knew something, and was not telling them. Right now it felt as if he was playing with them. He knew a lot more about the case than he should, and now he was playing some sort of game with them.

He finished his wine and stood by the table. Things were swirling in his head and it wasn't the wine. They had no momentum with this case. They seemed only to be cleaning up after the killer. He and Frank worked so well together but Carl was at a loss, and he wasn't sure if Frank knew what to do next.

He looked down at the pool table and the scattering of balls. He took a deep sigh and wandered upstairs to bed. Tomorrow was another day.

◊

Frank laid in bed thinking. Did they do the right thing with Alex Frey? They just couldn't jump right in with it. Both he and Lethgate had their doubts about Frey. Why did they bother even going to see the man? Frank thought about it and figured it beat sitting at their desks twiddling their thumbs.

But they had video of the killer, which was being cleaned up so they could get a clear shot of the man. They had fingerprints and hair samples in addition to a description. They were finally starting to roll, but Frank had a feeling of tension and anxiety around the case. Even with all the new evidence Frank felt the case was doomed. Something did not sit well with him. He felt it and he was sure Lethgate felt it, yet neither would ever admit it. Something big was happening and they were stuck in the middle of it with blinders on.

Frank listened to the soft breathing of Jill beside him. He rolled over hoping to find sleep.

◊

The police officer made his way through the station. No one would recognize him because he did not work there, but at 3 a.m. the place was busy with bookings. People only looked at the uniform and not the face. If he was stopped he had a story ready, and if things got too suspicious he would jab the person with a small needle causing instant cardiac arrest. When people started gathering to help he would slide away. He did not expect any problems tonight.

He had never been in the station before but he knew by heart the blue prints and video surveillance of the building. The front of the station had the greeting area that had Plexiglas sealing it from the counter to the ceiling, with gaps where officers could talk to members of the public without it appearing too cold. The booking area was located at the back of the station with a private exit. The suspect would be ID'd there, photographed, and taken to the holding cells which were downstairs. In the middle of the floor were countless cubicles with offices surrounding them.

He worked his way downstairs towards the evidence room. He met a couple of officers coming up the stairs but he just whistled as if he belonged and nodded at them. They returned the nod and went on their way. At the bottom of the stairs was a bulletproof Plexiglas wall, which held a small office behind it. The night officer would sign officers in and out to the holding cells and to the evidence storage rooms. The officer went up to the speaker, which was used to talk to the night officer. The man pushed the button but only nodded at the night officer. The night officer pushed the button and buzzed open the door which led to the evidence rooms.

The man walked down the hall noticing all the cameras. He had no worries about them because at the moment all video images were being erased. With computer surveillance, all it took was a world class hacker to break into the system and disable it for a short time. The hacker would also get into the main police terminal and coroner's office and destroy any information on the vampire case.

The man walked towards the evidence rooms where the toughest part of the job was coming. When he came around the corner there was the evidence clerk alone. He didn't worry about anyone following unexpectedly because the night officer was not going to let anyone past until the man was finished. He would come up with some sort of excuse. A big payoff to the night officer allowed entrance and exit of the area with no distractions. The night officer didn't have to do anything else. It was easy to bribe people with the right amount of money held under their nose. The night officer made sure it was under the provision that no one was hurt. The intruder agreed, knowing the night officer would be dead the next day of an apparent heart attack or a car accident—whatever the Organization decides. A dead man tells no tales.

The evidence clerk looked at the officer and did not recognize him. The officer pulled out what looked like his flashlight off his belt and shined it in the clerks face. The light was a pulsing beam, which rendered him temporarily blind. Before the clerk could do anything the officer plunged a needle into his neck knocking the man out.

The officer entered the code into the control pad to enter the room. It of course worked. He knew exactly where to go in the room. He put the boxes in the middle of the room and poured powder over and inside of them. He then poured a small vial of liquid over the powder. In a quick puff of white smoke, an intense white flame came to life. It quickly ate through the box destroying the hair and fingerprint samples and any pictures collected at the scene. The fire had little smell and created little smoke but had extreme heat which could melt the strongest of metals. The heat detectors would have picked up on it, but they were disabled along with the security footage. The man made sure nothing usable was left. In a matter of minutes all hard evidence was gone. The man went to one of the shelves and placed a small device behind an evidence box. In thirty minutes it would go off sending a huge fireball through the room destroying everything.

He left the room and placed another syringe in the clerk's neck, killing him. He did not want to kill him right away just incase the files were moved and he needed to find them again. The officer walked back down the hall towards the night officer and was buzzed through again. He climbed up the stairs and left the building. He slid into the car where he was driven to the airport. He was jetted off across the ocean, never to be seen again.

15

When the Vampire arrived in Europe he was sickened by the state of the land. He had made his way over in one of the merchant ships. As an Indian passenger he was kept in the bowels of the ship with the other poor souls traveling over.

During the first two days of the voyage he killed five people, three passengers and two of the crew. Talk of a cursed voyage quickly spread.

The crew immediately searched for wild animals who may have caused the wounds to the necks of the dead. The only animal they suspected was the Captain's dog. The Captain assured the crew the dog didn't do the killing. After the sixth victim they were anxious to get rid of the animal.

The Captain's dog was his pride and joy. It was a large breed poodle, but the Captain always told people not to be fooled by appearances that it was a hell of a hunting dog. The dog would dig into animal burrows as big as ground hogs and tear them apart. Many times the dog would trot home from a hunt alongside the Captain with blood stains around his muzzle and down his chest.

The crew knew of these stories, and many figured the dog had gotten the taste of blood in its system and wouldn't think twice about killing a man. The crew also hated the dog. It seemed to know the importance of its owner, and it thought it had the same standing as his master. It would come up on deck and take a shit right in front of the men cleaning the deck. It almost appeared to have a smile on its face when it did it. When it was finished its business it would walk a few steps and sit there watching the men, waiting for them to clean its mess. When the mess was cleaned up with a lot of cursing under the men's breath, the dog would go back to the spot sniff around and lift his leg, pissing on the now clean deck then prance away with its head held high.

The Captain told his officers the dog was locked in his room and would only come out when supervised by himself personally. The crew was told, but they still muttered under their breath about a curse and the dog was the cause.

That night the Vampire took victim number seven and made the attack very gruesome. He ripped out both sides of the throat and left the body partially hidden. Later that night the body was found, and there was a huge commotion on board. Matters only got more severe the next day.

Sometime during the day while the Captain was busy, somebody broke into his quarters, bludgeoned the dog to death, rolled it into a blanket and threw it overboard. When the Captain came back to his room and saw a small puddle of blood with no dog—he went out of control.

He ordered a full investigation and lined up three members of the crew. The passengers were called up to witness the event. The Vampire squinted at the light and looked around. There were no rich passengers on this ship just poor relics like himself who scraped up enough savings to make the voyage.

"Someone has broken into my quarters and has taken my dog. I demand the man who did it steps forward." The Captain eyed each member of the crew. No word was muttered. "Tie them!"

The three men that stood by themselves with scared expressions were tied to the rails of the ship. The officers took out three cat-of-nine-tails and ripped the men's shirts off their backs. "I want to know who did this! Every man on this ship will be flogged until I find out who did this!"

When there was no response from the crew, the Captain nodded and the whipping began. The Vampire watched the whipping with disgust. To rip open a man's back, just because of a dog. The white man was a brutal one.

Most of the passengers turned their heads, and could not watch. Many were afraid they would get whipped, but the warning only went out to the crew. The Captain knew it was one of his men who did it.

The Vampire didn't kill anyone for the rest of the voyage, and the floggings continued. Shortly before they arrived at port, the Captain went missing, obviously overboard. Some of the men reported they saw him staggering drunk on the deck the previous night crying over his dog. It was assumed he fell overboard in his drunken state. Some of the officers believed it was murder. When the Vampire and the rest of the passengers departed the ship the crew was lined up on deck, with a full investigation on the voyage to take place. Six men would hang on suspicion of murdering the Captain.

The Vampire hated London. There was a dirty smell to the city, and when he walked down the cobblestone roads he saw the bricks in the buildings were stained black from the soot that the chimneys pumped into the air. Some days he could hardly breathe when the fog rolled in. It almost had an eerie yellow, greenish appearance to it. He killed three people and left town, never wanting to see the filth-ridden city again.

He made his way over to the continent and hated going into the major cities. The smell and filth in parts of the city made him light headed and sick. It was a beautiful land, but the cities were like a rotten tumor. Each night he would kill. Every time he looked around and saw the city that surrounded him, he imagined his own land being turned into this filth. His own people were being destroyed so this could be built.

He would take one or two victims a day, but when he arrived in Spain he let his vengeance out. The Spaniards were well-hated by his people. They came to the new land and showed no mercy. They gave blankets riddled with disease, disease that was common to

Europeans such a small pox, but were new and devastating to natives, killing entire tribes—genocide.

The Vampire killed at random, each kill an act of revenge. At night he would cry himself to sleep. He lay under the stars looking up, wishing his life were different. He didn't want to be a vengeance warrior, he didn't ask for this, but he felt it was his duty. The killings didn't bring peace to him, they added to the heaviness of his heart. But he killed for the spirits of his fallen kin, the land he loved and for Aiyana. For weeks he ravaged Spanish villages and cities. The people spoke of evil walking the land and that the devil had come for their souls.

The days felt like they caught up to the Vampire. He was feeling tired, in need of a few quiet days were he could just sit down, relax and catch up on his sleep. But he knew he had to keep walking and put distance between him and anyone who might be following him.

He knew he was being followed. He had left a path of blood and tears behind him, and people wanted him dead. That day may come, but they won't find him sitting down relaxing when they do. He will be on the move, and they will have plenty more bodies to climb over before they reach him.

But for this day, he allowed himself to slow down just a bit. Not just to rest his body, but it was a beautiful day. Surrounding him were rolling hills and fields with beautiful shady trees lining the dirt road, it helped relax his mind. There were birds hopping in the tree tops singing to each other and the steady hum of insects in the grass.

Amazingly he didn't see the man until he was about 20 feet from him. The man was lying under a tree with his head resting on his traveling bag, and his hat lowered down over his face. The Vampire stopped in his tracks and watched the man. He could hear a slight snoring coming from him.

But it seemed just as the Vampire stopped to watch, the man started to stir and he quickly lifted his hat off his face and looked around with a groggy look on his face. He looked towards the Vampire, blinking a couple of times, then quickly made his way to his feet, brushing any leaves or dirt off of his clothes and wiped a hand across his mouth. Probably wiping the drool off his mouth, thought the Vampire.

"My friend, my friend! So nice to meet you sir!" The man approached him. He had a bright purple dress jacket on, which appeared to be one or two sizes too big. He had a dirty hat on his head and dirty shoes on his feet. For as long as the Vampire had been walking, this man had been walking longer by appearances.

The man took his well-worn hat off and did a deep bow in front on the Vampire. "My friend, I am Bo. I happen to be one of the greatest entertainers to have ever graced these, or any other parts." Bo threw his hat up in the air and Bo, with eyes up and feet dancing underneath him, moved a couple of inches each way before the hat landed perfectly on top of his head. Bo celebrated the feat with another exaggerated bow and a bright smile on his face.

"For years I have entertained thousands and I want to entertain you now! During the day I have entertained fathers and children while at night I entertain the mothers!" Bo gave a mischievous smile. "I have performed for countless kings and princes and I have bedded countless queens and princesses. My cock is practically royalty!" He tipped the hat off his head and it rolled down to his hand, and with a flick of his wrists, it flipped in the air and landed neatly on top of his head.

"My hand is faster than the eye," said Bo as his hand shot up his sleeve and it quickly came out holding a gold coin. The Vampire doubted it was real gold, considering the condition of the man's clothes. With his hand held out, the gold coin danced from knuckle to knuckle, faster and faster across the back of his hands. "The only thing quicker than my hands is my tongue, just ask the ladies." He gave another shrewd smile.

He clapped his hands together loudly and the coin was gone. For a moment the birds in the trees were silent, startled by the sudden noise, but quickly continued in their happy, musical gossip. The insects in the grass never ceased their buzzing.

Bo's hands quickly disappeared up his sleeve again and in a shot came out a long colourful handkerchief. It was no wonder the man's jacket was a couple of sizes too big. Most of the man's act was probably up his sleeve.

"My friend, I admit I am not a rich man. I kindly accept the generosity of strangers." The handkerchief floated from hand to hand. He would scrunch it up in one fist, open his hand and it would be empty, for it to only appear back in the other hand. "If you have any spare coins, or perhaps some food or some wine or ale?"

He twirled the handkerchief in his left hand spinning it lazily while he politely begged. The Vampire doubted this man performed for a living, yet alone to rulers. He was more likely a con man or a pick pocket. Neither of which concerned the Vampire because he didn't have any money to be stolen or conned away from him.

"I'll be even happy to call you friend," Bo said as the handkerchief continues to spin in his left hand.

The Vampire started to raise his hands to gesture he had nothing when the smile on Bo's face left. The Vampire had no time to react when the handkerchief was wrapped and twisted around his right wrist. In a flash he was pulled off balance and from Bo's right sleeve a sharp knife came out, looking for its target.

Instead of pulling back the Vampire moved in the direction of where he was being pulled, moving himself out of the way of the knife. Bo gave a small growl, obviously upset that he had missed his target.

With a twist of the wrist the Vampire got a good grip on the handkerchief so he could no longer be pulled off balance. Bo might have thought he had an advantage of holding a weapon, but the Vampire had experience. In many of the tribes he was in, they would play a game, tying two men's wrists together with the purpose of being the first to take the other person to the ground.

He didn't want to take his attacker to the ground—not with a knife in his hands. Bo the entertainer was fast, but he could handle that. His advantage of surprise was over. Weapon or not, the Vampire was in control.

With the next thrust of Bo's knife, the Vampire pulled the handkerchief hard, pulling the man off balance slightly. That was all he needed. The Vampire kicked out and connected to the front of Bo's knee, hyperextending it. Before the gasp came from the attacker's mouth, the vampire's free hand grabbed the knife hand, twisted and shoved the hand back towards Bo, blade first. The knife entered just above his heart.

In a fluid motion the Vampire kept hold of his wrist and raised his elbow above the man's head and spun behind him. Bo was now in the position of hugging himself with one hand holding a knife, plunged into his chest; while the other was pulled across his body, still attached to the Vampire, by the handkerchief.

The Vampire didn't wait for him to bleed out, as he bit into his neck, and tore the side of his throat open. As Bo dropped, the Vampire stood over top, the only one still holding the colourful handkerchief. The Vampire watched as blood darkened the bright purple coat the man wore.

He let the handkerchief drop as he continued down the road, with the birds hopping and singing in the trees, while the insects buzzed in the grass.

Over the next couple of days the Vampire laid low, and didn't kill. He was obviously being watched, and if there were any more, they wouldn't be far behind. He left Spain, *leaving fear and panic behind him. He wasn't sure where to go next; he just started walking wherever his feet would take him.*

They eventually led him to Italy, where he planned to start killing again. He found a beautiful place called Lake Como and sat by the hillside, looking over the beautiful blue waters with hills rolling in the background.

He was startled when he heard a voice behind him speak up.

"You are in danger my friend," the man said in a soft voice.

The man was plump and short, with stocky arms and legs. Too many fights flattened his nose by the looks of it, and there was a scar below his hairline. His eyes were bright, a beautiful blue which seemed wrong on the ugly little man, but his eyes were that of a rare crystal.

"What are you talking about?" the Vampire asked wary of him.

"When there is a lot of killing, and you my friend have been doing a lot of killing, they come and ask us."

"Who is us?"

The man looked down at the lake and took a deep breath clearly enjoying the fresh air around him. "There is a group of men whose job it is to police us vampires. They hunt and kill us when we kill too much, making too much of a mess. They don't have a problem with a victim here and there, but they do have a problem when we kill four or five a night like you were doing.

"When they suspect a vampire, they start asking a lot of questions. No one knows of you, so you are new to them. But trust me, by now they know a lot more. They have probably tracked where you have been, and know the exact route of where you came from."

"You're a vampire?" the ancient Vampire exclaimed.

"You truly didn't know I was a vampire?" The stranger asked with surprise. "Most of us can recognize each other immediately. And considering you are an ancient vampire..."

The Vampire tried to shrug it off.

"At first I thought you were ignoring me as I approached you. Did you even hear me coming up behind you?" He asked slightly squinting his eyes?

The ancient Vampire was ashamed to admit he didn't hear the other vampire. He was so immersed in the beauty of the lake and mountains around him; he kind of lost himself in the moment. The thought about not recognizing another vampire also troubled him. How many times in his life had he met one of his own, and just walked by them? He felt a queasiness in his stomach and his mind seemed to be racing at the idea.

"Who are these men?" the Vampire asked quickly changing the topic, remembering Bo the entertainer.

The stranger looked into the ancient's eyes. He was shocked to find this vampire was mentally weak. He wanted to press the issue about not being able to recognize another vampire, or that he was so easily crept up on. The one thing this vampire knew was you do not anger an ancient. This ancient could more than likely tear his throat out before he knew it even happened. He decided not to press his luck.

"They don't have a name, but that is not your worry. Your worry is that they are after you, especially if you have killed one of their own. My point is that you stick out like a sore thumb around here. We do not have too many Indians walking around these parts." The stranger said with a grin. "My advice to you is to go back home where you can blend in better. Over here it will only be a matter of time. These people have many friends and a lot of power. They will find you."

"I am not afraid of them. Whoever they send I will kill."

The man just nodded. He took another long look over the lake and took another deep refreshing breath. He didn't try to convince the Indian. The Indian had already made up his mind and would probably die because of his stubbornness. The man was risking his own life by warning him. He extended his pudgy little hand to the Vampire and the Vampire shook it.

"Good luck, my friend." And he left.

The Vampire sat by the lakes edge for a long time. He didn't fear being hunted, but there was no point in being sloppy and getting himself killed for his own arrogance. He would stay away from any towns or villages for the next few weeks. Let the trail behind him cool before he planned his next move.

16

Ryerson showed up at the station to see a couple of fire trucks outside. This was not the first time he had seen trucks at the station. Sometimes fire alarms were pulled, and fires set in had been set in the cells. But what appeared strange was seeing Thomas there. He never showed up at the station. They would always have to go see him. There was a lurch in Frank's stomach—something didn't feel right

"Hey Thomas, what are you doing here? And what's with the fire trucks?"

"Fire in the evidence lab. It nearly gutted the whole place. The sprinklers didn't even go off in the room."

"Anyone hurt?"

"The evidence clerk, Al Clarke is dead. Maybe a heart attack," Thomas shrugged, "maybe not."

"Oh my God!"

"All the evidence for your case is gone. And a whole load of other evidence. A huge setback for a lot of cases. Let's step over here."

The news was incredible. A lot of high priority items were lost, most importantly a life. Ryerson didn't know Clarke all that well but they were friendly. Death was a hidden truth shared between officers. Clarke may not have been on the street, but he shared the same uniform as the men, making him family.

Ryerson followed Thomas to one of the interrogation rooms and shut the door. Ryerson could see something was wrong.

When they entered the room Thomas squinted towards the two-way mirror. There was no way he could possibly tell if anyone was behind it, but there shouldn't be. He also looked up at the video camera in the corner. It stayed off, along with audio until it was turned on in the viewing room. Thomas sighed and hoped they were alone.

"What is it?" Ryerson asked.

"All of the evidence in your case is gone, Frank."

"Well I am sure we can get around a lot of it. We have the hair and finger prints on file and the DNA results."

Thomas lowered his eyes, "No, we don't"

"What are you talking about?" Ryerson said raising his voice.

"It's all gone."

"How can it be gone? It is in our system. The fire didn't burn out the computers did it? We have backups, check them."

"This has a strange feeling to it, buddy," Thomas said raising his own voice. "I know a guy who is really good at computers. I mean if you need info fast, even illegal info, this guy can get it. But there should be no way he could get into your stuff. It's all gone," he whispered. "All the files have been deleted. All primary and backup files. They are all gone."

"How can that be?" Ryerson stared stunned.

Thomas just shook his head. "I don't know. When the case is still open, it can't be deleted. Frank, someone got into the police system, which is nearly impossible I've been told, and got rid of every bit of information. I don't know who, I don't know how." Thomas looked around the room as if he was expecting to see someone suddenly appear. "Whoever did this, did it for your case. As far as I can tell nothing else was touched. Nothing. Higher profile cases were untouched. Frank, nobody knows about your case, at least not in the public. Something like this just can't be done. What they did was impossible."

Thomas leaned in to Ryerson and whispered into his ear. "All my files at my office regarding your case are gone." Ryerson just starred with his jaw slightly ajar trying to gather all the information in his head. "The stuff on my computer, all the hardcopies, gone. Both your stuff and mine. This is not a coincidence."

Ryerson's mind went directly to Alex Frey's warning about a higher power being behind this case. He put his hand on Thomas' shoulder. "Don't theorize to anyone else. Just keep it under your hat."

"Keep it under my hat? Do you realize the magnitude of this? What just happened is...well impossible. Do you know anything that you're not telling me about this case?"

"Not a thing," Ryerson lied. "We didn't have much on evidence and even less on leads." He didn't want to drag Thomas into this. He loved the man too much, to risk Thomas's life too.

Thomas looked into Frank's eyes and held his gaze. "There is something there, I'm sure of it. You tell me to keep it under my hat and that there's nothing there. Whoever did this, figured there was something there. Too much of something."

Thomas let out a deep sigh and put his hand on Frank's shoulder. "Listen, I've always been there for you, and I want to be here for you now. Something is going on. I think you and Carl stumbled into something and it's huge."

"Listen," Frank replied wishing he could tell him everything, but knowing he couldn't. "You've seen the evidence we have. It's all crazy, it doesn't make sense and Carl and I are racking our brains trying to make heads or tails out of this thing.

"I can't explain what happened to the evidence, but it's serious and a threat. But we are working in the dark here. I have nothing to share with you, because there's nothing." He slowly shook his head and gave a shrug hoping Thomas was buying this. "As of now, the case is pretty well dead—and it was barely alive to begin with. I'm being totally honest with you."

Thomas could tell Frank was holding something back, but he couldn't figure it out. He was lying that the case was barely alive—any kind of evidence was vital and they finally had some. But what could he and Carl have found for all this to happen? Whatever it was, Frank wasn't talking.

Reluctantly Thomas had to let it go. Either Frank was telling the truth and had no idea what was going on, or he was in over his head. Either way, someone with a lot of power and resources was keeping a close eye on this case.

When Lethgate showed up a few minutes later Ryerson quickly filled him in. Things were hectic, and it would take a few hours before it turned into the controlled chaos they were used to.

"What happened is impossible," said Lethgate. "With all the surveillance and back-ups on the computer..."

"I know, I know. There's nothing we can do about it now. Let's just organize what we do have and we'll start over again."

"You seem to be handling this pretty well."

"Well to be truthful, we were kinda banging our head against the wall regarding this case, and if it stays unsolved, we now have an excuse."

17

The Vampire knew he was being sought. He knew the police were working diligently trying to make heads and tails of it all. He also knew about the hunters. Unlike the police, if they caught him, he was dead.

He had known about the hunters for many, many years. Hundreds of years ago they would chase vampires in disorganized groups with torches and farm implements as weapons. The groups were not very successful, many getting killed. It was not until a man named William White came along that they became organized. He would huddle the groups roaming the countryside's into a larger more organized group. When a vampire was found they would surround the vampire as a group and destroy it.

White would then claim the vampire's property and use the vampire's fortune to train a select group and hire them full time to hunt vampires. Soon the Organization became very skilled in hunting down vampires, but the Organization was barely making a profit. It was White who came up with the idea of vampires paying the Organization not to kill them. He would set up a large monthly fee and charge the vampire. With many of the vampires walking around the earth over hundreds of years, accumulating a fortune became easy.

If a vampire ran out of money, they would go into town and rob landowners while feeding on them. When a town or city would quietly come to the Organization and ask for help with a vampire problem, White would put forth a service tax. He would charge for the Organization to show up, and if the vampire were killed there would be a second fee. Many times he would convince vampires to go from one town to the next to cause havoc, and the Organization would come in and collect the money, promise the vampire a safe passage out, and move on to the next town.

By the time White died the, Organization had quickly become one of the most powerful businesses in the old world. White had bought legitimate companies to invest the Organizations money. A truce came between the vampires and the Organization. No more fees would be levied on the vampires, but the Organization had full policing rights on vampires when one got out of control.

Secrecy also became very important. If people knew there was money to be made then there would be competition. No one knew of the Organization. If another vampire hunting group started up, they were quickly snuffed out. If an Organization member had a loud mouth about what he did, he would soon be eliminated. Only certain people within the world's governments knew about the Organization and vampires. They would pay annual fees to keep vampires quiet and keep them subdued. They still pay the fee today.

Many vampires were scared of the Organization. Even though they stopped taking fortunes away from vampires, they knew how powerful and organized the hunters were. If you had hunters after you, then your life expectancy was curtailed. It had been many years since the Vampire had been sought out by the Organization. He would disappear for years at a time, but it wouldn't be long before the hunters would start to close in on him again.

The Vampire was not afraid of any hunters. He had many years of hate built up inside of him ready to be unleashed. He had seen his land raped and people killed while the white man made money off it. He would allow the hunters to follow him and when he came across them, they would die.

Dazinski and Patrick now had control over the situation. The police were dealt a huge setback, a blanket was being placed on the media, and the case would not be making news. Both Patrick and Dazinski knew it was time to reel in the vampire. The vampire was getting bolder and the more audacious he got the more difficult it would be to keep this under wraps.

They climbed into the car and headed north to the suburbs to talk to a vampire.

The neighborhood looked like any typical middle to upper class development. Trees lining the streets, sprinklers set up on the lawn to keep it green, gardens decorating the front of every house, and the odd person in the middle of them pulling weeds.

Patrick pulled up to the house. It did not differ from any of the houses around it. It was not a black house with inverted crosses on it. It was a simple Cape Cod design with light blue siding and white trim. Hardly the house you would expect a vampire to live in.

They knocked on the door and it immediately began to open. The vampire was expecting them.

He led them into the living room and they all sat down. Not a word was said. The vampire did not offer any drinks, and he was not about to.

There were numerous pictures on the walls along with a couple of original oil paintings. One of a sunset, and one of a cliff with the water crashing on the rocks below. Dazinski liked the paintings and wanted to know if the man had painted them, but he was not there to talk about art.

"What can you tell us about the vampire responsible for all the killing?" asked Dazinski.

The vampire looked thoughtfully at the two hunters. He was not afraid of being killed by them. Hunters only killed when a vampire started talking too much or started killing. He was safe, but he still felt uncomfortable looking at the two killers.

"Word is that he is a Native American Indian."

"We already know that, tell us something new," this time Patrick spoke up. Patrick did not like his time being wasted. If he had his way he would waste this vampire too.

"You're chasing an ancient."

There was a pause between the hunters, neither said anything, they just stared at the vampire.

The vampire in front of them was Jesse Hughes. He had been dealing with the Organization for nearly 20 years. The Organization found him and asked him to be their eyes and ears. In return Jesse was untouchable. As long as he didn't arouse suspicion, he could live a king's life.

Hughes enjoyed the simple life. He liked being a part of a community. He loved talking to neighbors and inviting them in for a beer and to watch the game. He was the same as everyone else in his community, just a couple of extra strands of DNA.

"Have either of you ever hunted an ancient?" the vampire asked.

"We are asking the questions," said Patrick in an even tone. He would not let his voice express emotion. "Do you know where he is holed up?"

"No. This guy is dangerous. I had one guy trace him. I hired a private detective to search him out."

"Why wouldn't you do it yourself?" This time it was Dazinski.

"We are talking an ancient vampire here. I'm not going to go after an ancient vampire by myself, or with anyone else for that matter. If he'd have known I was following him, I'd be dead."

"What did your private detective find?"

"Eternal peace, I imagine. I haven't heard from him in weeks. He's missing and probably will never be found."

"We want you to offer the challenge," said Patrick.

Jesse just looked at him.

"Did you hear my partner?" asked Dazinski.

"Yes, but..."

"Good, here is the information you will need." Patrick passed over a piece of paper to the vampire who reluctantly took it.

"But what if... if I can't..."

"You better issue the challenge," said Dazinski with his eyes flaring up. "If not, we will be back and we will stake you to the front of your house so everyone in this fucking neighborhood can see you. Understand?"

Jesse just nodded his head. He would deliver the challenge.

18

"Hey Frank!" One of the cops flagged him down. "Just to keep you up to date on the guy you asked us to flag. He is being released tomorrow morning. He was being held for domestic violence."

"That son of a bitch. Keep this under your hat, you don't know shit about this."

"Know shit about what?"

Shannon Chambers reached for the Tums. He didn't have breakfast and his stomach wasn't in the mood for it. He was an experienced drinker, but he still didn't know the cure for a hangover. He would sometimes grab a couple of beers to numb the pain, but this morning, he knew he shouldn't. He would have to wait until the churning died down.

He walked into the living room and dropped into his lounge chair. He turned on the TV and scratched his hairy stomach. Amber was not home, she was at her sisters. She would be home soon, she always came back.

The front door bell rang. Fuck. A man could not even watch TV without being bothered by some asshole trying to sell you books or sell you religion. Fuck them. He was just going to watch TV all day and order a pizza and watch the game at night.

The front door was being pounded. Fuckers. "No one is home!" Shannon yelled.

The door was pounded on again. "Fuck you, asshole! Don't make me get up or I will seriously kick your ass!"

The door pounded again. Shannon was getting a serious headache on top of his existing headache. The door rattled as it was kicked.

"That's it, you fucker! You better run because you are dead!"

Shannon stormed to the door and opened it.

"Who the fuck are...?" Shannon's voice lowered. He knew this man, but his face did not click. He looked into the man's eyes. The recognition made his stomach lurch. "No... no I... don't you... I'll..." The rage in the man's eyes was primal, like an animal. The man burst his way into the house knocking Shannon down. The man shut the door, spun around and kicked Shannon in the ribs. Pain and nausea tore through him.

The man picked him up by the hair. "I told you, you son of a bitch, that I would be back but you didn't listen!"

The man held the back of Shannon's head and punched him repeatedly in the face. With the fourth blow Shannon heard the snapping of the cartilage in his nose. He felt the blood flowing freely and his face swelling. He put his hands up to try to deflect the blows. He tried to scream for help, but all that came forth was vomit.

"If you tell anyone about me or if you think someone will be able to help you, you are wrong! I will have you killed! Do you understand what I am saying? Tell *no one*!"

Covered in blood and vomit he just nodded his head.

Shannon dropped to the floor only to be kicked repeatedly. The man kept kicking and yelling at him until everything went dark. With Shannon Chambers laying in a pool of his own blood and vomit the man stomped down on his body a couple more times. He walked calmly over to the phone and dialed 911.

Frank Ryerson left Shannon Chamber's house to go clean up, and get back to work. His lunch hour was over.

19

The Vampire looked out his hotel window. He was ready to take to the streets and was ready to make the city take notice.

Janet Becker just finished leaving Humphrey's department store, having finished her shift as a cashier. Janet had been working there for nine years and enjoyed her job. She liked meeting new people, although some people were rude, but that is society in general. Tonight she was anxious to get home, to set up for her son's birthday.

Danny was turning six and she wanted to get home and decorate the house. It was just after 9:30 pm, so he would be asleep. She was going to put streamers all over the house, balloons, and a big banner with his name on it. He would be shocked. He was a great kid, right now her mother was looking after him. Mom had been great ever since Jeff walked out on her and Danny.

The marriage started on rocky terms. They had known each other for six weeks before Janet got pregnant. Jeff didn't want to have a child and she broke down crying. After a couple days he lightened up on the idea and was looking forward to having a child. Janet knew she was wrong crying like she did, she shouldn't have cried in front of him. Jeff had a soft heart and it really tore him up seeing her cry like that. She realized that she'd trapped him. At the time she forced it out of her mind and told herself it was a mutual decision.

Two weeks later in her apartment, Jeff got down on one knee and proposed. She was shocked, things were spinning out of control. He explained he didn't want his son or daughter born without having married parents. He wanted a stable home environment for the child.

They talked things over all night. All that mattered now was their love and their unborn child. Regardless of how little time they'd had together, their love was strong and true. They said they felt as if they had known each other their entire lives. It was a terribly romantic notion, a young couple being forced down by society with only their love to shelter them. She said yes. They would make it work.

Three months later, both 18, they promised each other their love for the rest of their time on earth. Janet and Jeff moved into a two-room apartment both of them could barely afford. But they would make it work. Like their love.

When Danny was born Jeff picked up his son and cradled him in his arms. Tears streamed down his face as he looked at what the two of them had created. When visiting hours were over, Jeff bent over gave his wife a kiss on the forehead, and kissed his newborn son. He walked out of the room and out of their lives.

He cleaned out the apartment leaving only dishes and a kitchen table with no chairs. Janet was crushed. She had to give up the apartment and moved back in with her mom. Two months after he left, Jeff mailed a letter with a cheque for $250. He said he was scared and could not think straight. He was sorry for what he did, but he just needed time to find himself. He said he loved his son and would help support him. He promised a cheque every month. That was the last letter and cheque she ever received from him.

Jeff had left, but she still had a new son. She promised to be a good mother and she had kept her promise. Danny was a kind-hearted young boy. He seemed to be an old man in a young body. She tried to make him laugh every day. She would always kiss and hug him and tell him she loved him. He was her angel sent from heaven.

She walked down the street with a smile on her face. She knew this part of the city well and she was not afraid to walk down it at night. There was only a two-block walk to the bus stop and she passed right in front of the police station. It was the safest street in the city. She was also fortunate the bus stopped right in front of her mother's house.

She was thinking of where in the house the balloons would go when she felt the sharp pain. It was a quick feeling of pain that went away as quickly as it started. A spinning feeling and light-headedness came over her. She felt, as if she was going to pass out. A strange feeling of peace and love came over her. A feeling she'd never felt so strong before. She looked around her and noticed she was floating up. She looked down and saw a woman lying on the ground with a man kneeling beside her. He got up and quickly ran away. The woman had her bags on the ground beside her, a package of streamers sliding out. She took a closer look and saw it was her. She was floating above her body.

The realization she was dead suddenly came to her. She did not feel pain, it happened so fast. Maybe she died of a brain hemorrhage. She thought of Danny. On his sixth birthday he would find out his mommy had died. He did not deserve this. She tried to go back to her body but she could not. She kept floating away. Tears started to come to her eyes when she heard voices she recognized. Her tears of sorrow turned into tears of joy as she heard the voices of departed loved ones. She looked back to the body and whispered, "Mommy will always love you Danny. I will always look over you."

She disappeared into the light while her body lay dead on the sidewalk.

20

When Carl got home that night he and Dawn wanted to spend some time by themselves. They want out to dinner at a fine Greek restaurant, and followed it by going to the movies. It had been a long time since they had gone out for dinner and a movie. Dawn found it romantic. But for Carl it was a way to escape.

Earlier that day he had heard about the beating of Shannon Chambers. The name was whispered around the station. Most of the guy's on the force knew a cop did it. When Chambers was waking up in his hospital room, the nurses and doctors said he was mumbling about some crazy cop who was trying to kill him.

When the nurse tried to gently nudge him awake he said, "Please Officer, don't hit me anymore! I promise I will never touch her again."

It took a few minutes for Shannon to realize where he was. When the doctors asked about what happened to him he refused to talk. It was about an hour later when a police officer came in the room to take his statement.

He just kept on saying a gang attacked him. He can't remember what they looked like, he doesn't remember a thing.

"They attacked you in your house?"

"I can't remember."

"And they didn't trash your house or steal anything?"

"I can't remember."

That was his answer for the rest of the interview. The police officer took that as his statement and was not going to press him anymore. He had better things to do with his time, besides, he had been called out to Shannon's house a couple of times on complaints. The bastard deserved everything he got.

Even if no one else at the station knew who did it, Lethgate did. He just couldn't understand why.

When they arrived home from the movies they sat in the living room and talked. It was a great relief to talk about something other than work or vampires.

Carl and Dawn had met seven years earlier. She was previously married at a young age, to a brutal and cruel man. On their honeymoon, he hit her for the first time and knocked her unconscious. She never thought she was a person to stay in an abusive relationship, but she did for three years. The beatings were terrible and her self-esteem was nearly gone. He beat her so bad she was hospitalized for a week, and he was arrested. When she was discharged, she moved far away and filed for divorce. He tried to find her, but she found out a couple of years later he killed a girlfriend, taking a knife to her. He was serving a life sentence. She couldn't help but think that poor girl could have easily been her.

She met Carl and was afraid to get into a relationship. She wasn't afraid of men, she was afraid of getting hurt again, emotionally. Carl was the most wonderful, caring man she had ever met. He made her feel beautiful and made her feel loved. He never raised his voice to her, let alone his hand. She thanked God every night for sending her an angel.

They were walking up the stairs to the bedroom when his phone went off.

"Shit!"

"Don't answer it, Carl. Just say the battery died and you forgot to charge it."

Carl stood in the middle of the stairwell looking at his wife and then down to his phone. He let out a big sigh, "I have to take this."

Dawn watched him walk down the stairs and into the kitchen to use the phone in a whispered voice. She knew she sometimes came second to his work. She knew it when they got married, and she knew it now. But sometimes it still hurt.

When Lethgate pulled up to the back lot of the station he knew something was seriously wrong. He had seen the police tape in front of the station and the on-lookers trying to gawk at the scene.

He walked into the station where he saw Frank and Thomas talking.

"What is going on?"

"Thanks Thomas, we'll talk later," Ryerson said.

Thomas walked away scanning the room to see if anyone had been watching or listening. Paranoia seemed to be the flavour of the week.

"What's up?" Lethgate asked again.

"We'll walk and talk. There was another attack, this time in front of our building. No one saw a thing. Thomas said he saw the body, and it was like a mummy. He said it appeared like all the blood was removed from it. The autopsy will probably show a small amount of blood remaining, but he said he saw a bite to the neck."

"Jesus Christ!"

"We can't keep this one under wraps anymore. The press will be beating down our doors, and the city is going to go insane with panic."

"Well, Alex Frey said higher powers will be keeping this quiet and so far he has been right."

"I don't think anyone can keep this one quiet."

They arrived at the scene and walked under the big temporary tent, which had been set up. The road was completely blocked off, and people were being held back nearly half a block away. The tarp also blocked any attempts by news helicopters to take pictures of the scene.

The woman's face had a serene expression. It was almost a look of puzzlement instead of pain or fear. There was a bite on the side of the neck, no other injuries. No sign of a struggle, much like the other victims.

They collected some samples from underneath her fingernails, and took some prints off her neck. Ryerson couldn't help but think the prints would go missing soon again. He would keep a set for himself.

After nearly two hours, the body was removed, and shortly the tarp would be pulled down.

When Ryerson and Lethgate got back to their desks there was a message waiting for Ryerson.

"Shit!"

"What is it?"

"Mark Dekins from the Tribune called. He is going to be in his office all night. He wants me to call."

"What are you going to say?"

"I'm not sure."

Ryerson called up the Tribune. There was no use of trying to hide.

"Dekins."

"Mark, it's Frank."

"What the hell is going on over there?" Before Ryerson had a chance to dance around the question, the anxious reporter kept on talking. "I heard there was a murder, but as soon as I put the phone down the publisher came to my desk. Just to give you an idea Frank, I have only met this man in the halls, he has *never* come to my desk. He tells me there was a woman dead from a heart attack in front of your station. There was no need for me to go there, and any calls regarding a possible murder were pranks. He said for me to hang up on any calls saying it was a murder. He told me to write a brief piece about it. He passed me a story already written. Already written! He just wanted me to type it up and send it to the central computer for printing."

Ryerson just sat there stunned by what he was hearing.

"Frank, he already had the name! A woman just dies of a heart attack, and he already has a name and a brief written about her? What the hell is going on over there?"

"I don't want you to look into it. You're getting paranoid, Mark. Nothing happened, we just wanted to take precautions with this, and we weren't sure what happened at first. When we knew it was a young woman, we thought there might have been foul play involved, but the poor girl's heart just gave out."

Lethgate was looking very strange at Ryerson but he had his finger up letting him know to hold on. He had things under control.

"Frank?"

"Hey, do ya want to grab a coffee? You know that fishing resort I told you about that I went to last spring? Well I have some pics if you finally want to see them. That is if you're not too busy to grab an early morning coffee?"

Mark sat at the phone numb. He never talked about a fishing resort before, not to mention that it was nearly 2 a.m. He decided to play along.

"Oh great, I would love to see the pictures. My brother and I plan on taking a vacation and if the pictures look good enough we'll go. I guess I can make it out for coffee. I guess it was the hound in me, trying to look for more of a story than there really was. Oh well, thanks for clearing things up Frank. See you at our spot?"

"Sounds good, Mark. See you later."

They had met at a small 24-hour diner a few times in the past to talk about stories. They would meet again, but in secrecy.

When Ryerson hung up the phone, Lethgate watched him closely.

"It seems someone got to the Tribune. Told them it was a heart attack. It will probably be buried in tomorrow's paper."

"So what's going on now?" asked Lethgate.

"I'm going to talk with Mark, then in the morning I thought you and I could go visit Alex Frey again."

21

Mark Dekins sat down at the booth with a steaming cup of coffee in front of him along with a dog-eared magazine. He had been flipping through the articles but he was not reading. His mind kept on wandering back to the day's events and the cloak and dagger routine Ryerson was now pulling. But, he trusted Frank. Ryerson had been a good source over the years and neither had broken the others trust. Ryerson would give Mark leads regarding cases, and Mark would let him know about any investigations into the department.

He also knew Ryerson was not a man to play games. Whatever this was about was *big*. To go through all this trouble he also knew it was dangerous, and Mark felt as if he was walking in the middle of a minefield.

He heard the bell on the front door to the diner and he jumped. It was only a couple of young people looking to grab some late night munchies. Probably coming down off of something, thought Dekins.

"Mark!" Someone whispered from the corner of the room.

Mark looked around, shocked anyone would know his name. He didn't write a column for the paper so his picture was never in it. He looked behind him and saw Frank Ryerson sitting in a booth.

Dekins got up and slid across from the detective.

"I didn't see you come in."

"Backdoor," said Ryerson. "Us cops have a pretty good relationship with diners and coffee shop owners, you know."

Dekins gave a little smile but it felt totally false on his face.

"What the hell's going on here, Frank? What are you not telling me?"

"Let me save your life Mark. Don't ask any more questions. This is too big for you, hell it's too big for me."

"I'm the press, Frank. I can expose the truth to millions."

"You'd be dead before the ink ever hit the paper. Stay away from this. Work on other stories, act if nothing is up. You start to ask too many questions, or don't look your usual self, they may kill you."

Dekins felt as if his heart stopped beating. He always dreamed of being in the middle of a big conspiracy, but now the threat of death made everything too real and drove the Hollywood-style fun right out of his mind.

"Who are they?"

"I'm not sure. That is the honest truth. It goes deep, Mark. I can't trust anyone at the department... they just have a lot of power and I have no idea where I am in this. I just know I'm in trouble, and I know if I don't warn you, something may happen to you."

"But..."

"No! Listen to me Mark, no more questions and for God's sake don't do any snooping. You may have other sources from the police force besides me. I don't know. But you ask too many questions someone will shut you up. Leave it. I don't think these people want to hurt anyone, but they will stop people from exposing certain secrets."

Dekins wanted to ask about the secrets but he knew better. Ryerson looked scared which scared Mark even more. He made his pledge.

"I promise I'll stay out of it. I swear to you."

Frank looked into his eyes for a moment, studying him. He simply nodded his head, stood up and patted Mark on the shoulder and walked out through the back door.

Mark Dekins sat at the booth shaking, scared for his life.

◊

The Vampire looked out his window and watched the messenger leave. He was going to be facing very dangerous men. The time and place had been arranged, it was just a question of how the challenge would be resolved. By fist or by mind.

He would find out tonight.

✖ 22

As much as he hated to admit it, the Vampire was on the run. Since arriving upon European soil, it has been a blood bath. He reluctantly admits to himself it was too much, too fast.

The run in with the man named Bo confirmed that. He knew he was being tracked by men who knew he was a vampire and they wanted him dead. He didn't believe though that Bo had been tracking him. He believed this group of men had people scattered with the hopes of accidently coming across him. If Bo had known the Vampire was coming his way, he would have had a group of men with him, ready to ambush.

The Vampire terrorized villages by striking, leaving behind body after body and making his way to the next village or town. To add to the terror, he would double back after a few weeks and hit the villages again. Local search parties started up, but without luck. Even though the land was new to the Vampire, he had lived off the land for generations, and no person on the earth knew how to live on it better, or avoid people better than he.

But carelessness can get one killed, regardless of experience. They were more familiar with the land, and he underestimated their ability to organize a proper search party. It became clear to him early on that he wasn't just being followed by angry and scared farmers and villagers.

After time, he realized it was the psychological terror that was the greatest weapon. He had the right idea when he would return to a town and kill at will, but with high numbers of victims, brought higher numbers in search parties.

But by killing one at a time, spaced out, and gradually decreasing time between victims, it created more of a frenzy in the population. As much as he wanted to lash out at the white man, he had to be smarter. Unfortunately, he learned his lesson too late, and now was working his way down to Africa. He had heard about the wildness of Africa, and it seemed like the perfect place to hideout and refocus.

It was when he was being hunted by a group of men, he discovered their true identity. He doubled back on his pursuers and managed to pick off one of the men who separated from the group much like a wild animal taking down its prey.

Like a wild cat hunting a rabbit, the Vampire waited patiently ready to strike, and when the hunter wasn't looking and had his guard down, he struck. When the white man saw the Vampire the fear was apparent in his eyes. When the Vampire spoke the man again couldn't hide the look in his eyes, this time of surprise, he spoke his language. The hunters thought they were chasing a man who was a mindless animal.

"Who are the men you travel with? You are not farmers or peasants." The Vampire kept an eye for the other men. As careful and skilled as the Vampire was, there was no way to predict a fluke or blind chance in being discovered.

The man refused to talk and seemed to be contemplating screaming out for help. The Vampire took no chances. With one hand he covered the white devil's mouth and quickly bit down into the man's shoulder. It only took seconds for the ancient Vampire to drain enough blood to remove any amount of fight that was in the man. A few seconds more, the man would have been dead.

"Again, who are they?" The Vampire only slightly released the pressure from the man's mouth, because with the other hand he dug fingers into the bite on the shoulder. There was a whimper of pain, but not enough to draw the attention of anyone close by. The

Vampire could see from the man's eyes that he would get the information he needed. The will to live over-powered any will to keep secrets.

The white devil told him he belonged to a group that knew of him and other vampires, and that it was their job to keep them from power and to kill them when they killed. He wasn't sure how many other men were hunting the Vampire, maybe 100 or 200, he didn't know.

The number of men chasing him stunned the Vampire. Regardless of his ability to hide and to avoid detection, he was now on the defensive. He has now being hunted and with that many men after him, he was certain it would only be a matter of time before they would close in.

What if the men offered a challenge to him? He didn't believe they would be honourable enough to abide by the rules—sacred rules older than him.

When the Vampire pressed for more information, the man knew very little. It seemed this was the man's first time out with this hunting party. Useless to the Vampire, he snapped the man's neck and worked his way from the others.

He had a couple of things going against him at the moment. Both of which he had no control over. The first being his appearance. Dressing in the white man's clothes was not going to change the fact that he was an Indian. The hunters after him were looking for an Indian—make up and a new hat wasn't going to be enough to hide his facial features.

The second problem was that he wasn't aging, or getting any younger. Ancient vampires had the ability to grow old, and when they reached a certain age, they reversed the aging process starting to appear younger to that of a young man. When the age reversal stopped the body would reset and begin the aging cycle again. They would continue this process for many centuries. But for reasons unknown to the Vampire, his appearance would sometimes stay the same for many years. Sometimes it may have been for a few years, or sometimes 30 to 40 years.

Eventually, the aging process would happen, but as of now he would remain the same age since leaving the 'new world'. Any sketches of him from earlier sightings would look similar to any taken today, not that it mattered much. Even though there wouldn't be more than a handful on the continent, the hunters would kill any Indian, without even looking at a sketch.

He would travel south to the Mediterranean and find a port town. It wouldn't be hard to find someone to take him to Africa. He had accumulated some of the white devil's money, which seemed to rule them. They lusted and killed over it so he was sure any Captain would gladly take it, for the voyage.

He had to be smart about things. He had to keep a low profile, which he was used to, but he couldn't kill anyone—something he had become quite efficient at. He wasn't sure the number of people who were involved in suppressing vampires. They could be anywhere, observing and collecting information.

He had no idea why vampires in this area were controlled like this. If just a few hundred or a thousand vampires were to form an army and attack the masses like he had been doing, there would be uncontrolled panic. No group or army could stand up to them. But instead of being the wolves, these vampires were the sheep.

Before the white devil came to his land, he was happy and complacent with his life. Hopefully the vampires in this area wouldn't wait for their friends and families to be slaughtered before they stood up for themselves.

◊

Africa was more incredible and exotic than he was ready for. Outside the populated areas, the vastness was incredible. He could walk for days without seeing signs of civilization. But this was a much more dangerous land with many strange and dangerous animals. The deeper the Vampire made his way into the continent the more relaxed he was from any threats of being followed. He would still double back to make sure he wasn't being followed, and he wasn't.

He continued to see the white devil in many parts, but kept his distance. Typically the white devil would appear in small villages or towns taking advantage of the dark man by trading useless trinkets for valuable gold or gems. If the dark man wasn't impressed with the trinket, they would use their modern weapons as trade bait. At that point, the dark man's eyes would open wide with the possibility of owning something as powerful as the white man's weapon. When that didn't work, many times the white man would just turn the weapon on them, and take it by force.

He followed a river and came upon a settlement. The village consisted of mainly mud huts. Any wooden structures were made by the white men, only for white man use. A few new buildings were being erected by the dark man of course, even though they would not be able to go into them. Very few white men departed ships that made their way down the river, mainly just supplies.

After watching for a couple of days, the white devil would gather up some dark men, and they would walk into the wild with the white devil carrying his weapons of death, while the dark man loaded up with back breaking amounts of supplies. He saw some white men come back at the same time and he realized they were forming hunting parties. The white man enjoyed killing animals for fun, seemingly to tame their blood lust.

It was while watching from a distance that he saw a young dark man approaching him, with wide shocked eyes, but also with a strange smile on his face.

The tall dark man approached him with his hands open and out to the side, speaking something he couldn't understand. After a few more words, he heard the African man say "vampire." The man's face lit up with a large smile, obviously seeing the Vampire's reaction to the word.

"I am very honoured," the black man said with the smile still on his face. He looked back over his shoulder to where some white men were laughing and he motioned the Vampire to step back, more out of sight. The Vampire, always on edge, ready to deal with any possible attack, took a step back out of the way of any wandering eyes.

"Those men have been drinking," the African said in very strong English. "When men drink there is always a chance of trouble." The tall African looked down at the Vampire, and with a slight look of concern said, "You, my friend look like a man who wants to avoid trouble. There are three more boats that are supposed to arrive this afternoon, and forgive me for prying into your business, but I think you don't want a lot of...attention. Come with me, I'll take you away from here."

The Vampire turned his gaze back in the direction of the loud laughter. Although he just met this man, he was willing to put blind faith towards this dark man than any white devil.

"Is there somewhere safe I could go?"

Again, a large white smile appeared over the man's face. "My village is about a week away... by foot. It has been a couple of generations since we were blessed by the appearance of vampire. It would be my honour to take you there, and my village's honour."

Having again to rely on blind faith, the Vampire was cautious. He knew he couldn't rely on his survival skills in this land. Besides the animals being strange, he didn't recognize any of the plants. He would test them slowly to see what was edible, and how he reacted to each one, but sometimes it took only one single plant to kill a man. If he were to survive, he had to put his trust in someone else.

The man's name was Padda. He went by the name Paddy—a nickname given to him by the white man. The Vampire told him he should honour his given name, and never accept anything else from the white man.

"Padda, in my language means frog. Believe me, I like the name Paddy, over being called a frog my entire life."

A frog was the first thing his father saw after his son's birth, and took it as a sign. Countless time Paddy wished his father would have seen a hawk or a fierce animal. He often told his father later in life, that he didn't look hard enough for another sign.

Paddy had been away from his tribe for what he guessed, a few years. He didn't like being in one area for too long because he got restless. When he was old enough he asked permission to travel and see what was around him. He knew of the dangers, animals and tribal wars. He acknowledged them with a smile, and the next day began his journey. Every few years he would return home until the call of adventure lured him away. The Vampire was an excellent reason to return home.

As they walked mile after mile Paddy told his stories while at the same time teaching the Vampire his language. They would occasionally stop and hover over plants while Paddy taught him which were good for eating, for medicine, and which could kill. The Vampire was a sponge with information, taking all of it in.

He also learned of the horrors of the slave trade. Sadly, a lot of it was done by Africans themselves. The Vampire could relate, as some of his own people turned their back on their own culture and people only to serve as the white man's lap dog. Dark men, working *on behalf of the white man would go deep into the country finding small villages and attacking.*

They would tie up the villagers, killing many of the elderly knowing they had no value and would never survive the march. Men, women and children would be marched, crying and pleading for their freedom, to slave ports. They would be shackled in irons and put on huge ships, taken forever away from their homes.

Escaped slaves would tell of the horrors on these ships. Cramped together, having to sleep in filth and disease. If the person they were chained to, got too sick or died, they didn't bother unchaining the people when the dead were thrown overboard. Sometimes 5 or 6 would go overboard with the dead. If the slaves fought back they would be thrown overboard. And sometimes the ships were in such disrepair many sank due to ocean storms. The ocean became watery graves for countless hundreds of thousands possibly millions of Africans.

The voyage turned many Africans insane living in claustrophobic conditions with no promise land at the end of the journey. They became slaves and if they had children, the children would be torn away from mothers when they were old enough, to be sold themselves.

Nighttime in Africa was easily the worst for the Vampire. The noise of the animals big animals would be hard to pinpoint a location. He and Paddy would make noise to scare the animals off if they sounded close, and they were armed with weapons if one approached the camp, but holding a long spear brought little comfort.

On a quiet night with a small fire, the heavens above them and animals far in the distance, the Vampire had something on his mind that had been bothering him. "Padda, how did you know I was a vampire?"

"I'm not a frog, call me Paddy," the tall African replied with a grin.

The Vampire couldn't help but smile, and asked again. "Seriously, how did you know?"

Paddy's face turned into a slight frown, thinking about it. He shrugged, "I guess, after meeting one, it's easier to spot another."

The Vampire was taken back. "You mean you've met another vampire."

Paddy poked the embers of the fire and watched the sparks dance into the air and fade into the night. "Yeah I worked with one a few years ago. I was carrying gear for the white man who wanted to hunt. We had four men carrying the supplies, but we needed more help. I've never seen so many bags and trunks for a hunting expedition.

"The guide told the men we would have to wait until more help arrived. The white men looked around and saw a black man sitting at the base of a tree napping, and demanded that he should help. The guide started to protest right away and there was mumbling and a nervousness among the other men.

"When I questioned a man beside me what was wrong, he whispered to me that the man was a vampire."

Paddy's eyes shifted back to the fire and was quiet for a short time, before starting back up. "One of the white men went up to the vampire and kicked his foot waking him. The other men around gave out small gasps. The vampire immediately got to his feet and was face to face with the white man. The white man told him to grab some bags and to help with their hunting party.

"The vampire looked over at us and smiled. He bowed his head to the white man and came forward and grabbed a bag. The other men in my group tried to take the bag from him, offering to add to the loads they already had, but he just smiled not saying a word, and picked up the remaining bags. He was smiling, but I could see danger in his eyes."

Paddy looked back up into the Vampire's face studying him. "Your eyes are different," he said. "You have very old eyes. There is danger in your eyes too," he paused unsure if he may have crossed a line.

"Tell me of this vampire," the Vampire said understanding what Paddy had said.

"There were three white men, and they were loud and they were rude. We never got close to hunting any large animals because they heard us from far away. They ended up shooting birds and small animals."

Paddy took a deep breath, the stick he was poking the fire with, now still in his hand. "One night the three men were drinking and were very loud. They yelled at our guide to bring them another bottle of whatever they were drinking.

"I guess in their minds he was too slow and one of the men pushed him down and spat on him."

The Vampire noticed Paddy's breathing becoming shallower and the joy which lived in the man's eyes disappeared with the telling of the story.

"Our camp was a short distance away from the white man's and when they sat after knocking the guide down, the vampire rose. One of our men stood up and put a hand on the vampire's chest trying to stop him. The vampire just parted his lips, and all I saw were sharp teeth—the teeth of an animal."

Paddy realized what he had said, but the Vampire made a motion with his hand conveying he wasn't offended and to carry on.

"The vampire walked over and the guide who was walking back stayed clear of him. We all knew what was going to happen, except for the three white men. The three white men were sitting around a fire... slightly bigger than the one we have.

"He walked behind one of the men and kicked him hard, head first into the fire. When the man landed on the fire, the Vampire jumped onto the man's back holding him

there. Surprisingly there wasn't much of a struggle. I think when the man landed he probably inhaled smoke and hot ash, knocking him out.

"The vampire jumped off and faced the other two men. Neither man made any attempt to help their friend who was now on fire." Paddy took a deep breath, reliving the events of that night. "I don't think they had any idea what was going on. They were in shock and couldn't react.

"When one of the men did step forward...I don't think he was going to do anything, he just had a pale stunned look on his face." Paddy continued, "When he did step forward the vampire lashed out and bit into the man's throat. He jerked his head back and all I saw was blood. The man's throat opened up and... and there was so much blood."

Again there was a pause and the Vampire let the young man take a moment to gather himself. He could tell he was reliving a nightmare he couldn't forget.

"The final man," Paddy continued, "the man that did the pushing, found his feet and started to run. But it was no use. It took only a small chase before the vampire caught him and jumped on top of him. They stayed that way, the white man on his back, and the vampire on top of him.

"The men around me started to get up and leave. One man started to go through the white men's bags, but the guide told him no—it now belonged to the vampire. We started to leave in the middle of the night—a very dangerous thing to do, but none of us wanted to stay. It is doubtful the vampire wanted to harm us, but nobody wanted to stay and find out.

"The worst part of it, the part that will always stay with me, which sometimes wakes me up at night," he was staring into the fire, his eyes wet, and the corners of his mouth twitching. "We had to walk past the vampire and the white man. I didn't want to look. I was determined not to look. But I heard a muffled cry. I tried to keep my head down, but I glanced over. It was only for a second, but it was enough to be locked into my mind until the day I die.

"The vampire bottom teeth were under the white man's chin and his top set were dug in above his lip. I have no idea how his mouth could stretch like that, but I swear upon what I saw. The white man's mouth was clinched shut, unable to open it, giving a little whimper. The worse is that I saw the white man look into my eye's pleading for help. They were wet with tears, and scared. They were pleading with me to help him.

"I must have slowed because the man behind me pushed me along and said, 'we must leave. He is already dead.' Of course he wasn't dead, that wasn't what he meant. There was just no saving him.

I have no idea how long they stayed there...minutes, hours....days."

He let out a long, deliberate breath. I would like to think it was only minutes, because the vampire would be afraid of attracting animals with the smell of burning flesh, and freshly spilt blood. But, part of me, in my mind's eye sees him biting down harder and harder, eye to eye, until the white man died"

The Vampire could understand this man's hate and rage. He knows what he would have done. "Did you ever see the vampire again?" He asked, startling Paddy. He had been so wrapped up in the telling of the story, he seemed to have forgotten about his audience.

With this question Paddy hesitated. "I think so," he said confusing the Vampire. "A few weeks later I was working carrying bags for another hunt when we came across a smell. About 20 steps away, tied to a tree was the body of a man. A dark man like me, but his head was missing and his arms had been cut off. Only the legs and the body. There was no way to say for sure if this was the vampire that killed those white men, but my heart says it was."

The Vampire thought of the men chasing him. They stretched far, because he was sure it was this group that was chasing him, had made an example of this other vampire.

"It is late my friend, it's time to get some sleep." Paddy didn't question the Vampire and laid down to sleep. Sleep was hard to come by for each man.

Paddy had the white man's pleading eyes etched in his mind, and a little voice in the back of his head telling him that there was a very real and dangerous secret the Vampire was hiding from him.

During the voyage to Paddy's village, the men took a long detour of two days around another tribes land. "When I left my village we were at peace with them, but just in case we aren't let's just play it safe." He looked down at the Vampire and with a grin said, "I like having my head on my shoulders."

The Vampire knew this too well with his own people, always warring and fighting over hunting grounds and sacred land. His people and Africans had much in common it would seem. They were both exploited and punished by the white man, they have no way to match the white man's fire power, and they both can't seem to unite as one to fight for the common good or against a common enemy.

After many miles one day Paddy looked around, a giant smile appeared on his face and he took a deep breath through his nose. "My friend," he said putting a gentle hand on the Vampire's shoulder, "we are home!"

When they finally saw the village in a distance Paddy started talking faster, obviously excited to be home. After a short time the Vampire had to laugh and put his hand on the tall African's arm. "My friend, I might be a fast learner in your language, but you still need to talk slower with me."

Paddy tilted his head back and laughed an infectious laugh. "Sorry my friend. I'm more excited than I thought I would be."

When they arrived at the village, Paddy and the Vampire were greeted royally. Paddy was the returning son, and the Vampire was a good omen. The people of the tribe lived in mud huts, close together forming a circle with the fire pit and cooking area in the middle. The outside of the village had thorny brush built up around it to keep wild animals out.

The villagers had never seen anything like the Vampire before. He was short and his face much lighter than theirs, although not that of a white man. But he was a vampire, and he stood beside Ediganuio as a friend, and any vampire, even one as strange looking as this one, was welcome.

They had a big feast for the two, but Eddie knew it was more in honour of the Vampire. The people of the tribe were shocked and honoured when the Vampire started speaking in their tongue. He made some mistakes, but the tribes-people never took notice of them, impressed with the effort.

The chief of the village made a speech welcoming the Vampire saying while he was there he was one of them. The villagers all nodded in agreement. Standing before the fire, the chief gestured towards a young woman and when she reached his side, he looked at the Vampire.

The Vampire didn't need Eddie to translate what was being said. The chief was offering his daughter as a wife for the Vampire. The Vampire stood up, walked over to the chief's daughter taking her hand and placed his hand over the chief's heart, which showed he was honored. He escorted his new bride back to where he was seated. An eruption of cheers went through the village.

The Vampire wasn't looking for a wife, but he knew if he had said no, even with good intentions, it would have been an insult to the tribe and the chief. Even if he was a vampire, such an insult could have cost him his life.

When the feast was over, and stories were told, the Vampire took his new bride into one of the huts, which was given to him—it was pleasantly cool inside.

It had been many years since he was with a woman, and he took his new bride hungrily. They made love with a wild animal passion, his new wife matching every thrust she pulled him closer and wrapped her legs around his waist tighter. During their love making, the Vampire could hear giddy whispers outside his hut. The chief and some of the elders were making sure the marriage was consummated. They didn't return any of the following evenings.

It didn't take the Vampire long to adjust to his new life. Suni was the name of his new bride, named after a flower that blossomed on their lands. She was full of life, laughing with the other women in the tribe and always stealing a look at her new husband. She was insatiable in bed, with plenty of pent up energy.

The Vampire would go off hunting with the men in the tribe. They would split into small groups and circle a herd of grazing animals, staying downwind, and always mindful of other predators that might be hunting the same herd. Letting your guard down is an easy way to end up dead in the wild.

The men in the tribe used a series of hand signals to indicate their strategy. The Vampire was very familiar with hunting, the only difference was the signals, and the prey. When the signal was given to strike, the men in the tribe were amazed by the speed of the Vampire. He was a small man, smaller than most of the women in the tribe, even some of the older boys were taller. But this small man was dangerously quick, and his hunting techniques were remarkable. The Vampire was catching a hairy beast that seemed like a distant relative of the buffalo.

He lunged and drove the spear into the back of the beast's neck. The animal uttered a brief cry and dropped to the ground. He pulled out his knife, a metal one—the others in the tribe used sharpened rock, and slit the animal's throat. The other men gathered around the Vampire smiling and laughing at the Vampire's success. He was a true warrior of the tribe.

The Vampire did not smile back at the other men. He placed his hand into the beasts torn throat. Removing his hand it was covered in dark, almost a blackish coloured blood. The men stopped laughing and joking and watched the Vampire with a fascinated interest. The Vampire placed his hand over his heart.

He bent over for more blood and placed his bloody hand on each of the men's chests. They understood—they were now part of his tribe.

When they arrived back they would clean the animal, readying it for the evening feast. In their hut Suni would rub his shoulders with oil. The oil smelled unpleasant, but was warm on his muscles. She would start rubbing his lower back and start kissing the back of his neck. Her hands would move around to his stomach and work their way down. The Vampire let out a small moan as her hands worked enthusiastically over him. He turned to face her, held her hands getting some of the oil on his. He laid her down and started to run his oiled hands over her body. She arched her back and shivered in delight. He gave her a small kiss and slid easily into her. They moved gracefully over each other with only a thin layer of oil between them.

The weeks and months passed and the Vampire felt at home. But as much as he wanted to stay he knew there were dangers. The men who were hunting him through Europe into parts of Asia were still probably searching for him. He loved these people, and he would not bring any danger to them.

One day he asked to speak with the chief. The chief, sensing something wrong, asked the Vampire to walk with him. They walked to the west of the village for three hours, making small talk. They climbed a ridge and came to its crest. The view ahead took the Vampire's breath away. They were on a high cliff, and it seemed the entire world spread out in front of them. The blue sky seemed to go on endlessly with birds circling high in the sky. The Vampire thought the view must have been more breathtaking to the chief. Only he and Eddie had ever travelled, while the others in the tribe stayed where they were. To them, this would seem like the whole world.

They sat down and stared at the view for a few moments before the chief turned to the Vampire. "What is troubling you, my son? Your face says all is fine, but your eyes tell me something different."

The Vampire gave a small smile which the chief returned. Being called son lightened his heart. It had been many, many years since he had been called that name. He loved the old man like a father. "There are men who are after me," the Vampire said looking back over the magnificent view. "I believe they will not stop looking for me," he looked back at the chief, "and I will not stop my war with them. There are many but I will not stop. My people died fighting for their land and beliefs, and I will do the same."

The chief figured as much. He had heard certain stories told by the Vampire. He wanted to ask an important question, but he knew to wait. Impatience shows ignorance.

"I may have to leave some day. I don't want to bring danger to my people." It was the chief's turn to feel warmth in his heart—he still waited.

"I love Suni very much and she makes a wonderful wife." This was what the chief was waiting for. What was the fate of his daughter? "When I decide to leave she will come with me. We have talked about this, and she will respect any decision I will make. I cannot give a time, we may have to leave in the middle of the night with no warning." The Vampire *wanted to say more, but he just returned his gaze to the world stretched out in front of him. When they first arrived it looked peaceful, now it looked like there were a lot of shadows for his enemy to hide in.*

The chief was silent for a while. He didn't want his daughter to leave, and if the Vampire wanted to take her he would. The Vampire would fight every man in the village if it came down to it. He would probably die, but he would spill an incredible amount of blood in the process. But the chief could not do that. He loved his daughter, and he loved the Vampire. He thanked the gods every night for bringing him to them.

"If you must leave," said the chief, both men looking into each other's eyes, "then you need to leave. And if that means Suni leaves with you then I understand. I see the love you have for her, and she for you. But remember your wars are now our wars. Your enemy is my enemy. I will give my life for you, and I know you would give yours for mine. You do not have to keep running my son. We will stand by you."

The Vampire just nodded at the chief. Inside he fought back tears. His love for these people and his new father grew, believing his love for them was higher than the clouds. The two men turned back to the view, not speaking, enjoying the view and love between them.

The season changed and every morning the chief was pleased to look over at his daughter's hut to see her and the Vampire. They may leave some day unannounced, but it was one more day he would spend with them both.

During the time the Vampire was with them, he showed the villagers new farming techniques, that he had learned over his many years. His knowledge showed in the bounty of the garden's harvest, easily doubling their previous best.

The timing could not have been better. It was made known that Suni was pregnant with the Vampire's child. The Vampire was stunned when she told him. Over his many years, he had never been a father. It was rare for an ancient vampire to impregnate a human woman. The Vampire assumed he would lead his life childless, unless he was to mate with an ancient female vampire. The odds for conception were slim even in that situation.

Upon hearing the news, the chief announced a feast, which would last for three nights. The village was excited with the news of the coming child—it was a good omen. They had been blessed with good fortune with one vampire, and with vampire blood running through the baby, their fortune could only get better. Preparations for the feast were underway, and were to take place in one week.

The Vampire met again with the chief and told him he would be leaving. The chief's eyes bulged out, and he stammered, looking for the words to form a plea. The Vampire placed his arm on the chief's shoulder, smiled and said, "I will only be gone for three days."

It was a long forgotten tradition of his people to leave the village for three days when the man found out about the coming of a child. He would walk into the outdoors with no supplies and pray to the gods for a healthy child, and for the baby to survive the birth. He would pray for the health of his wife and ask for prosperous years ahead, taking only a single weapon for protection.

The chief was concerned for the Vampire's safety, but he didn't bring it up. The Vampire would fend off the gods if need be to see his first child's birth.

The Vampire would leave the next morning. He grabbed the ivory walking stick with the clubbed foot. Any animal that dared get close to him during his prayers would be brained by a single blow.

The Vampire heard a commotion outside his hut and walked out. A group of three traders were outside selling their wares. This was only the second time the Vampire had seen traders in the village. He was told sometimes they did not show up for years, and other times many visits during a season.

The three men were from a tribe in the north. The tribe was known for their skills as labourers and craftsmen. They would sometimes offer their assistance in building and farming or sell their goods of skins, clothes, pottery and some weapons.

The three men were showing their skins when one glanced over and saw the Vampire and his jaw dropped. The Vampire looked back, used to this reaction by strangers. He knew these men had never seen a man with his colour skin and facial features before.

The Vampire felt hands run down his shoulder and made their way into a hug around his arms. Suni gave him a kiss on his head and whispered into his ear. The Vampire smiled and saw the man's jaw drop even more if that was possible. The Vampire walked back into his hut with the men outside trading their goods, and probably looking for information about the short, strange man who lived with the beautiful woman.

The Vampire left early the next morning with a smile on his face. He never imagined he would have the opportunity to live this tradition, and even though it could be physically taxing on him, and dangerous, the joy at becoming a father was stronger than any fear or concern.

He walked for one day solid and when the morning light arose, he sat down and started his prayers. For hours he prayed, keeping his ears alert for any approaching animals, but nothing disturbed his session. It was as if the animals around him knew of his journey and respected his space, and understood the joy of parenthood that was emanating from him.

He didn't sleep through the night, continuing his prayer. The Vampire tried not to think about the feast that would be waiting for him. He would make his way back to the village in time to clean-up and get ready to celebrate the soon arrival of his child.

As he prayed he felt himself slide away from his body. The Vampire's spirit soared and the Vampire didn't resist. He floated above the clouds and circled like a bird. He couldn't see ground below him, just the tops of the clouds. He circled faster and faster, staying at the same height, the thick clouds not allowing him a peek through them. He realized he was sitting on a bird, with its dusty feathers under him. The feathers seemed fragile, but the muscle underneath was pure power.

Like a thunderbird sent from the heavens, he suddenly dove through the clouds racing towards the ground. His stomach seized, not believing the speed he was reaching. He was racing towards a settlement, no doubt his new home. The speed increased, the wings of the bird tucked onto its side, and its head straightened out in front, increasing its speed.

The Vampire knew the vision would not let him die, he had faith in the bird to deliver him safely. As the ground approached he wanted to shut his eyes, but he refused. His vision was blinded from the watering of his eyes against the air whistling past him.

He blinked deeply to squeeze the tears out of his eyes and he saw a bed in front of him. In the bed was Suni, and in her arms was a child. His child. The baby had beautiful dark skin like its mother, and he could see the slanted forehead and jaw line that was his. It was a boy—his boy. Suni lowered the baby to her breast and stroked the baby's head while he fed. The Vampire's heart felt as if it was going to explode in his chest with joy. He blinked tears out of his eyes again, but these tears weren't caused by any wind.

A flash and he saw the boy older sitting on the chief's knee. The proud grandfather bouncing him slowly, looking down with pride and love. The boy pointing and talking trying to say out loud everything he saw. His grandfather smiling, correcting the boy when he was wrong. The chief gave him a hug, and kissed his head the smile never leaving his face.

Another flash, and the Vampire saw himself and the boy walking. The boy was no longer a boy, but a young man. Muscles just starting to fill in his frame. The boy looked up with wonder at his father as told him stories of his past. The Vampire couldn't hear what was being said, but the young man was interested, with love and awe for his father fresh in his eyes. Pride filled the Vampire's chest, and he fought back the tears, not wanting to miss anything.

A bright light appeared, but no other vision followed. The brightness started to fade and turn into a slow reddish colour. The Vampire opened his eyes and realized it was the morning sun he was seeing. He reached for his face and felt the fresh tears. He thanked his gods, and started his journey back to the village.

He saw the smoke, miles away from the village. Sunset would be in a couple of hours and his people seemed anxious for the festival to begin. They would not start until the Vampire arrived, but the children in the village were no doubt begging for things to start early.

The Vampire smiled, but it slowly started to fade from his face. The smoke was a dark black colour—it should have been a whitish plume. There should have only been one fire but the smoke was slightly separated. His heart dropped and he started to run even before he knew what he was doing.

His feet carried him the distance in a short time, but he willed himself to go faster. There were numerous fires, and he knew it was the huts smoldering. He stopped dead in his tracks. Ahead were spears in the grounds with objects on them. He knew what they were.

As he approached he could see the faces. Decapitated heads were placed on the spears. Men from his village, men he considered brothers. He walked along the trail of heads and saw the chief. The Vampire uttered a small cry. The chief's eyes were closed, and his mouth remained closed. In death he retained a proud look. Two spears over he saw Ediganuio. His eyes were slightly open looking down, and his swollen tongue hung out of his mouth.

The Vampire dropped to his feet and cried. "I am sorry. I am so sorry I brought this to you." He cried on his hands and knees, all energy gone from his body.

As if shocked, he jumped from the ground, feet slipping underneath him, trying to find traction. He ran into the heart of the village screaming for Suni. He ran past the garden which was trampled. In the middle of the village where the feast should have taken place he saw the carnage. Butchered limbs being burned in a pile. He ran to the smoldering remains of his hut looking for Suni but she was not there. He turned back to the pyre and knew she was in there. His wife and his son. It was a boy, he knew it. The spirits had shown him his son. Damn them for showing him his son. After many long moments the Vampire went to the edge of the village and grabbed the spears. He placed them and the heads on top of them into fire. He said a quick prayer and left the village—his home and followed the tracks of the bastards who killed his family.

It took the Vampire two days to catch up to the men responsible. There were two camps placed about four hundred metres apart. The first camp held three natives, the same three men that had traded with his people only five days earlier. The men were sleeping by the fire.

The Vampire walked into the camp holding his ivory walking cane. He raised it high over his head and drove it down upon one of the sleeping man's skulls. He pulled the clubbed end out of the man's skull and raised it again. Once again the cane came whistling down into the other man's skull, breaking it open like a melon. The last man, the Vampire recognized. It was the man from the trading party who visited his tribe before he left for his three day quest, whose jaw dropped open when he saw the Vampire. He recognized the Vampire, and recognized the intent to kill in his eyes. The Vampire pounced on him. He covered the man's mouth and proceeded to bite off his nose.

When the screaming turned into a moan the Vampire compelled him to tell him what happened. The Vampire promised a quick death.

With blood pouring down his face, the man tried to tell his story. The man was told many months ago to keep an eye out for the Vampire and was given a description. Any information on the location of the Vampire would be rewarded in gold and other riches. When the man spotted the Vampire he immediately raced out and came across the white men who were only half a day's journey away. It was not the same white men who gave the description, but they were associated. As he understood it, there were many groups of these men, throughout the land from coast to coast. They were spaced to make travel time as minimal as possible.

The three natives led five white men back to the camp, and the white men opened up on them with guns. The villagers tried to fight back when they realized what was happening but at that point it was too late. The tribe was too deep in their work to notice they were being stalked like prey. Incredibly outnumbered the five were vicious fighters, armed to the teeth. In the end the villagers had no chance.

The Vampire lowered his head. They were preparing for the celebration of his coming son. All the villagers were killed, even the children. No one was spared. They went around with machetes cutting off limbs and cutting off the men's heads and placing them on spears.

The Vampire snapped the man's neck not needing to hear more. He proceeded to the second camp, this time much more carefully. With all his stealth he made his way to the edge and saw five men inside. He took a deep breath and with hate in his eyes, charged in. With an uncanny speed he charged the men, who were caught off guard. He didn't kill any of them but crippled them by smashing out their knee caps.

He proceeded to tie the men up, and over the next five days he tortured them. He didn't ask them questions, did not even say a word. He peeled their skin off their bodies, and applied every method of pain he knew—and having lived for many hundreds of years, he knew many. He would torture them to the point of death and then treat them. He would repeat time and time again until their hearts gave out. When their bodies were eventually found, no one would ever understand the hell they went through.

The Vampire left the dark content never to return to the place his father, brothers and sisters, wife and son were murdered.

23

Lethgate and Ryerson stood outside of Alex Frey's apartment. They looked at the door but neither knocked.

"You think we are doing the right thing by coming back?" asked Lethgate.

"I don't know, but we are running out of options aren't we?"

Lethgate reached out and knocked on the door. A short time later the door slowly opened. Alex did not seem to be surprised to see the detectives. He stood at the door but did not offer to let them in.

"Can we come in," Lethgate finally asked.

"I told you gentlemen when you first came over. I cannot help you."

"But maybe we can ask you some new questions, maybe you know *something* that could help us?" replied Frank.

"I am not the type of expert you are looking for."

Puzzled, Lethgate asked, "Why not?"

"Because I don't work with animal control. Maybe you should go talk to a vet or something."

Frank thought he must be on some sort of drug. The man's eyes were clear, and he couldn't smell booze on him. Frey also looked dead serious. Finally after an awkward pause, "What are you talking about?"

"The pictures. You don't need my help."

After a short pause it all made sense to Lethgate. They did not bring the actual crime scene photos. They had gathered pictures of animal attack victims. They were not sure if Frey was legitimate, and they did not want to show pictures to just anyone.

"We're sorry about that, Mr. Frey," said Lethgate. "You have to understand we have an extremely classified case here. We just couldn't come around and flash you the entire case file."

"So you come here and waste my time and try to take me for a fool! It takes another death before you come back and ask for my help again. How can I trust you will be honest with me this time?"

"What do you mean 'another death'?" Ryerson asked stunned.

"Come on now. Right in front of your own station. The street is blocked off for a number of hours, a one-block police barrier and a tent to cover the body from any eyes in the sky. All this for a heart attack? I don't think so."

"Can we come in, Mr. Frey? No games this time. We will tell you everything we know." Lethgate looked over at Ryerson and he nodded in agreement.

"We promise," said Ryerson.

Alex Frey stood silently for a moment and stepped back opening the door to the detectives. They stepped over the threshold, not knowing what they were walking into. Alex closed the door and only a hollow echo was heard down the hall.

They sat down at Alex's kitchen table, each with a cup of tea or coffee in front of him. Ryerson felt the tension building up in his throat and stomach. For a brief moment he just wanted to bolt from the room, but he just took a deep breath and tried to relax. Frey very patiently just sat at the end of the table sipping his tea.

"What can you tell us?" asked Lethgate finally.

"First off, can I look at the police file?"

"I wish I could." Alex tilted his head to the side showing confusion. "All our files are gone. Everything."

"Is this going to be another waste of my time?" Alex said ready to rise out of his seat.

Ryerson raised his hand to him, gesturing him to sit down. "No it is true," said Ryerson seeing his frustration. "Someone deleted and destroyed all information we have on the case. Everything we have is from the last crime scene and that's not much."

"Ah, the higher powers are already at work? Just be careful you two. You know too much already, but if you keep tight lipped you should be alright."

"Should be?" Lethgate asked sounding concerned.

"Hey, what else can I say? I don't know what they are going to do."

Ryerson decided to push the topic off the table. No point in worrying about what may or may not happen. He figured if they were going to do it, it would have been done. If they can get deep enough within the department to destroy classified files then they could easily pop a couple of detectives regardless if they were expecting it.

"So it is a vampire we are facing?"

Lethgate felt embarrassed by the question. Although he and Frank had talked and revisited the notion of vampires, hearing it said out loud to somebody else sounded insane.

"There are vampires all over the world, looking just like you and me. Different colours, with different religious and personal beliefs.

"One thing you have to do is get past the vampire, and look at the man. That is who you will ultimately face.

"The fixation with many people was the teeth and the consumption of blood. Some had normal teeth, but the older the vampire, the more 'pure of blood' it was, the more of a difference would be noticed." Frey didn't want to get into it with the detectives; he was in danger of putting more doubt into their minds.

With and older vampire the jaw could extend and open wider than regular people, but it was the teeth that would have been the main focus.

Older vampires had a set of teeth where the upper set would lower in front of existing teeth. Their regular teeth would recede back, while the vampire teeth, which in some vampires would be longer and deadlier, or maybe just a small set of sharp, razor looking teeth, would move in.

For years Alex found this the most interesting facet of vampires, and had the privilege of talking to a very old vampire in South America. The vampire said he was close to 400 years-old and although not a pure blood vampire, he was very close.

Alex started asking him questions regarding his teeth, and how they worked. If they were controlled by the vampire or if it was a subconscious response. The vampire slowly shook his head and looked at him with a solemn face.

"I have lived a very long time, and I have met a lot of unique and wonderful people. I have seen beautiful days and also days of great horror. I have tasted wonderful drink and have eaten many delicious meals. I have learned so much in my years, which I could fill many books and teach so much, yet you just want to know about my teeth?

"What of the world will you learn, by learning about teeth? Will that bring wisdom? Will it help you look at your own life differently? Will you wake tomorrow morning looking at the world in a different light because you learned of my teeth?

"I gave you too much credit my son. I thought you craved knowledge. You sadden me."

It was a life altering moment for Alex Frey. It was the worst he had ever felt, but at the same time it was the most important lesson he had ever learned. The vampire walked away and would not talk to him further.

"Vampires can be very similar to you and me," he continued on. "Older ones have developed their muscles to respond quicker and grow stronger than ours. That is from life times of experience. But when their primitive instincts kick in, that is when they are at their most dangerous.

"During World War I, for example, groups of five or six men would be pinned down in a bunker with bombs dropping all around them and bullets whizzing overhead. When it all stopped, fellow soldiers would come upon the bunker with all the men slaughtered. All but one, of course. The dead men would just be torn apart, not by a bomb or by bullets, but by the man left cowering in the corner of the bunker. Many times the vampire didn't know he was a vampire. He thought he was Joe Blow fighting for his country, but under the extreme stress, when it was time for fight or flight, the vampire in him came out and attacked any threat around him. Regardless if it was his own men or not."

"What do you mean some people don't know they're vampires?" Ryerson asked, hardly believing he was hearing this.

"In some cases. I wasn't exactly truthful in saying all vampires are alike," Frey continued ignoring questions and comments. "While physical traits may be the same for a vampire born in Europe and may be very similar to one born in Africa or Asia—there is a difference in vampires from one part of the world, which is vampires of the Australian aborigines. I'm pretty sure you are not dealing with one of these. For some unknown reason the Australian is the most vicious of the lot. They have long razor sharp teeth and a mean streak a mile wide. They tear and rip and leave very little behind. They are very aggressive and very messy. He raised his hand to his chest giving it a slight rub having a strange look on his face. He found his focus and continued

"Human attacks are very rare," he said running his fingers through his hair temporarily looking away from the detectives. "The attacks are usually done on animals. Australian sheepherders have seen many of their sheep slaughtered. I have no idea why they are so different from the rest. They seem to have a hair trigger. Others in the aboriginal tribe make sure to keep the vampire away from populated areas, and out of the way of trouble, but sometimes trouble cannot be avoided.

"I travelled to Australia nearly 12 years ago and happened to talk to an Australian vampire."

"You actually talked to one?" asked Lethgate, not sure if he was buying all this.

"He was a quiet fellow. I just wouldn't want to be around him when he turned into a vampire. Anyways, he said he didn't know why the aboriginal vampire was more savage than the other races. But he did say when he changed, his mind changed. Almost to a primitive state. He said self-control was very difficult. In my research on vampires it seems only Australian vampires have that problem. The others I have talked to said they are totally aware of what is going on."

"At least when we take him to trial, he can't plead temporary insanity," said Ryerson.

"Oh, you would never get a chance to take him to court. He would fight to the death and..."

"I was kidding, Mr. Frey. Sorry. Please continue."

Alex decided to let that one go. He hated jokes and especially being the butt of jokes. He took this seriously and if they came to him for advice, then they should be serious too. He knew the two men in front of him were signing their own death sentences if they decided to go after the vampire. For their sakes, he wished the vampire would move to another city, but he had a feeling this vampire wasn't looking to run.

"You have to realize some things," he continued. "The stereotypes you have heard about vampires are false. Yes many do need blood. It's a biological need for them. They may need blood once every few months. It doesn't need to be human blood, but folklore always said there is more energy in drinking blood from a live human. No, vampires do not come out only at night. They can come outside just like the rest of us. No, they are not afraid of crosses. I even knew of one vampire who was a minister.

"Yes, they can die with a wooden stake in the heart. So would you and I. You could also kill one by drowning it, by shooting it in the head or a vital organ. Vampires have amazing healing abilities. Their injuries knit and heal much quicker than you and I. But if you stab or shoot one enough or in the right spot, they will die like you and me."

"We believe this vampire to be a Native American," said Lethgate.

"The most important piece of information you will need to know is his age."

"His age?" said Ryerson puzzled.

"To know if he is an ancient vampire or not."

24

Jesse Hughes, part time vampire messenger, returned from delivering the challenge for the two men. He was shaking and scared. He was nearly 200 years old. He did not know any other vampires around older than himself. Until today.

He had never met an ancient vampire before. When he saw the ancient his blood turned cold. The ancient had such a look in his eyes, and power in his aura. The vampire knew the ancient could kill him if he wanted. The ancient was very powerful, easily the strongest he had ever seen.

He delivered the message and the ancient only nodded. His expression did not change, did not show any fear. Jesse was sure the ancient knew whom his opponents were, and he did not seem to care.

The two men didn't stand a chance. Regardless if they were from the Organization or not. For a moment he thought he would tell the men whom they were facing, but he didn't. Fuck 'em. He was sure the men did not realize it was an ancient, well that was their own damned fault.

The vampire walked to the phone and called the men. He said the challenge was issued and he hung up. He tore up the phone number the men gave him, he would never call it again. He hoped he would never see the men again.

Jesse climbed into the shower to try to warm up. The cold flashes went through his body. The warm water would not warm him up. It was the ancient's eyes, and the memory of those eyes, that kept him cold.

The two men would die, this he knew. He just hoped no more men would come to his door. He never wanted to see those cold eyes again.

Dazinski received word the challenge had been accepted. He knew it would but now it was time to prepare. Dazinski sat down in front of the TV and turned on the football game.

"Lazy piece of shit!" thought Patrick.

One of the most dangerous situations either of them had ever faced was coming up in a few hours, and the lazy bastard was watching football. The prick just needed a beer and he would fit the bill.

Dazinski might not be prepared for it, but Patrick was. He mentally pictured the fight in his mind. Every situation, with him reacting brilliantly every time. Neither man really knew what to expect. They worked for a powerful group, but they knew little of the Organization's history other than what the Organization told them. They had no idea if one of their own had ever challenged a vampire and lived to tell about it. Information was on a need to know basis. They were not there to learn history but to fight. The men who served the Organization were natural killers. They were trained to win. They could kill a man with any weapon.

With the challenge ritual, weapons were not allowed. But Patrick did not give a shit about rules. He was going to carry a piece, and if he had the chance he was going to use it. He wanted to shoot the bastard in the head and have brain spray on the lazy fuck Dazinski. He could just imagine Dazinski' reaction. He would be angry talking about honoring tradition. Patrick would shrug it off and blow out Dazinski' brain.

He would dispose of the bodies and would report back the vampire killed Dazinski, and it was he who killed the vampire with his bare hands. He looked at Dazinski sitting on the couch.

"Lazy fuck, your time is coming." He kept the thought to himself and went into the bedroom to clean and oil his gun while thinking about Dazinski and the vampire's death.

25

"There are many different ages of vampires," continued Alex Frey. "It is interesting how the life span works. The oldest are ancient vampires. It is interesting how the life span works. Ancients can live over a thousand years. The vampire is born from its mother of course and grow like you and me. They go through the typical stages of life—puberty, young adult, middle age, old age, but this is when it gets really interesting.

"The ancient vampire will actually start to get younger. They may reach 80-years-old and they start to go back and other times it may be around the age of 40. There is no real explanation of the occurrence. Life expectancy with all the conditions and illness, people did not always reach 70 or 80-years-old, so 40 was actually 'old' hundreds of years ago.

"They reduce in age appearance to approximately 15 years old or so. They never repeat puberty again, so it ends in mid-teens. When they reach this age, they begin to age again. They will live for hundreds of years like this. The vampire grows old like everyone else, and when they start getting younger it is important for them to keep on the move.

"If people see you getting younger year after year, well, they would kill the person fearing witchcraft or some evil means. When they stop getting younger they can return to the town or city, and nobody would recognize them. The vampire already owns some land there, and can say they are the heir to the land. By the time they get old again, no one recognizes them because all the people who last saw the vampire as an adult are long dead.

"Sometimes a vampire can tell when the cycle is about to end. Eventually a vampire will begin to grow in age and it will just keep on aging until it dies. The cycle eventually does end," said Frey.

"What if this one happens to be an ancient vampire?" asked Lethgate.

"Just pray that it is not."

◊

The Vampire showed up at the warehouse district. This is where the challenge was to take place. He showed up nearly an hour before the confrontation was supposed to begin. He wanted to familiarize himself with the surroundings. He knew the men would already be there, probably in the shadows watching.

That was okay with the Vampire. Let them look, it made no difference to him. He was going to win the challenge. He would kill them if both got involved. Of course, more men would show up and hunt him down. He didn't care. He would kill them too. He would lash out at the world and drink as much blood as he could. Feed until the world was cleansed by his mouth.

He saw the movement in one of the windows. They were watching him. It was okay, let them watch because he would be the last image they ever saw.

◊

"It is important to note that only ancient vampires come from a pure blood line," Alex took a sip of his tea. He had the detectives' full attention. He could see they were still having some problems believing it all. They better start though, it could save their lives.

"For an ancient vampire to be pure, both parents need to be pure vampires, their grandparents pure, and so on and so forth. Ancient vampires are very rare.

"I met a colleague who once met an ancient vampire." The detectives were surprised to hear there were actually other people in this field of study. "The vampire was in the last stage of her life. She had lived nearly 850 years. My colleague met her in South America. The vampire was a native to the rain forests. What a life she must have led. She had seen many births and deaths, and was the tribe's medicine woman, an honour considering the position is usually filled by a male of the tribe. Her people told my colleague it was the destruction of the rain forest, that was killing her. Maybe they were right, maybe her time was just up. She was weak and feeble, but her eyes were strong. They held a lot of power and there was wisdom behind those eyes.

"One thing the vampire said was if she was younger and healthy, she would go to the edge of the forest and kill any man who burned and cut down her land. She would have waged war on the invaders. Maybe this is what your Native American vampire is doing. Let's say he is 200 years old. In that time he has seen *a lot* of destruction to his people and his land. Maybe he has had enough and is fighting back. I don't know.

Alex looked at both men studying their faces, hoping he hadn't lost them. Fortunately he still had a captive audience, albeit one that was struggling with the reality of the truth.

"To finish up on the ages, say an ancient vampire mated with another vampire that didn't have a pure blood line, their offspring may potentially live to 500-600 years or so."

"Why do some vampires not have a pure blood line then?" asked Ryerson.

"Because somewhere in the past a vampire has mated with a regular human. Don't look too surprised! Think about the plantation owner mating with the slaves. It happens."

"What happens when a vampire mates with a normal human? How long does the baby live for?" asked Lethgate.

"Maybe 150 years or so, depending on the blood line of the vampire. For a vampire to live hundreds of years, it needs both of its parents to have vampire blood. Some people may have a small trace of vampire DNA in them and not even know it. Why do you think some people can live to 100 plus years while the rest of us die in our 70s and 80s?

"How would you know?" asked Ryerson

"Some come about it by accident. They might be in the heat of the moment with a partner and they attack their partner by biting at them trying to taste blood. They are born with it in their blood and at a very young age they just know. It is like some young people today who go to these fad goth bars, and dress like vampires. Some may actually be vampires and some are just followers.

"Like some of the soldiers during the war, many do not realize they are vampires. It is not as common as you may think. There are not too many out there, not for the lack of trying. Reproduction for vampires is very difficult. It may take many, many years before a pregnancy can occur."

"How do we kill it?" Lethgate asked.

"I don't know if you can."

◊

Patrick and Dazinski watched from one of the windows in the warehouse. They watched the vampire walking and looking around.

"Is he looking for us?" asked Patrick.

"No, I doubt it. I just think he is looking around getting familiar with the area."

Patrick put his hand on the slight bulge of the hidden gun. Tonight he would be the hero. And Dazinski and the vampire would both be dead.

"Well let's go do this," said Dazinski heading for the stairs. Dread raced through his system. Something was not right. The Vampire was walking casually, and he was sure the Vampire saw them watching. There was no fear in him, and the Vampire knew who he was facing. The Organization was very dangerous to vampires who strayed from the flock. The Vampire knew this threat and did not appear to care.

Something was just not right. It wasn't a trap. Vampires are very traditional, and this was a matter of honour. Then there was Patrick. Earlier in the day he was antsy, and now he seemed cool and calm, almost excited. There almost seemed to be a different smell to Patrick. It smelled of danger.

Something was just not right.

◇

"I don't know if you really want to face the vampire," said Frey.

"Why not?" asked Ryerson getting a bit angry.

"You are facing something you are not trained to handle. Do you realize how far over your heads you are?"

"Listen, Mr. Frey. We have to do something," Lethgate toned it down a bit because in his own ears he heard a bit of pleading. He wanted to display strength and control. "I don't want to have to go to any more families consoling them while in the back of my mind I know who is doing the killing. We joined the police force to be able to help people. We have been trained to deal with all types of problems and situations. Maybe not like this, but we are going to handle this. We just need your help."

Alex took a look at both men. He didn't know how much of the 'joining the force to help people' line he believed. He did know they didn't have any idea how dangerous this situation really was. He looked around the room and glanced out the window looking for inspiration but found none.

"You can issue two challenges. Challenge of the fist or challenge of the mind. These are their terminologies, not mine. Wait and I will explain," he said seeing the looks on their faces.

"Challenge of the fist is pretty much what it is. It is a fight. The two men fight, but it is not 'til one goes down, it is to the death.

"The only problem with this one is the fact that you are human. Vampires prefer a challenge of the fist, and *always* if it's against another vampire. It's been known that sometimes a vampire will challenge another vampire, but it's rare. Vampires are quicker and stronger than us. Some are much more stronger and faster. The longer the vampire has lived, the more time he has spent fine-tuning his reflexes. Do either of you have boxing experience, or with weapons, other than guns? There are no guns allowed."

Both shook their heads no.

"I am sure you have had training from the force in self-defense, but to face a vampire you must have stamina and strength. Boxers are trained to fight for a long period of time, but the only problem here is there are no three-minute rounds. If both of you want to fight it is one at a time. When one of you dies, then the other one takes over. But then again, that is up to the vampire. He may accept both of you for the fight, or he may allow only one. It would be his choice, not yours.

"Only natural born killers should ever face a vampire in a challenge of fists." Frey paused and thought about what he said. "To be truthful, no one should ever challenge a vampire. It will only result in death."

◊

The Vampire saw the two men walking towards him. The two came within a couple of feet of him. One standing right in front and the other slightly off to the side.

"Hello," said Dazinski.

"Hello," replied the Vampire.

"I really wish we didn't have to do this but I am sure you understand why."

The Vampire just nodded.

"We've been tracking you for a long time. And my understanding is, we've had an eye on you for many, many years." The Vampire just looked at Dazinski. "For a while now my partner and I have been trying to track you all over the place, you don't stay in one place too long. It was like following a shadow. Why now? We didn't find you because of anything we did, you let us find you. Why?"

The Vampire just kept eye contact. Dazinski knew he wasn't going to get anything out of the vampire. It was time to start the challenge.

"I don't want to seem naïve but this is my first time doing this." Dazinski admitted.

Off to the side Patrick held back from shaking his head. Dazinski was such an idiot. Why was he wasting time talking. He would have just walked up to the vampire and pummeled him. He had an urge to pull out his gun now, but he waited.

"Of course," said the Vampire. "First, what challenge do you issue? Fist or mind?"

"Fist."

The Vampire nodded and looked at the other man. "One or both?"

Dazinski replied. "One. Me." Patrick looked over at Dazinski. This was never discussed. It was to be the both of them, at least that is what Patrick thought.

Fine then. Let the dumb fuck get killed. They had a much better chance of killing the vampire with both of them. Oh well. As soon as the vampire killed the stupid slob, Patrick would pull out his gun and place a shot right between the bloodsucker's eyes.

The Vampire looked deeply at Patrick. Almost as if he was trying to read his mind. He turned his attention back to Dazinski. "Shall we start?"

"Sounds good to me."

Patrick looked in disbelief as Dazinski put his hand out for the vampire. The dumb fuck actually wanted to shake the bastard's hand. The Vampire seemed a bit surprised, but reached out with his own hand and shook the hunter's hand. When he released he took three steps back. He took a deep breath and stepped forward. He was going to kill the hunter, and then he was going to kill the devil-eyed partner.

◊

"What about when they die?" asked Ryerson. "Do they turn into a pile of dust?"

"No. It is just the same as we are. The body starts to decompose, and all that is left is a pile of bones."

"Yeah, but an autopsy should show that they are not entirely human."

"You are forgetting one thing though Detective, and that is the powers that be. These people do not want anyone to know about vampires. If anything is found out, it is immediately quashed. I have found out the majority of medical examiners are linked with these people. When an autopsy is required, and they see something vampire-like, they just don't record it.

"The Organization would never allow a vampire in a high position of power. They will allow a certain amount of wealth, but not to the point of where they have any type of influence or power. I've heard rumors of vampires coming into political power as a leader, but with that much influence on people the Organization would snuff it out. So when there is a coup going on, or a political leader is killed, there may be more behind it."

"Do you think these hunters have found *our* vampire?" asked Lethgate.

Alex got up and went for more tea. He offered more to the detectives and they declined. He sat down and sipped on his drink.

"With the vampire coming out in the open I'm sure they will soon. They have an amazing amount of resources at their disposal.

"It seems your vampire wants to be discovered, and that is something that worries me. I'm sure this vampire knows about the Organization, either from other vampires or experience. He knows he is facing killers, but he is willing to draw attention to himself."

"And they will try to kill him?" Ryerson asked this time.

"They don't have a choice and the vampire knows it. There will be no negotiations. They may decide to take him out with a sniper or a challenge will be issued, and the vampire will accept."

"What if the vampire does not accept the challenge," said Ryerson.

"Honour is a huge thing with vampires. They believe for someone to live for so long, and to live that long without honour is a sin. Vampires consider themselves blessed to be vampires. It is a blessing from God."

Ryerson and Lethgate looked strangely at Alex.

"Hey, listen guys, this is what they believe. I wouldn't think it was a blessing. Living that long, seeing friends die while you go on. There's a lot of things you can learn living hundreds of years, but there is a lot of pain you can see and feel, too. I don't think I would like having blood as part of my diet."

"But what if you are only part vampire, do you still need blood?"

"You may get an urge for it. Rare steak might even be good enough. Depends on the person."

"You mentioned two challenges," said Lethgate. "What was the second one?"

"There is the challenge of the fist and the challenge of the mind. With a challenge of the mind, there is no draw. One person lives, one person dies—end of story."

◊

Dazinski charged at the Vampire. He had his right arm slightly cocked. He had no intention of hitting with the right. The Vampire could possibly be one of the most experienced fighters in the world. Living hundreds of years a vampire could learn a lot of fighting techniques, and could be lethal if they kept in training.

Dazinski knew he was facing a killer, but he believed in himself, and sometimes that is what was important.

The Vampire saw the man closing in on him. He had abnormal speed and strength compared to a human. He would not use it. He would fight at the man's level. He would pull some of his punches and try to slow down his movements, he always tried to fight at his opponent's level, not wanting to show all his skills at once.

Dazinski faked with the right and shot out a straight left. The Vampire did not block the punch, merely stepped to the side. Dazinski ended up punching thin air, and his momentum sent him past the Vampire.

The Vampire kicked the back of the man's left knee putting the man on one knee. He had a hold of the man's head, but let go and backed off. The man got up and looked into his eyes. The man understood. The Vampire could have killed him, either by breaking his neck or biting him. This would be the only mercy the Vampire would show.

Dazinski got up and looked off to his left. He couldn't see Patrick anywhere. The bastard was up to something. Patrick wouldn't run, he was an asshole, but he wasn't a coward. Dazinski pushed it out of his mind, he had more to worry about. The Vampire was quick, much quicker than he expected. This one was old, very old. He took a breath and circled the Vampire. He was over his head in this. The Vampire could have killed him and doubt was lurching in his stomach. He would try to fight defensively and try to get a feel for the Vampire's style.

The Vampire moved towards the man. He spun and attempted a leg sweep. The man jumped over the low leg. The Vampire followed with a back punch, and then a high kick. The man was able to block both; he was very well trained. But the

Vampire could smell the doubt and fear coming off the man. He knew he had won. It was just a matter of time now.

Patrick had walked into the shadows during the fight. He thought he wasn't going to get a chance to pull out his gun when he saw Dazinski go down the first time. Stupid idiot. Why would he go through with the challenge? If Dazinski was smart he would have pulled out a gun when they were only a couple of feet away and emptied the round into the Vampire's chest.

He had the gun out and was just positioning himself. The Vampire was getting more aggressive in the fight. With every blow that was being blocked, one was landing. Dazinski' face was bleeding, and his shoulders were starting to haunch. The dumb bastard was tough, Patrick would give him that. Patrick was originally going to wait until the Vampire had killed Dazinski before he would take him out but his plans had changed. This vampire was playing with them. He was playing with the hunters! Vampires never fucked around with hunters, ever. Patrick figured out this one must be an ancient. It was the first ancient he had ever seen, and it was probably the first one Dazinski had ever met. And he challenged it. Dumb fuck.

He was going to shoot the Vampire and if there were any bullets left, he might give one to Dazinski. He lined up the gun with the Vampire. Patrick took a deep breath, exhaled... and shot.

Dazinski heard the blast and jumped. He saw the Vampire drop. His mind was all confused until he remembered Patrick. Patrick the son of a bitch had shot the Vampire. Asshole! Dazinski knew he was losing and would die, but it was a matter of pride. He had challenged the Vampire and they were fighting man to man, the two of them. The way it should be.

But Dazinski made a fatal mistake when he turned to yell at his partner. He forgot about the Vampire. In what seemed to be lightning reflexes, the Vampire kicked out from on his back landing the blow squarely on Dazinski's knee cap. There was a loud popping noise, and a quick blur in the corner of his eye. Before he had time to collapse, the Vampire threw a punch which crushed Dazinski's windpipe and muffled the on-coming scream. The Vampire kicked the hunter in the direction of the man with the gun.

Dazinski's spirit did not float over his body, he did not see a light. Life just ended for him, in a series of gasping sounds. There was only blackness and silence. Cold black silence.

Patrick did not know what had happened. He shot the Vampire, and was walking in to shoot again then... the Vampire appeared out of nowhere. For a second Patrick thought there were two of them. The Vampire got up quick. Lightening quick.

Dazinski's body came flying towards him the result of a powerful kick. Patrick had to point his gun away because Patrick's body was in the way and he didn't want to shoot his partner. He wouldn't be able to explain that to his superiors. The Vampire ran off, so fast. For the first time in his life, Patrick was dumbfounded. He didn't get a chance to pull off a second round.

He looked down at Dazinski and blood poured from his mouth. It appeared that his throat was caved in. The body seemed to be staring at Patrick. The glossy eyes had a look of surprise and sadness in them.

Patrick ran for the car. He had no idea where the Vampire was, but he had to get out of there. He ran with fear coursing through him. The Vampire was now the hunter. No one was ever allowed to interfere with a challenge. The penalty for interfering was death.

The Vampire would hunt him down, so would any other vampire who heard about it. The Organization would also hunt him down. He ran to his car and got behind the wheel. While fumbling for the keys he knew he would have to track the Vampire down again. He had no choice. Killing the Vampire was his only out.

Killing an ancient Vampire who was now hunting him. He shivered and drove off.

25

"The challenge of the mind is very dangerous and supernatural," explained Frey. "It's just what it says. It is a challenge of mind versus mind. A challenge of belief versus belief.

"I am not sure when this ritual started. Some I talked to said ancient Egypt, some ancient China. It always seems to be a mystical setting. Personally, I think they are just romantic answers, saying it was created in some small country in Europe or South America just doesn't have the same flare.

"Regardless of where it started the people I talk to all agree, it is a dangerous challenge.

"Basically what happens is the two opponents will stand face to face. They will both expose a wrist to each other. They grab the opponent's wrist and each take a bite and draw blood. Now this is when it gets interesting." He leaned in when he talked, his voice getting a little louder, obviously enjoying teaching the detectives.

"When the blood is mixed in each other's system, so do their minds, with both man hearing each other's thoughts, they battle with their beliefs. They may believe their God is better, they may believe they will win the challenge, they may even believe their city has the best baseball team."

"Best baseball team?" Ryerson was not buying any of this. They were wasting valuable time and this kook was talking about baseball. "Come on, this is getting silly."

"Please let me explain further. You believe or at least accept the possibilities of vampires, but you won't accept this?"

Ryerson looked over at Lethgate. He also had a look of doubt but he just slowly raised his hands from his lap just to indicate to Ryerson to hear the guy out. Alex Frey continued.

"It doesn't matter what belief you have. It could be that you love your wife, believe in UFO's, it really does not matter. As long as you truly believe it. The danger is when doubts sneak in. You may believe you have a great job, but if in the back of your mind you think your boss is a pain in the ass then it will weaken your belief. You may believe in God, but if you think if there is a God why doesn't it show itself, it will weaken your belief.

"The battle of mind is a battle of doubts. When you start doubting your ability it can kill you."

"Kill you? You mean you can die from this," Lethgate asked.

"There are no draws. One man will live, one will die."

"But you said earlier that vampires do not challenge each other in this? Why is that?" Ryerson asked slowly starting to get interested in the subject but not totally sure if he believed it.

"From what I can discover, it is too dangerous for both. Their blood mix, and their minds just... explode I guess. Both die. No one knows the reasoning behind it. Every vampire I have talked to say they would never battle another vampire that way. Who knows maybe it is a vampire 'boogie man' story, who knows. They just won't do it.

"The problem you guys are facing is if this is an ancient vampire or one who has been around for hundreds of years, in all likelihood they've trained their minds for this. Vampires train both their minds and their bodies. They take these challenges very seriously."

"There must be more options than that," Ryerson said. "Either we get into a fist fight or a battle of minds? Why can't you help us find him and we can get a SWAT team to bring him in?"

"I have no idea where he could be staying. Anywhere in the city."

"Well if he is an Indian, there are not too many pure blood Indians walking around the city."

"But if you find him he will not give himself up. He is fighting right now. He didn't start killing these people for feeding. He is sending a message. He will not give up to you, you'll have to kill him."

"Well we could challenge him and when he shows up we could kill him." Ryerson said plainly.

"You could, but I wouldn't help you. This is an ancient, honorable tradition and I will not set up an ambush. Plus, your vampire may see right through it anyways."

"So what you are saying is that we don't have too many options?" This time Lethgate.

"Your best option is to stay out of it," Alex said looking at both officers.

"What!" Ryerson was almost ready to burst out of his chair. "We come here for you to help us, and all you can say to us is turn our back?"

"I don't think you can win this."

"Well I have a very strong belief that this is my job. I won't turn my back and watch innocent people get killed. We came to you asking for help and that is what we want."

Alex exhaled. He liked the two detectives. He didn't want to see them die, but he had to try to help them. They were walking towards their death he knew, and he was helping lead them down the path.

"I don't think police work will help find him. I'm sure if you gentlemen had any leads you wouldn't be desperate enough to come see me." Both Ryerson and Lethgate had accepted that fact earlier. "I don't think you can defeat a vampire in a battle of fists. You could use a weapon like a knife or club, but like I said, they probably know more fighting techniques than any martial arts master.

"Of course there is a chance of landing a lucky blow which knocks him out, so don't forget that. As far as battle of minds, I would recommend that only if I knew what kind of vampire you were going against. If I knew it was an ancient, I would tell you to look the other way. But it seems neither of you are going to take that advice.

"If it's a younger vampire, say a couple of hundred years old, there is a chance they have not prepared their minds for this challenge. There is no real way to train for this. A person can physically train for a fight, but there is no way to train your beliefs. Being cocky in this kind of challenge is dangerous. If it is a young vampire you may be able to take him because he may think he is ready. During the challenge if a bit of doubt starts to cross his mind, a cocky attitude will certainly lead to death."

"What happens after the challenge?" asked Lethgate. "If we have vampire blood in our system do we become a vampire? What about our minds? Will they be the same? And what if the vampire is sick? What if it has Aids or something?"

"Good questions. First off, you can't be turned into a vampire, that is all Hollywood. You can only be born a vampire. As far as your minds, what I have found is that you will feel completely drained. It may take you a couple of weeks to get your mind strong again, maybe even a couple of months. There is no permanent damage as far as my research has found. Plus, you will not catch any illnesses either. Vampires are not afraid of Aids because they can't catch it. Vampires have an amazing filtration system. When blood is ingested, and they can ingest enormous amounts, the body can filter out disease or infected blood. Vampires can get sick but not from blood.

"I am very sure you are facing a vampire with a strong blood line so don't worry about it."

"What is the first thing we should do then?" asked Ryerson.

26

Patrick arrived back at the hotel room and was pacing.

The room was tastefully decorated with solid wood furniture and marble floors. Beautiful art pieces stood out on the wall and a huge window with a walk out patio overlooking the city. It was the most beautiful room the hotel had, covering 3500 sq/ft and Patrick took no notice to any of the glamour around him.

He couldn't calm himself down. First of all he didn't know what happened. He was sure he got the son of a bitch. The image of Dazinski throat being caved in ran through his mind. He wasn't shaken up by the actual event, Dazinski deserved what he got. It was just that the image in his mind had his own face replacing Dazinski's.

The thing of most concern was the phone call. They were supposed to call the Organization after the meeting. He didn't know what he was going to say. For the first time in years his mind was reeling and he couldn't get control of a single thought.

He thought about getting a drink, but he was not a drinker. It made the body weak. So he just dropped to the floor and started doing push-ups. He was doing knuckled, one-armed push-ups. He stopped when he was exhausted. He laid on the floor staring up at the ceiling. What was he going to say?

He decided he would take a long, hot shower. The water would clear his mind and help him relax. He started to undress when the phone rang. Patrick just stared at the phone. He knew it wasn't the front desk. What was he going to say?

He gathered himself and took a deep breath before answering the phone. "Hello."

"Status?" the monotone voice on the other end asked.

Patrick rubbed his forehead. "This is Juliet, Romeo is dead."

"Big bad wolf?"

"Alive."

"Hold for connection."

There was a series of small beeps as the monotone voice transferred to another secured line. The line they were on was secure, but the one they were transferring to would take the most modern tracking equipment an hour to trace, and the traced number would only lead the tracking device to a scientific base located in Antarctica.

If there were any listening devices on either phone line, a high pitch tone would blast through affecting only the intruding party. It was the safest phone line in the world.

"What happened Juliet?"

Another deep breath. "Romeo and the big bad wolf started in on the ritual. Romeo on his own accord went alone. When Romeo was starting to falter he pulled a gun. He shot the big bad wolf in the left arm. The big bad wolf then... killed Romeo."

"We have a clean-up crew on its way. What did you do?"

"Big bad wolf ran away. Must have been hurt worse than it looked. I wasn't able to keep up."

There was a pause on the other end. Patrick had his eyes closed hoping nothing else would be said.

"We will be bringing you in Juliet."

Patrick's heart skipped a beat. This was serious. The voice on the other end was not buying this.

"Give me four more days. In our time we have been able to establish contact and I will be able to contact the big bad wolf again. The situation is under control."

"The situation is not under control Juliet. Romeo is dead."

"Romeo was a rouge!" Patrick said angry at the fear stirring in his belly. "I was not included. It was Romeo's decision. I was not even told until the challenge began." That part was true.

There was another pause.

"Four days. I can handle the situation."

If the voice called him in again, he would not be able to talk his way out of it. He would be a dead man.

"Four days." he repeated with authority in his voice.

"Four days Juliet," the voice said and hung up.

Patrick dropped to the floor. He hung up the phone and started to take slow, steady breaths. He crawled across the floor into the bathroom. The marble floor was refreshingly cool. He opened the shower stall which had room for at least six people. Patrick turned on the water and crawled in when the mirrors started to fog over.

He sat against the shower stall wall letting the hot water pour over his head. It was difficult to breathe, but the water helped clear his mind.

He thought about returning to see Jesse Hughes who set up the meeting, but he knew the vampire was either out of the city or would refuse to help even if it meant death. When Hughes saw only one man return after the challenge looking for information he would know something terribly wrong happened. Hughes would want nothing more to do with the ancient.

His options were slowly fading. He let the water rush over him, hoping the water was ideas, and by osmosis, the answer would just pop into his head.

◊

The three men sat in silence. Alex Frey was giving the detectives time to think, and they were trying to justify it in their head.

"Excuse me gentlemen," Alex said rising from his seat. "I have to use the washroom, it can give you both a chance to talk."

They watched the lanky man leave the room. Lethgate was unsure of the whole visit.

"I guess we should set up a stake out at some restaurants," he said.

Ryerson looked at his partner confused where this came from. "What are you talking about?"

"I think anyone eating a rare steak should be considered a potential suspect."

Ryerson gave a small chuckle. He got up from the chair and walked into the attached kitchen. Obviously Alex didn't care too much about decoration. All the walls were painted white, but in the kitchen he had a black fridge and yellow stove. He opened up the fridge door and grabbed a pop near the back.

When he cracked the can open he could hear the toilet flushing down the hall. He gave a snicker thinking back to Archie Bunker and remembering he always laughed when the toilet flushed.

Alex came back to his seat and looked into the kitchen and saw Ryerson drinking one of his pops. He had no problem with the detective drinking it, but he would have preferred if he would have asked.

Alex was hoping when he returned from the washroom the detectives would have had a deep conversation regarding what they had discussed. It appeared as though neither man was going to talk about it in front of him. He also knew they were hooked by what he had said. Although both men were silent, they were not leaving. They were struggling with what was said, but were staying for more.

It was finally Ryerson who broke the silence.

"So this challenge of the mind. Do we both do it? Does this guy choose who he wants to go against?"

"Only one of you will participate. Whoever it is, is up to you. However, you must know that once the challenge is over and if one of you dies, the other cannot do anything. The challenge is over, the winner leaves. The winner will be very weak, but if you lose and the one of you who didn't participate tries to arrest him afterwards, his survival instinct will kick in. Just remember the story of the soldiers in the bunker."

Lethgate was slowly shaking his head. "So let me get this straight. As soon as you think a negative thought you die, and if this bastard wins, he walks away no questions asked."

"First of all, sorry if I confused you. A negative thought will not kill you, but it will weaken you. Just picture it as a boxing match. You drop your guard and you get hit. You'd feel weakened by the blow. That's what this is like. You allow a negative thought in your mind and it is like dropping your guard. But, if you don't start to counter with thoughts you believe in you won't win. There is no rope a' dope in this.

"And these are not just simple rules. For thousands of years they have been honoured. And don't think after thousands of years you can suddenly change them. To this vampire you are just men, not police detectives. The badge means nothing to him."

For the first time Alex Frey started to raise his voice, "And if, *if* you do arrest him after the challenge you will have vampires from all over hunting you down. It is like a religion to them. Never mess with their traditions. They will hunt you down and kill you and your family."

"Hey, don't you threaten me or my family," Lethgate said leaning forward. "Anyone who tries to get close to my family is dead." There was a steely glare behind his eyes. Alex was taken back, not intending to stir up the officer like this.

"I am not threatening you, I am only telling you the truth. You will be hunted down with your family. You are not dealing with regular people!" Alex started to raise his voice again. Ryerson was at first shocked by his partner's stern warning, and the look in his eyes was serious and frightening. It was the first time he had ever seen that look.

"What you detective," Frey said pointing at Lethgate, "are dealing with are vampires. Vampires! They are killing machines. They kill thousands of people in this country every year. All these missing people, do you really think they are all missing? It is true that most don't like to kill humans, but they sometimes do. We don't need blood to live, they do. Medically I do not know why but I know it is true. They are a proud race and very traditional. If you break their tradition and rules for their challenge, they will make an example of you and your family. They will go for your family to make sure others will get the point and not try it again."

"How can there be thousands killed every year and we don't know about it?" Ryerson asked this time.

"Men have been trying to police vampires for a very long time. After many years they soon realized vampires couldn't be policed. It was almost a one-sided compromise. Vampires were asked to feed on animals if possible, but if they had to feed on humans, to not make it too noticeable.

"A missing person can be accepted by society, but when there are a series of bodies with blood missing, that is unacceptable. The hunters who are after your friend are here because he is starting to make news. They do not want any news. They can't kill every vampire, but they will pool their resources and take out the rouges.

"I know I am jumping all over the place here," he said running his hand through his hair, "but I want to emphasize one point again about negative thoughts. I know I said it before but you need to understand. The challenge of the mind is a challenge of beliefs. If doubt enters your mind it weakens you, it will not kill you. Think of it as an arm wrestling match. Doubt starts entering your mind, your arm drops a couple of inches. To get back up, you must rely on your strong beliefs."

"How long does it last for?" Lethgate asked. He was still trying to calm down from earlier. He was not mad, just embarrassed he did that. Every time he saw Ryerson react like that he felt angry with him for acting like such a fool. Now he was the fool.

"On the outside watching, I hear it is only a few minutes. To let both of you know I have never seen a challenge first hand. This is all what I have gathered in many interviews. On the outside it is only a few minutes but inside it feels like hours, at times days.

"Think of it this way. When a situation happens on your job, and I am sure there are many situations which need a split second decision. Well, think of how much can run through your head in a split second. You think of what different actions you can take, at the same time you have the inner voice telling you to hurry up and make a decision. What seems like a long period of time is hardly any time at all. The mind works at such an amazing speed, and we can keep up with the thoughts most of the time.

"In the challenge of the mind, you will be thinking a hundred maybe thousands of thoughts which may seem like hours, but in reality only a few minutes."

"Can we win this challenge?" Ryerson asked bluntly.

"Sure, I've heard of challenges where humans have won. It can be done. The strength and speed of your opponent is not a factor."

"How do we find the vampire to do this?" said Lethgate leaning forward.

"You must first issue the challenge."

Lethgate looked down at his watch. They had been sitting there for two hours and they still had matters to attend to. As if reading his mind Ryerson stood up and did a small stretch.

"I'm sorry Mr. Frey," said Lethgate. "My partner and I have to attend to other matters but would it be possible to talk to you tomorrow around the same time?"

"Certainly, I know this is a lot of information to try to absorb in one day." He walked over to their coats and handed them to the detectives. They thanked him and he opened the door for them.

After shutting the door Alex walked to his bedroom which was always kept immaculate. He paced the room and thought about the conversation he had with the detectives. They still had no clue what they were up against. If they were seriously considering doing a challenge of the mind, they would have to get ready. And which would it be?

The black detective, Lethgate, was a very emotional man, based on the reaction about his family. It could be a strength because of the strong feelings and need to protect them, but emotion could potentially be a bad thing in the challenge. Things could slip away quickly.

Detective Ryerson was harder to read. There was something under the surface with him, something that troubled Alex. He was scared inside when Lethgate blew up at him, but that feeling of fear crept into his belly when he would see Ryerson just sitting there listening. He didn't know what was at the root of Ryerson and he wondered if Ryerson even knew. He could be their best bet. Whatever doubts he has may be supported by a deeper persona. Regardless of who went, if they were facing an ancient vampire, they were dead.

◊

Patrick was looking over some notes of his, checking line taps and doing some research. He felt better than he had in hours. He felt his strength coming back. He was no longer worrying about the Organization or the Vampire. He would deal with both.

The Vampire would be killed or he would be killed. Either way it was going to be resolved. The Organization was different. He could kill the Vampire and when he returned, he may either return to a handshake for a job well done, or a bullet in the head.

There was no point in worrying about it now. If he were to return to face death he would look his executioner in the eye and show no fear. But in the back of his mind he thought what if the Vampire was his executioner? Could he look him in the eye—in the face of death? He avoided the question and pushed it out of his mind. Even with all his military training, he could not escape being human. The thought kept popping into his mind making him feel weak.

He put on a fresh suit and headed for the door. He was going out to ask some questions and get his strength back.

27

Jill Ryerson saw her husband come home and he went straight to the basement. Over the years she had gotten used to this occasional behaviour.

Being married to a police detective can be a job of its own. She was not only his wife, but also a psychologist and priest. When Frank wanted to talk he would confess his fears and his doubts. At work a detective needed to show he was positive and sure in his work, but was just as human as anyone else.

She knew he faced a lot of horrors. Every day he could walk into a horror movie, but Frank would always walk in at the end when the killer was gone. He was left with blood and a body. The victim's family would look to him for answers and help in catching the killer. It was an enormous stress for anyone to handle.

Frank was worrying her lately though. He seemed unusually distant. Frank would hide from her usually for a few days, gathering himself, taking time for himself. It was something she could never understand. When she had problems she would always open up with Frank. Talking her problems out made her feel better and she felt it strengthened their relationship sharing not only their happiness but their pain as well.

She stood at the top of the basement stairs, pacing nervously back and forth. Jill always gave her husband space, but he had been acting strange for a few weeks now and she knew it was work related. Frank always took work related problems to the basement. Bills, money and other problems he would deal with upstairs.

She took a deep breath and walked downstairs.

"Frank honey?"

"What!" He snapped from across the room.

"Is everything okay?"

"I'm busy! What the hell do you want?"

It hurt. Jill bit down on her bottom lip.

"Ah, I just wanted to let you know dinner will be ready in 10 minutes. I know you are busy so I will just keep it warm in the oven for you."

"Oh right. Okay. Thanks."

She walked back up the stairs fighting tears. She had developed over the years a thick skin. She knew Frank had a tendency of blowing up easily when he was like this. Jill knew he did not intend to aim the anger at her. It seems you always lash out at the people you love.

Nevertheless, it still bothered her. If the situation were reversed she would not yell at him for caring. She understood a man needing his space, and she had given him that but a woman needs reassurance at times. She needed a hug to say thank you for understanding and that he still loved her.

Again, she wanted to call Carl and asked him what was going on, but she would never be let into that boy's club. Carl would shut her out quicker than Frank. If Frank ever found out he would explode. It was a side she would not want to bring out.

Jill Ryerson sat at her kitchen table, set for two, and would eat alone.

28

Alex Frey was sitting at his kitchen table eating some pizza he had heated from the freezer and thinking about the day.

He could not help but wish he were more articulate. In the movies and TV shows, which were based around vampires the experts had a certain aura around them. When they talked people listened to every syllable. They never rolled their eyes and looked at the expert as if carrots were growing out of his forehead. He felt he was being too repetitive and not convincing.

He wasn't sure if the detectives believed what he said. Regardless, it was out of his hands now. It was a risk to talk to the two. This case had gotten really big, and Alex was sure the detectives were being watched closely. He may have just gotten himself into a huge mess, and the detectives may not have believed him.

It was alright though. He felt as though he had done the right thing. Sometimes you need to take a stand and do the right thing for other people even if you don't know them and even if there are repercussions.

A rouge vampire was very dangerous and he couldn't get that point across. He felt he didn't stress how dangerous it was. There was no way he was going to get further involved in this. He would not face the vampire himself... ever, under these circumstances. He would love to pick the vampires mind and see for himself what the vampire was like. Was he an ancient vampire and why was he striking out? He would be very interested in talking to the vampire, but it was being hunted. Frey was sure the vampire knew it too. That would only make the vampire more cautious, and more dangerous. The vampire would be more acute to its senses and would fight with more speed and strength.

He chewed on the end of the pizza and dropped the crust back onto the plate. As a civilization they could send a man to moon, they could send pictures back from the surface of Mars, but they couldn't make a frozen pizza with a good crust.

One of the greatest lessons he learned was from an Inuit vampire he had met in northern Canada. The vampire was very nice always with a smile on his face. He had a wife but was not able to have children. It was his dream to be a father yet he and his wife could not conceive. Instead of leaving his wife and trying with another woman he found the positive out of a negative. The vampire was a father figure to all the youngsters in the community. He would spend countless hours with them teaching and listening to them. He would tell them old stories of their people and myths and legends, which were nearly forgotten.

"I have no children with my blood, but I am a father to many," he had told Alex. "If I had a child I may have only told him the stories. Instead all the children hear now about our people, and they will spread it to their children. Our people will continue to live in those tales."

Alex smiled when he relived the moment. The knock at the door startled him back into reality. He walked to the door with a smile still on his face. He opened the door and saw the man standing there with a crisp, clean suit. He knew he was in trouble.

29

Hype was used to walking the streets with his brothers. They were not blood related, they were closer—they were gang members, brothers for life. Hype had walked the streets since he was young. His older brother lived in a gang and eventually died from it. Hype knew his life would mirror his late brother's. In the inner city there was strength in numbers. The people in the suburbs would never understand of not knowing if you'd wake up to see another dawn.

Poverty with blacks had always been an ignored issue in society, unless you were poor and black. The cops treated them all the same—like criminals. In the sixties this community had hopes and dreams. Today the dreams remain, but hope had faded. The new attitude was, some had to break heads to make it in the world, or bury your head in faith praying God would bring salvation. Soon many in the good flock would stray because the cops thought all black teenaged males were gangbangers, and they would rough them up as much as the youths who bared gang colours.

Hype thought they all deserved it, and knew there was no such thing as God, or at least not for the black man. The whites had a God and it showed. If he were to walk through a white neighbourhood people would be watching him as if he were going to steal everything, and the cops would come by, pick him up, and rough him up in private. It had happened in the past. White people always viewed cops as nice men and women who rescue cats in trees or what they see on the TV show *Cops*. They don't see the mace to the eyes and the beatings.

It didn't matter to Hype if the cop who questioned him or if the judge he stood in front of was black. They were an Uncle Tom. The only reason there are black cops and judges is because quotas had to be met. There had to be a certain amount of brothers hired in the white fraternity. The black cops would hit harder than the whites because they had to beat the reality out of what they saw. They would beat out their anger and frustrations so they could sleep easier at night.

The only time blacks were looked kindly upon in Hype's mind was when they were dunking basketballs, catching touchdowns, hitting home runs. Yeah they got cheers, but if some black athlete was ever invited to some rich white guys home, you could bet out of instinct the white guy would keep a close eye on the black guy just in case he tried to steal something.

Black music scared the white man. They think rap is shit and just a bunch of noise, yet their kids are listening to it. These middle class white boys with their silver and gold chains, hats on backwards, bobbing their heads to some nigger talking about having to kill a man because he disrespected the brother. Hype wondered how these white boys thought they could relate. If they had to live in the real ghetto they would piss their pants and cry for their mommas.

Life was fucked up in the city, and Hype and his boys knew it. Hype and four of his brothers were walking the streets that night looking for some action. They kept an eye out just in case they crossed paths with any enemies. It was Dodger who pointed him out. Hype smiled and looked at his brothers. The dude was walking on the other side of the street sticking out like a sore thumb. It was time to fuck the man up and release some anger.

◊

Ryerson and Lethgate were driving to the hospital with lights flashing. They had received the call from Alex himself lying in a pool of his own blood. He called the detectives after he called 911, and told them the story while he waited for the ambulance.

He was able to knock the phone onto the floor from the table and managed to press the buttons by using one of his knuckles. The intruder had broken all his fingers, along with one arm and both his legs. Blood was stinging his eyes from the deep gash along his hairline, and he kept coughing up blood. It was hard for Alex not to throw up. He held the bile down despite the taste of his own blood seeming to fill his stomach. The man had repeatedly smashed Alex in the mouth knocking out most of his front teeth. Alex tried not to swallow any more blood, and breathed out the corner of his mouth very slowly. He could feel some of his teeth were broken with exposed nerves. When he breathed the cool air would just attack the nerves sending bolts of pain through his head.

Talking to the detectives helped him stay focused. He was afraid he had a concussion, and did not want to pass out for fear he would never wake up. The detective's business card with the cell number on the back, which lay on the floor beside him, was saturated in blood. "Look at all the blood!" Alex thought. The room seemed to spin and blackness crept in front of his eyes.   "Alex are you still there? You okay?" Ryerson asked. Alex was slightly slurring his words and Ryerson could tell the man was seriously hurt. Seriously hurt and he still managed to tell them what happened. A man dressed in a suit had come to visit Alex. When the door was opened a fist struck Alex on the side of the head sending him to the floor. The man shut the door and proceeded to kick and stomp him.

Alex covered his head and tried to endure the blows. The man picked him up and threw him onto the recliner. Alex remembers the man punching him in the mouth and grabbing his tongue and trying to rip it out of his mouth. With all the blood the man could not get a proper grip, so he continued to rain blows upon his face.

He believed he passed out for a short time but the smelling salts woke him up. "The man actually came with smelling salts," Alex wept into the phone. Ryerson did not know what to say.

One thing Alex did remember was the man grabbing each of his fingers, twisting and bending them until there was a sickening crack and pop. With each finger he said, "You're done talking."

Alex knew the man was from the Organization and the man must have either had a tap on Alex or the detectives. Maybe both.

"You'll be okay Alex, we are going to meet you at the hospital alright?"

Silence. "Alright!" Ryerson yelled.

"Jesus Christ I heard you the first time. I think the paramedics are here." There were some groans and a strange breathing sound. On his end Frank could hear the front door being opened. There were a chorus of voices then the phone was beeped off. It was amazing Alex could even talk after the beating.

It had been 10 minutes since the phone call and they were slowly making their way through traffic. They had called dispatch and found out Alex was headed to Saint George Hospital. Lethgate sat quietly through most of the drive trying to think of how to question his partner.

"Did you know Shannon Chambers is at Saint George?" Lethgate asked.

"Who's he?" Ryerson asked still looking at the traffic built up in front of them. They had turned off the police light because it was not helping them get there any faster.

"He was the guy we had to visit a couple of weeks back. The domestic call you wanted to take, the wife beater."

Ryerson looked up as if trying to picture the call. "Oh yeah, right. Is he a friend of yours?"

"No," Lethgate said patiently. He did not want his emotions to take over. He wanted to ask Ryerson about it calmly without accusing. "No, I found out from one of the guys who had to respond to the call. Shannon was held overnight because he beat his wife again. The next day he got home, and someone came to his house and beat the shit out of him. Severely beat him."

"It was probably her big brother. He got sick of it and decided to teach the guy a lesson." Ryerson was no longer looking ahead. He was looking directly at Lethgate and it was sending a cold chill down Lethgate's spine.

"Saint George's, huh," Ryerson continued. "Do you remember when Steve Drury got shot a few years back during that break and enter?"

"Ah, yeah. He fully recovered." Lethgate said not understanding what this had to do with Shannon Chambers.

"I remember Donny Blake his partner staying by his side for the first 48 hours. When Steve showed up he was in critical condition and Donny made sure he was there as soon as Steve came out of surgery.

"He made sure that when Steve woke up he saw two faces—Steve's wife and himself. After Steve was downgraded to serious Donny made sure he visited every day. It still brings a lump to my throat. The bond that two partners have is almost... well, a brotherhood. I know if anything ever happened to me you would be by my side no matter what and I would be by yours."

Lethgate now understood what this had to do with Shannon Chambers.

"Why were you asking about that Chambers guy anyway?"

"No reason," Lethgate said. "Just wanted to let you know the peace of shit got his, that's all."

They drove down the road and Lethgate could not focus on the road. Buildings went by in a blur and other people seemed to be oblivious of their existence. He lowered the window to allow some fresh air into the car. City air is far from fresh but it helped. Lethgate did not look over at Ryerson but could still feel his partner's eyes on him. Ryerson finally looked away and started talking about the game he had watched the night before. Lethgate had no idea what sport he was talking about because his mind was in a different place, a different universe.

He took a small breath inhaling the air from outside. A smell of change in the air? The change had been happening for a while, and Lethgate had known it. He just continued driving, hoping the change would not get them killed.

◊

Hype felt like a lion tracking down its prey. When he went to school he did not feel special like this. He felt stupid and small. On the streets he knew the answers and in school he felt lost. He remembered when he was really young going to school, waking up early having his mom tell him to go back to bed because it was still too early. He enjoyed school. He had met a bunch of new friends and he enjoyed learning, he was good at it and it was fun.

Hype, or Freddy Andrews back then, would gather with his friends near the end of the playground and would play with their toys. Sometimes they would bring in toy cars, but more often than not, they would just bring a tennis ball and make up games. They would have a few simple rules to start, but usually the games would just happen and they would figure out the rules as they went along.

One day in early October, Freddy and his friends were playing when some older kids came along. They had always avoided the older kids. They played too rough and they always seemed angry. If they got too close Freddy and his friends would quietly move away trying not to get anyone's attention.

The boys came over and took their tennis ball. Freddy knew he should just stare at his shoes and let the boys take the ball, but he spoke up. He said it was his ball and they had no right taking it.

The boys were three years older than Freddy and his friends and they started punching and kicking the little boys. There was no way they could fight back. Some of them tried to run but it only made the boys more aggressive in their beating. Freddy just dropped and covered himself the best he could.

The beatings continued throughout the rest of the year. When teachers got involved, the fights started happening on the way home off of school property and out of the teacher's view. Freddy did not have a father and his mother simply told him, "Stop bothering them and they will leave you alone." If his older brother was around he would have done something, but he was in 'Juvie' according to his momma and was not coming home anytime soon.

School became hell for Freddy. He hated his friends because they reflected his weakness and he hated his teachers because they were supposed to help him. One day Freddy decided he would be a victim no longer. He would lash out at kids in his class and started bullying kids younger than him. It helped give him back some of the power the older kids had taken from him.

The older kids still continued to beat him up and on one occasion broke his arm. The next day the older boys saw him in his cast and started to tease him but they did not touch him because they got into a lot of trouble over it. It would only be a matter of time before they struck again, and Freddy would be waiting for them. He knew they would likely ease off for a week then start back up.

Freddy was walking home when he felt a slap hit him on the back of the head. There were four of them. If Freddy saw them alone they would leave him alone. They were only tough in numbers. They started pushing him around and kicked him in the ass a couple of times.

"Hey Freddy how is your arm?" they would ask and would smack his cast.

They pushed him to the ground and started laughing. They always started off light and would work themselves up. On the ground Freddy turned his back to them and reached into his cast past his wrist. He had loosened the cast as much as he could and was able to keep a small hunting knife that might have been his father's, or belonged to one of his mom's many boyfriends.

He locked the blade and made his move. One of the boys leaned in and he slashed the boy right across his cheek and cut into the boys lip. The boy immediately screamed in pain and the other boys just stood there. The power the boys had over Freddy seemed to be gone and even at a young age Freddy knew this. Freddy lashed out at one of the other boys and cut him deeply on his hand. The boys fled and immediately went home telling their parents some kid attacked them for no reason.

Freddy got in trouble when he got home because the police were called. His mother beat him that night but it was a small price to pay. Freddy had the feeling of power and refused to give up the feeling. As Freddy got older he got a bad reputation, which was a good reputation for him. He was not to be messed with because he was a crazy son of a bitch. He dropped his given name and took on his street name— Hype. And he lived up to the hype. He started hanging out with older kids who wanted to recruit him into their gang. Now with power in numbers Freddy started to get revenge on the four boys who beat him. They were part way through high school when the gang bangers Hype was hanging with started to beat the boys. They killed one during a drive-by shooting and beat another into a coma he would never awaken from. Hype would not let the other two get away. In time, their lives would be his.

Hype saw the short man walking ahead of him. He was slightly hunched over and walking fast—for whatever reason this bothered Hype. The image of his childhood beatings ran through Hype's mind psyching him up. He was ready to steal the man's power. They were only five feet behind the man.

"Where the fuck do you think you are going?" Hype yelled out with arms flailing in front of him.

The man continued to walk as if he did not even hear them. He figured the man was hoping if he ignored him they would go away. Hype looked down at his foot and saw a drop of blood on the pavement. He glanced behind him and saw other fat drops of blood on the sidewalk. This dude was hurt. Hopefully who ever hurt him didn't already rob him, because that is what Hype was going to do.

"Hey motherfucker! I'm talking to you!"

"Fuck off," was the reply.

Hype stopped in his tracks and looked at his four friends, his brothers. Who did this guy think he was? "Fuck off." No one talked to him that way especially in front of his fellow brothers. What was just going to be a beating and robbery was now going to turn much more serious.

The five of them caught up to the man and followed close behind. L'il Stevie, one of four guys, stepped forth and lined up as if he was going to kick a field goal. L'il Stevie always wore steel toed boots, his shit kicker boots he called them.

He was lined up to the small guy's ass and was going to kick him a new shit hole. He kicked as hard as he could and his friends looked on with big smiles on their faces, they couldn't wait to hear the little guy yell out in pain. But as quickly as his foot went, the injured man turned around and caught his foot, holding it. He looked straight into L'il Stevie's eyes. Stevie would have fell back but the man pulled him forward a bit so he kept his balance. The man's expression did not change at all. He moved really quick and the guys heard a loud snap and a pain filled scream. L'il Stevie's foot was pointing in the wrong direction, sickly hanging from the end of his leg.

Hype's boys had been in many fights and their biggest skill was reacting, and they did not let him down. The remaining members attacked the small man with their hands and their feet.

But the little man's reaction was quicker than any of the thugs expected. The man turned and blocked all of the punches and kicks with only one blow hitting him below the knee. The small man grabbed the closest attacker and there was a loud snap. Then the injured man had grabbed the kid's wrist and with his other hand he landed a palm strike to the elbow, not hyper-extending it but completely dislocating and breaking the elbow. There was a nauseating bulge in his sleeve where the bone was sticking out.

Hype had no idea what was happening. The little man who looked like an Indian was striking out with incredible speed and force. The only noise was the snapping of bones and the screams of pain. All his friends had dropped around him, leaving Hype with this little man.

For the first time in Hype's life he could not react. His strength was his street sense and his ability to strike out with his fists without thinking of what to do next. It was what kept him alive, and now the hunter became the prey trapped in the headlights.

The Vampire started to walk towards Hype. Hype had faced guys who had known martial arts and had managed to hold his own, but he had never seen this particular style and nowhere near the speed.

There was a distant wail of a police car, Hype hoped for the first time in his life for the police to show up. But he knew the car was not headed in his direction. He had spent most of his life avoiding the sirens learned to determine from a distance what direction they were headed.

The streets never looked more menacing to Hype. He had spent his entire life in the graffiti lined streets and always considered it home. Now home had a different feel, it would be the only world he would ever see. Something in his gut told him this was it. He had heard it said by cops, teachers and his mom but he never took it to heart. Death was walking towards him and he knew there was nothing he could do. He would never experience love, sure he had bedded plenty of women but he never loved any of them. He would never experience the love of a child lying in his arms—his child. He never paid attention to sunsets or sunrises.

He let out a small breath and looked to the sky to take one last look at the moon and the stars, but the buildings and the glare of the city lights hid them from him. He raised his arms to the approaching man, trying to calm the man down.

The street warrior in his last moments went out a victim instead of a hunter. He felt the man grab the back of his neck and pull him close. He felt terrible pain shoot through his neck, feeling the teeth tear into his throat. He heard a slight gargle not realizing the noise was coming from him. The last noise he heard was the explosion. It sounded too familiar, but everything was slipping away, and then silence.

The Vampire spun around like a top but managed to keep his feet under him. The one who first attempted to kick him was holding a gun at the Vampire. Pain was wrapped around the kid's face as he held one hand on the gun and his other was on his leg trying to steady the pain, which was flaring up from his badly broken foot.

L'il Stevie was feeling very faint. He had lost consciousness shortly after hitting the ground. He remembered screaming and his head getting very light. He wanted to scream now because of the pain, but he knew if he screamed, it would make him even more light headed. He couldn't pass out. He saw what the man had done to Hype. The bastard bit his throat open and spit it on the sidewalk. He heard muffling around him. Some of his friends sounded alive, but he could not check. He had the little man in front of him, and the fucker was going to die.

Fear had blocked the pain in the Vampire. The encounter with the Organization went terribly wrong. He was not expecting an ambush, let alone getting shot. The last thing he needed was this. The Vampire was in survival mode and that meant certain death for his attackers. The bullet wound from his encounter with the Organization was in his upper right chest was bleeding steadily but he paid no attention. The loud blast behind him got his attention.

Unbelievably the Vampire was shot again this time in his right shoulder. He felt intense heat mixed with a cooling numbness. The Vampire dove to his right, he could not stand in the way of the gun. The shooter, he assumed had used guns before and even with the youngster hurt he didn't want to risk standing still with two serious gunshot wounds, he moved.

He rolled on his good shoulder but the pain exploded down his right arm and across his chest and the back of his neck. He didn't stop, even with the pain. He had to keep moving. He lunged on top of the shooter and with his good arm struggled for the gun. The shooter with his other arm came crashing down on the Vampires damaged shoulder. Lightning bolts of pain shot through his body, and dots started to blur his vision. He was close to losing the battle for the gun. Instinctively with his left leg he kicked the shooters broken foot. There was a muffled scream and the gun slipped from the kid's hand. The Vampire seized the gun and quickly got to his feet before the shooter had a chance to attack his injured shoulder any more.

The Vampire was very shaky on his feet and closed his eyes to focus on his balance. With a couple of deep breaths he cleared his mind and regained his footing.

He looked down at the young man with his crippled foot and looked into his hand at the gun. Many years ago he told himself he would never use such a weapon on an enemy. There was no honour or challenge to a gun. Hand to hand combat was the true test for a fighter.

The blood quickly soaked the Vampire's clothes and he was getting weak with every passing moment. He looked at the gun and pointed it at the young man. The Vampire was in no condition to finish off the man under his own power. He pulled the trigger.

Pain again shot up his arm due to the small kick in the weapon, but the Vampire paid little attention. He looked down at the smoking gun amazed at the power contained in the small weapon. He had seen plenty of guns over the years, it was what killed many of his people, but to feel the power in it was almost intoxicating.

He turned to the other young men lying around him and started to unload the gun into them. The last young man lay on the cement with what appeared to be two broken arms. There was a small puddle of blood leading from the back of his head. He had been knocked out when he fell. The Vampire pointed the gun at the young man's chest and pulled the trigger. There was only a shallow click. The gun was out of bullets. The Vampire looked down, upset he could not finish the job. He quickly shook his head and tossed the gun away as if it had turned into a venomous snake.

The gun had taken over the Vampire. The power inside of it tried to deteriorate his soul making him dependent on its power. Never again, he promised. He would die before he ever touched a gun again. He looked down at the young man. The gods must be looking over this one. The Vampire reached down and tore the shirt from the young man. He placed it over the wound on his shoulder trying to stop the blood.

The Vampire quickly left the scene, knowing he would need to tend to his damaged shoulder, and to try to shake the vibrating sensation that the gun had left in   his   hand.

30

When they arrived at the hospital it was the smell that struck Lethgate first. The smell of chemical cleaning agents was strong in the air, but it could not totally mask the smell of sickness. He hated hospitals. The white walls led down one aisle leading into another. It seemed an endless maze of white walls with patients walking with IV drips wheeled beside them and people visiting, keeping a vigilant eye on the signs on the wall in fear they would get lost or wind up in a restricted area.

The hospital tried to make the reception area warm with couches in front of the windows for patients to stare out of, and a gift store with teddy bears and flowers in the front display case. Lethgate looked at the teddy bears and thought one of them might be some child's last toy. He quickly tried to push the thought out of his head and walked towards the IC unit where Alex was roomed. In most cases, Alex would be lined up in the aisle just off the emergency ward waiting for a bed, but because the detectives called the hospital administration on the drive over, saying the beating was a serious police matter, they moved him into a room where the detectives could question him without disturbing other patients.

Ryerson and Lethgate had to wait for nearly an hour while the doctors finished treating Alex. They did numerous x-rays and a CAT scan to make sure there were no internal injuries.   They concluded there was no serious internal damage, but had to set the breaks he had received. While setting the bones Alex passed out due to the pain, and because he wanted to talk to the detectives he wanted only mild painkillers.

By the time Lethgate and Ryerson got to see Alex they were shocked by his appearance. His face was severely swollen, with his lip sticking out, stitches keeping it together. He looked like he had aged 20 years. His eyes looked tired and drained from all the pain he had experienced, both in the beating and in the setting of the breaks.

His head was bandaged, he wore a neck brace, and his arm had temporary splints and both legs in soft casts slightly elevated off the bed. The doctors wanted to wait a day or so to make sure all the breaks were properly set to see if any pins or screws were necessary and to check on any possible complications that might develop with the head trauma. The brain looked fine, but they wanted to make sure over the next 24-hours that no swelling developed.

"How do you feel?" Lethgate asked. He felt sheepish asking such a stupid question.

Alex looked down at himself using just his eyes. That alone seemed to be painful and draining. "I'm just peachy." He spoke with barely moving his lips. With his broken teeth any breath would rip into the exposed nerves. A dentist would be by in the morning to pull them.

"Do you know who did this?" asked Ryerson getting to the point.

"Yes. Well, in a way. I don't know who the man is, but I know who he represents."

Lethgate nodded understanding what he meant. "If we get someone in here, could you describe the man and we could make a composite of him."

"You'll never find him. The picture will be "lost" as soon as it leaves the hospital. The man will never be caught. Don't even waste your time."

"What do you want us to do?" Ryerson asked closing his note pad.

"Go after the vampire, detectives. You are close, the Organization is scared of what you know. You must continue."

Ryerson shook his head slowly. Lethgate took a step closer to the bed, but didn't say anything. He knew Ryerson had taken control of the case, he took control as soon as they had the talk about Shannon Chambers in the car. Lethgate looked at his partner. Did he have control over their work partnership? Lethgate did not want to answer the thought.

"How the hell do we go after *it* Alex? Tell us!"

"You must issue the challenge. You have to..."

"For fuck sakes, how do we issue the challenge? What, take out a want ad?"

Alex closed his eyes and it looked like he had fallen asleep. Beside the IV drip there was a heart monitor and both detectives took a glance to make sure he was still with them. Alex slowly opened his eyes looking at the two men. "You have to let the vampire know. You do not have a middleman to give him the message, so you have to find one."

Lethgate was getting frustrated with the conversation. It was the same shit, different place. Frey seemed to enjoy being an enigma, and even in the hospital after being severely beaten he continued the charade.

"Just focus on getting yourself better, okay? We'll leave our number with the nurses so if you need to get in touch with us we'll be here. Do you think the man will come back for you? We can get an officer assigned to stay outside your door."

Alex gave a slight moan and a twitch. Both men looked down concerned for him before realizing he was stifling a laugh. "The man wanted me alive so I *could* talk to you." He took a deep breath and released the air out his nose. "Be very careful. He is watching you closely, and he is very dangerous."

He? Though Lethgate. The vampire or the person responsible for putting Alex in the hospital? "We'll be okay Alex, just get better," Lethgate was going to touch him to give reassurance but he was afraid to touch him in case it would hurt him.

"Remember, he wanted me to talk to you."

The two detectives left the room and left one of their cards at the nurse's station. It had both men's cell phone numbers on the back. A muffled voice came over the PA while they walked down the halls looking forward to leaving the white crypt.

"What are we going to do," asked Lethgate.

"I have a call to make," replied Ryerson looking straight ahead of him.

◊

The Vampire just barged into the house barely able to keep his balance. The woman at the door let out a surprised scream but quickly kept her breath when she saw the Vampire. He had lost a lot of blood and was nearly out on his feet. She hooked her arm under the Vampire's arm and led him to the room at the back of the house.

This was a house many vampires knew. It was sort of a safe house. A place for refuge or medical care. The Vampire learned of it shortly after he arrived in the city.

"Robert!" She called upstairs. "Come downstairs right away."

She could not worry if anyone saw the Vampire come into the house, it was too late to worry about that.

"What is it? Why... oh Christ!" Robert said stopping himself. He had been a doctor for nearly 23 years. He had been a vampire for much longer.

"Rose get me an IV started and blood right away." It didn't matter which type of blood it was, vampires could ingest it all.

Robert went to the front door and looked up and down the street. Nobody was peeking through their windows or gathering on the sidewalk so the Vampire may have not been seen. He gently closed the door and walked back to his patient.

Rose was quietly working on the Vampire's wounds. She was not a vampire, but long ago she had learned the truth about her husband and other vampires. They did not frighten her, novels and horror movies did not prejudice her. She had met many vampires and she could honestly say she loved the company of each one. This vampire was much older than any other vampire she had ever met. He looked young in appearance but his eyes were very old. She just went about her job and kept quiet.

"You could have used the doorbell," the doctor quipped. "What happened?"

"Shot," was all the Vampire would say.

"By the police?" he asked. Rose lifted her head and made eye contact with her husband. She looked back to the wounds and tried to stop the bleeding.

"No, not the police," he looked at Rose who was packing his wound. "She is not one of us."

"No she is not, she is my wife. If you have a problem with that I suggest you leave and maybe get treated at a local hospital."

The Vampire looked into the doctor's face and settled down on the examination table. It had been many years since he had trusted a human.

The back room was set up as a small clinic. The doctor didn't have everything he wanted to treat the injuries, but it would do.

Rose picked up the needle and tapped the end. She reached for the Vampire's arm and he quickly pulled back. "What is that?"

"It is merely something for the pain. It will help you sleep," answered Robert.

"No sleep. I don't want any needles."

"This is going to hurt."

"I've experienced pain before."

Robert nodded at his wife and she lowered the needle. She stepped back from the table and let her husband treat the Vampire. She would stay if she were needed.

The doctor rolled the Vampire onto his side and examined the back of his shoulder to see if the bullets had come through. "There are no exit wounds." The doctor looked at both wounds and could tell they were from different guns. "The shoulder wound I imagine was a small caliber, but I think it hit bone. The larger caliber in your upper chest is what concerns me. I am going have to take a look."

The doctor got some forceps and got Rose to hold it to keep the wound open. The Vampire hissed in pain but just closed his eyes and breathed loud.

The bullet in the upper chest appeared to be a fairly clean wound. It missed his lung which had been a big concern. "A hospital would be the best place to treat this. I am not worried about infection, not with a vampire, but there is a chance it may have nicked something that I can't see."

"You know I can't go to a hospital." The doctor nodded in agreement. A gunshot wound would be reported to the police, and he believed this vampire didn't want the police involved. "Try your best, that's all I ask."

The Vampire reluctantly agreed to take a local anesthetic to help with the pain, so he didn't jerk his shoulder around during the examination. The doctor methodically looked around the inside of the Vampire's shoulder. He removed all the bone fragments and made sure no arteries were damaged. The bullet in the upper chest appeared to be a fairly clean wound. It missed his lung which had been a big concern. He took his time thoroughly checking the wounds and stitching him up.

"You should have a cast to immobilize your shoulder."

"No."

"How did I know you were going to say that? Anyways, here is a shoulder brace. For an injury like this it will provide little, but it is better than nothing."

He helped slip it on the Vampire with care. "Try not to move your arm too much. You'll pop the stitches and you could still do some serious damage to your shoulder. When you *can*, I would suggest going to a local clinic that won't ask a lot of questions, and get an x-ray of your chest and shoulder to make sure everything is healing alright and there are no hidden bone chips."

"I will thank you," said the Vampire. Robert heard sincerity in his voice and for the first time could see a genuine human side in him.

"Can I ask you a question," Robert ventured.

The Vampire let out a little breath and closed his eyes. He was tired just wanting to sleep if the pain would let him. He didn't like to show weakness. "Go ahead."

"Why are you doing this? The vampire community in this city is well informed and word gets around fast. You seem to have a lot of people looking for you. Why bring all the attention to you, and to the rest of us?"

The Vampire gently put on an old shirt of Robert's since his own was blood soaked. He hopped down from the examination table and his head started to spin. He had lost a lot of blood, and when he landed his shoulder flared up in pain, shooting sparks down his arm and up his neck to the back of his head. He steadied himself and looked at the doctor, always keeping eye contact.

"Sometimes enough is enough. I have seen a lot in my life, more death and hurt than I hope you will ever see, doctor." Robert could feel the strength behind the eyes. "I have seen my people treated like cattle and worse. I saw a beautiful land defiled, for no reason other than money.

"To tell you the truth doctor, I wish I was not a vampire. I wish I'd died years ago before all the killing. I tried to fight back but it was too late. They took everything I ever loved from me. I'd kill one and ten would come in their place. I tried to find peace and explore the world but hate and prejudice is everywhere. A man can only take so much.

"We as vampires are a suppressed people as well. It's okay to be one only if we don't let on. There are people around who would kill me if I decided to come forth and tell the truth. I am just tired of it. I will not be repressed like my people were. I will fight and I will fight to my death."

Robert didn't look away when the Vampire finished. The Indian was a small man, but Robert could see power in his limbs. He knew he shouldn't push the Vampire too much. Vampires have killed other vampires, and the Organization had no problem with that. But he had to ask though, "Are you trying to start a revolution? A vampire uprising?"

The Vampire laughed at the question. He didn't laugh too long because the pain in his shoulder flared every time he moved and his head would spin. He had no idea how he would get home, but he would worry about that when the time came.

"I'm not trying to start anything doctor. This is my fight. I ask for no help and I ask for no sympathy. You will never, or I hope you will never understand what I have been through. This is my battle and the battle will die with me."

Robert said nothing. The Vampire seemed to have shrunk before him. The wound had taken more out of the Vampire than he would admit. "First off, we will give you some blood to bring some strength back to you, and I'll get you some pain pills. We have a spare bedroom upstairs you could sleep in tonight until you feel strong enough to leave."

"No, I'll leave soon."

"So be it. I'll call a cab, someone I know. He will not ask any questions and will take you anywhere you want to go. Come, I have some blood in the back."

The Vampire followed.

31

Patrick sat in his room and just waited. Most of the day he had his headset on listening in on phone taps. He was trained for patience, but he was starting to sweat on this one. The Organization would not wait long to pull the plug on this. He had stalled them for a short time but they would push more regarding Dazinski's death.

Instinct told him to wait. The vampire was hurt but would reveal himself in time. He kept tabs on the police to find out what information they had—the less the better.

He was sitting in his t-shirt and slacks. The slacks were wrinkled and the t-shirt was the same one as the day before. There was two day's growth on his face and it felt dirty and itchy. He hated the feeling of not being clean, but he had more important things to worry about at the time.

How the hell did he miss the kill shot? He racked his brain trying to remember the incident. Did the vampire move at the very last instant? Could vampires even react that fast? Was it a shake in his hand? That was what scared him the most. The possibility that when it came down to it, he let his nerves get the best of him and he choked. His mind drifted back to RGC Logistics and shooting the vampire mother in the throat. He missed his target then too.

The light on the computer screen lit up indicating a call from the detective's phone. The call was being recorded and the screen turned a light red colour. Patrick sat back listening to the call when he straightened up he put his hands to the earphones holding them in place.

When the call was finished Patrick smiled and replayed the message. He wrote a transcript of the conversation and printed it off. The computer would automatically record any other calls made on his taps. Carrying the transcript he got up and went into the washroom to shower and shave.

Finally the break he was waiting for.

◊

Ryerson and Lethgate got back to the station and were stopped by the Captain when they got there.

"How are things going on the case, boys?" the Captain asked.

"It's going good, we're following up on a lead as we speak," answered Ryerson. Lethgate looked over at his partner. They had no leads, but they had to tell the Captain something.

"I know you guys are working hard on this case, but I also need some work done on your other cases. I want you guys to put this one aside for now and get some of the older ones finished up before we get a big backlog."

"But Captain, we still have a lot of leads and the media is still hounding us on the Cathy Ferguson murder. If they find out we have eased up on the case, we will be raked over the coals in the press," pleaded Lethgate.

"Right now the press is on to the new flavour of the week," said the Captain. "The only talk of the murder is in the local fashion community where she was well known. We're not closing it. I know this one means a lot to you, but this isn't your only case. We have other murder investigations that need to be handled."

Ryerson stepped in again. "But this is a serial we are dealing with, both Carl and I know he'll strike again. Let us follow up on some leads. Just give us a couple more weeks."

"For Christ's sake Frank, I don't have two weeks to give you. We have no hard evidence. What we did have has been destroyed or lost. To be honest I have no idea what we are getting into with this case." The Captain lowered his voice to a whisper. "We already had an unexplained fire and no one can explain how the computers got wiped. People are getting a bit nervous about this case and so am I.

"When something comes up again—something solid—you guys can go back on it. Until then you are working on something else. Understood?"

"You are wrong on this," Ryerson protested.

"Understood?"

"Understood," they both answered.

Ryerson and Lethgate sat at their desks and Frank picked up the phone and started to dial.

He picked it up on the fourth ring. "Mark Dekins speaking. Hey there Frank, I didn't expect to hear from you, what's up...Okay we'd love to get an official quote on it... Verbatim, you got it... When I say I'll write it word for word I mean it... No I don't need to record it, I'll just write it down. Trust me Frank I have been doing this for a while now... Ok, talk slow, but I'm telling you I will get each and every word.... Ok.... Ok.... Are you sure you want it phrased like that? ... Alright Frank, it just sounds kind of weird that's all... Yep, it will be in tomorrow's edition... No I don't know which page, why are you suddenly wrapped up in media attention?... Ok, well I'll make sure it gets in.... bye Frank."

Mark wrote the article in a few minutes and took it over to the city editor's desk for a quick edit. "Strange wording," simply said the editor.

"I know. I'd fix it up for him but when you start doing that they bitch about being misquoted."

The editor mumbled something and gave Mark the ok to put it in the computer files for the next day. The paper had not written anything lately about the Cathy Ferguson murder, so a quote from the detective working on the case was welcome.

He answered on the third ring. "Ryerson."

"Frank this is Lou," Lou had been a veteran of the force for nearly 14 years. "I'm down on Glen St. off of Nottingham. There has been some action here and it looks like your boy. We have four dead, a gangbanger with his throat torn out and the other three have been shot. We have one on the way to the hospital."

"Shot? Doesn't sound like ours," but the torn throat does, is what he didn't say.

"The kid who made it is on his way to Saint Francis'. The kid took a real shit kicking. Before we took him away he said some dude jumped them. He was beat-up real bad. But with this crew, I find it hard to believe they were keeping to themselves. They picked a fight with the wrong person or persons."

"Thanks Lou, we should be there in about twenty minutes."

"I'll bake a cake."

Ryerson got up along with Lethgate. Lethgate could tell from Ryerson's side of the conversation their vampire friend had been busy again.

Before they left the building Ryerson slipped his head back into the Captain's office.

"Our boy has struck again, Captain. We're going down to the scene now." Ryerson had planned on making a smartass comment, but he decided against it. He had known the Captain for many years and had respect for the man.

The Captain leaned back in his chair and slowly massaged his temples. "Frank?" he called out.

"Yes Captain."

There was a bit of a pause while he looked at Ryerson and Lethgate now appearing beside him. "I want you two to be really careful. I just don't want you two to get over your heads. Understand me?"

Both men understood. They could see in the Captain's eyes that even he was in over his head.

◊

When Patrick got out of the shower his skin was raw from the hot water and the scrubbing. For the past couple of days he was starting to lose control. Things were going wrong, and for a rare moment, he couldn't do anything about it.

He always credited himself with being a problem solver. If he couldn't think of an answer to the problem, he would eliminate the question with force. He was trained to be a killer, and he took pride in it. He was good at it—something he now questioned, and he didn't want anything to distract his instincts any further.

Dazinski had been a problem for a while, but the vampire took care of that for him. The Organization will be looking him over with a fine-toothed comb, but if Patrick could handle the vampire situation he might get through it.

If he failed, he would die. That was the conclusion Patrick had made in the shower, and nothing was a better motivator than the threat of death.

He went to the closet and picked out a fresh suit and laid it out on the bed. He checked his computer and noticed another call had gone through to the detectives. He put the headset on while rolling on his socks and listened to the recording. He was just about to pull his sock over his heel when he stopped.

A smile came over his face. The vampire struck again. He wrote the street name down and got onto a secured line to the Organization. He had to make sure the scene was looked over by one of their own, and make sure it was kept out of the newspaper. The murder would now get as much press as a purse snatching.

Patrick wasn't dead... yet.

32

When Ryerson and Lethgate showed up at the scene there was a sparse crowd. In this part of town the residents were used to police tape and flashing lights. Violence was a daily part of life.

The two detectives inspected the scene and got information from the officers who were first on the scene. There was one gun on the scene, which looked like the murder weapon used against the youths.

There was a lot of blood and Lethgate was sure one of the blood samples would be an anomaly showing a mixture of all blood types—that of the vampire. He was also sure the report and sample would go missing, too. He scanned the crowd and looked for someone suspicious. He looked at the officers around him. Someone on the inside was probably involved with the destruction of the evidence.

"By the trail of blood leading away from the scene it looks like our boy got shot," said Ryerson.

"The question is how bad," replied Lethgate. "By the amount of blood, it looks like a solid hit, and it would explain why he used the gun.

"Let's go over to the hospital and check with the kid that was involved in this. Maybe he can give us a bit more."

Neither detectives saw any trace of blood leading to the scene. The Organization had already cleaned the trail, making sure nothing would lead back to the location where the challenge took place.

◊

When they arrived at the hospital they went to the emergency room and got into one of the examination rooms where they just finished surgery on the kids arm.

Trigga, as he was known to his friends, was known as Gregory Kin to his mother. At the age of 15 he had no criminal record, which was surprising considering the crew he hung out with. Trigga was a very good student at school until last year. He started hanging out with Hype and the others and his grades started to slip along with his attitude.

His mother would beg and plead with him to give up the gang. He just brushed her off, and it broke his heart. He didn't want to be with Hype or the others, but it was a matter of survival.

At school he was getting picked on more and more. Being the smart kid in class came with a price, and for Gregory it meant a daily beating. Gregory's mother always preached to him to turn the other cheek and talk the problems out. The problem was the guys who beat him up didn't like to talk too much. The worse of it was they would terrorize him for a couple of days before beating him up. The threat of getting beat up was nearly as bad as the beating itself.

One day things went too far. He was walking home from school when he was jumped from behind and dragged into an alley. Of course there were seven of them, making it impossible for him to fight back. Instead of the usual beating, they starting pulling down his pants. Panic swept through his body, and he started to kick and bite anyone in sight. The struggle did not last long after he was pistol-whipped.

He woke up in horrible pain. All he heard was laughing and there was a painful flare in his ass. The guys beating him up were sodomizing him with a gun.

They were calling him bitch and whore and all he could do was cry. They had his arms and legs pinned and there was nothing he could do to get free. He could feel blood running down his legs. He tried to hide his face and wished he were dead. They removed the pistol and he thought the ordeal was over. A scream escaped him again and it was smothered by one of the guys arm. They started using a pop bottle on him, and he could feel his anus tearing and the blood was starting to flow freely. The arm was suffocating him, covering his nose along with his mouth.

Gregory didn't try to free his mouth and nose, he wanted death to come, but death didn't come. The gang members let him go and left him on the ground with the bottle still partially inside him. They kicked him a couple of times before they left. Gregory cried and wished they'd killed him. He removed the bottle gasping in pain. Somehow he managed to make it to a clinic and was rushed to the local hospital.

His mother never heard about the attack, but he did go to Hype. He told them of the beating, but he didn't mention the sodomy. He gave a blood oath to Hype and said he wanted to join his gang and he wanted revenge.

Weeks later when Trigga returned to school he saw the gang of boys that had beaten him. They were not laughing or taunting like he thought they would— they actually avoided looking at him.

Within a week of his return, three of the boys were killed in a drive-by shootings. Trigga was in the back seat of the car and shot at the boys. He wasn't sure if he hit them or not, but he kept telling himself they would never do that to anyone ever again.

Of the remaining four members of the gang that attacked Gregory, two went missing never to be found again unless a bulldozer exposed their rotting corpses. One got stabbed in the neck and died later in hospital and the last was nearly beaten to death, and would never again know how it felt to walk.

Gregory never wanted to be a part of Hype's life. He just wanted to make good grades and go to college. He wanted to live a good life and be happy. Now he was a gangbanger and his academic dreams were a thing of the past. Now he sat in the hospital, pain pushing out the tears. He was lucky. He felt the man's strength and he saw how he killed Hype. He tried to convince himself it was a dream and that his memory was foggy because of the pain, but it wasn't foggy. The man was more animal than man, and he would have killed them all if he hadn't been shot.

The curtain divider opened and in walked two men. He knew they were cops.

Trigga was in no mood for cops. He still felt very tired from the surgery. He wasn't sure how long, but it had easily been five or so hours. The doctors said they would have to operate on one of his arms again later. They said they were able to save it, and he should get some of its use back. "Save it," Trigga thought. He knew the break was bad, but not that bad.

"Gregory, we would like to ask you some questions," said Lethgate.

Trigga didn't say anything. He had had a couple of run-ins with cops, but they had been small compared to this. Hype and L'il Stevie were dead, but he didn't know what happened to the others. He blacked out after the Indian they attacked shot and killed L'il Stevie. If he was honest with himself, he fainted. How did he ever get involved in this?

"We want you to tell us what happened. What did the man look like?"

"I have no idea what you are talking about. We were walking along and we got jumped. I got hit first and all I remember is my arm burning in pain. I blacked out and the next thing I know I'm here." Trigga was impressed with the calmness he displayed. He was calm and cool outside, but inside he was shaking and feeling sick to his stomach.

Ryerson drew the curtain closed. Trigga thought they were going to beat him. Could they do that in a hospital? If he screamed out, shouldn't a doctor stop it?

Ryerson walked up to the bed where Trigga was laying and pulled up a chair. "Gregory, we want the truth. This is about some of your friends that died. We need your help."

"I am telling the truth, man."

Lethgate sat down on the edge of the bed. He looked very calm, actually both cops in Trigga's mind looked calm. They must be trying that good-cop bad-cop crap on him, but right now both seemed to be playing the good cop. The less he says the less trouble he gets in.

"Was the man an Indian, Gregory, a native Indian?" asked Lethgate looking at the boy.

"I told you..."

"We know what you told us," interrupted Ryerson. "First of all you are not in trouble, and you can go home after this. There will be no charges laid against you even if you guys did provoke the attack. This man, the Indian, we are talking about is very dangerous, Gregory. I'm sure you know that after what happened to your friends.

"Plus, you don't have to worry about the man pressing any charges against you. If he wanted justice, he would have torn out your throat."

Trigga grimaced and he hated himself for showing it in front of the cops. But he kept on seeing Hype's throat, and all the blood. The bastard had eaten his throat. He tried to hold the bile down that was rising in his throat.

"Tell us the truth," said Lethgate. "We need to know what happened so we can stop him."

"Bullshit," said Trigga looking back and forth to the cops. "You say that, and then I get my ass thrown in jail. Fuck you."

"For that one boy," Ryerson said, "the Indian bit him in the neck didn't he. And I bet he was the strongest son of a bitch you have ever run against."

"Look what he did to my arm. By what little I've heard from the doctors, I'll be lucky if I can still keep it, let alone use it properly again. The man was so quick, I didn't have a chance."

"Gregory, trust me. No charges will be laid, when you leave here we won't be seeing you again," promised Ryerson.

"Did you guys jump him or did he attack you," asked Lethgate.

Trigga's injured arm started to burn. He lowered his head and answered, "we jumped him." He was waiting for the two cops to get the handcuffs out.

"Was the Indian shot?"

"Yeah, but it wasn't me, you have to believe me!"

"I believe you," said Ryerson. "You were in so much pain with your arm, you probably couldn't have done a thing."

"Where did he get shot?" asked Lethgate keeping the questions flowing.

"In the shoulder, I think."

"Was he hurt seriously do you know?," Ryerson this time.

"Man, the guy moved so fast still after being shot. My head was swimming, I was trying not to black out, but the guy seemed to be moving... like he wasn't real or something. I just can't believe what happened."

The detectives asked him some more questions and quickly wrapped things up. They wished him a speedy recovery and left. Trigga was lying in his hospital bed all alone thinking things over. How had things gotten so carried away in his life? He just wanted to start over and have a life where he didn't have to worry about drive-bys and getting attacked.

Trigga thought about school. He was doing poorly but it was not too late to pull up his grades. He may have to take summer school but that was okay, it would keep him off the streets. He thought about his gang life, but it had died with Hype. Hype was the leader, and to leave, permission was needed from Hype and he never let anyone go. It was for life.

But Hype was dead now. Gregory, once upon a time known as Trigga, settled his head deep into the pillow. He would have to make amends with his mother, but he could not tell her what had happened and some of the things he had done. It would break her heart. He would make it up to her, and he would make it up to himself. Lying in bed, Gregory promised himself things would change.

33

Alex Frey, confined to his bed, listened to the newspaper. Both of his hands were in bandages so it was impossible for him to hold a paper. A volunteer at the hospital, her name was Sandy, sat by the edge of his bed and read out headlines, and Alex decided if he wanted the article read or not.

He had not yet looked at himself in the mirror and he didn't plan on it. His face felt very swollen, and he thought if he saw his reflection things would start aching more than they were.

"City drops the ball in new stadium plans?" Sandy asked reading one of the headlines.

"No. I hate headlines with puns."

Sandy chuckled and scanned for the next headline. She had been volunteering for only three weeks and loved every day of it. She was financially well off, and regular work didn't appeal to her. Sandy was reaching a spiritual time in her life where she knew there was more to her life than just work and money. She had the money but there was an emptiness that had been in her for a while, and volunteering at the hospital, it filled a void inside her soul.

The hardest part was getting close to some of the patients, especially the elderly and terminally ill. She had always been a people person and she cherished sitting with a patient, even if they didn't want to talk and only wanted to listen to the rain.

She looked down at Alex to see if he was in discomfort. The poor man had been severely beaten, but he had such a wonderful outlook on things. Even when he was in pain he would try to make light of it by making a little joke. He was a bit eccentric, but in a very charming way.

"Police plead for help in unsolved murder?"

"Yeah, could you read that one please, Sandy?"

She smiled at him. He was a very polite man.

Alex listened to the article and he asked Sandy to repeat one of the quotes. "Strange way of wording it, isn't it?"

"Yes. Please say it again," he said as he tried to raise himself higher in his bed.

She finished the article and Alex seemed to be in his own little world. "Now it starts," he whispered.

"What was that, Alex?"

"Oh nothing," he muttered. "Sometimes I just mutter to myself, but it never seems to be important."

"Oh, I know how that is," Sandy smiled. She looked at him again and something seemed to be troubling him. Very eccentric indeed.

◊

Patrick went over the report on the attack, which had happened the night before. It appeared the vampire was in a bad section of town, got jumped, and when he started to tear the guys apart, he was shot—again. But the bastard had got away again.

The report indicated the vampire used the gun on all but one of the gang members, seemingly running out of bullets for the one surviving kid. The use of the gun nearly threw off the Organization's investigators, because they had to make sure it wasn't a regular homicide.

Patrick knew the vampire must have been hurt badly if he used a gun. He smiled to himself because the news was getting better all the time. He glanced down at the morning paper open to page seven. "Police plead for help in unsolved murder." Even though he was privy to the conversation over the phone the night before, Patrick had grabbed a paper as soon as it hit the newsstand. The quotes were not changed as Det. Ryerson had asked.

Patrick sat by his computer waiting for the call to Det. Ryerson. The detectives would soon find the vampire.

By Mark Dekins

Tribune Staff

The police have hit a roadblock in the murder of a local woman and are looking to the public for answers.

Two weeks ago police found local fashion guru Cathy Ferguson dead in her home. After exploring all avenues and interviewing many people, the investigators have no solid leads.

Detective Frank Ryerson who had been covering the case says someone in the community may have seen something that night and pleads for any individuals to step forward.

"Many times it is the small clues, that break open a big case," said Det. Ryerson. "We are pleading for anyone who may have seen something to please give us a call."

Det. Ryerson knows the pain and anguish the Ferguson family is experiencing and promises the police department is doing everything in its power to solve this case, which appears to be an isolated event.

He believes the murder may have been a burglary gone wrong. It appeared Ms. Ferguson may have stumbled upon the intruder and was killed senselessly.

"Whoever committed this crime should step forward. I challenge the killer to step forward and give himself up. I challenge him to do this."

If anyone has any information or may have seen something they are urged to please call the police at 555-TIPS.

◊

The Vampire read the article. The challenge had been issued. It was a unique way of doing it, but the detectives didn't have a way of getting a challenge issued to him personally so they used the media to do it.

He called the number.

34

The call came through his computer. He put his hands over the earphones even though it was not necessary—he didn't want to miss any of the call.

Patrick jotted down notes while he listened. The phone conversation was being recorded but just in case there was any technical problems he wrote it down. It was better to be safe than sorry.

When the call was over, he smiled. He had a date, time and location. He would have to call the Organization, but not now. He kept smiling as he cleaned his gun.

◊

Both Ryerson and Lethgate took turns answering calls the next day. There were about 24 new leads, none of them would be of any use. They knew who the killer was, they just couldn't find him. A lot of the calls were hoaxes, some people had nothing better to do than call the police with "information".

The phone rang again, all calls coming into the TIPS line about the Cathy Ferguson murder were being transferred to the detectives. "My turn to get this one," Lethgate said and picked up the phone.

"Detective Lethgate," Carl answered.

"I believe you were looking for me detective."

"Excuse me?"

"The article, the challenge."

Lethgate gave Ryerson a look and he picked up the extension.

"Do I have both detectives on now," asked the Vampire.

"Yes you do, answered Ryerson. "Who is this?"

"I am the person you have been trying to find, the one responsible for the deaths you are investigating."

"They were murders."

"Regardless of what you want to call it, I have called to answer your challenge."

The detectives looked at each other not sure on how to proceed. Neither was sure if it was the man they wanted.

"What challenge is that?" Ryerson asked trying to sound matter-of-fact.

"The challenge to face a vampire." They looked at each other. They had their man.

"Maybe we should talk in a more secure manner," suggested Lethgate speaking for the first time and trying to keep a level voice.

"I know the line is tapped, they are watching you closely. It doesn't matter to me anymore. This will all end one way or another."

A chill went down Ryerson's back—*this will all end one way or another*—sounded like an omen. "That is what we want," Ryerson said sincerely. "We just want this all to end. We don't want any more people hurt."

"Where is the challenge?" the Vampire asked. The pain in his shoulder still flared. He knew he was in no condition for a challenge, but he wouldn't back down from one. A challenge doesn't show one's strength, it shows one's heart. It was a sacred belief to him.

Ryerson and Lethgate just looked at each other and shrugged. They had planned to contact the vampire and issue the challenge, they just never thought of choosing a location. It would be unlikely the vampire would agree to meet inside a secure prison.

"Ah, I, well we, haven't," Ryerson stuttered looking to his partner for help. Lethgate just looked at him and shrugged. Ryerson had a deep urge to laugh, but knew it would blow any opportunities of meeting with the vampire.

"Do you know the water tower at the old tire plant on Yorkshire Drive?" The Vampire asked cutting off the awkwardness. The detectives said they did. The Vampire described a section along the back where the challenge would take place. The area was secluded, the perfect place. They agreed on a date and a time and the conversation ended.

They hung up the phone not believing the conversation that had taken place. They got up from their desk and went to scout out the location. They wanted to be sure they knew the place. The challenge would happen tomorrow night.

35

The Vampire stood at the bow of the ship, the wind and waves threatening to send him overboard. The waves lifted and tossed the vessel, all other hands inside praying to whatever god would listen to them. The Vampire grasped onto the rails daring the storm to take him.

He was on his final voyage home, but there was no happiness to this. The home he had left, was many, many years ago and he could only dread what he would find. With the salt water soaking him, stinging his eyes and threatening to take his feet from under him, the Vampire knew he would not meet his end here. He was cursed to live on.

He was cursed to see the horrors of the world. To see good men die, and bad men prosper. Throughout his journey he had seen greed rule, and desperation populate. He was cursed by the men hunting him. Despite the distance he put between them, traveling by night over land no animal would choose, they would still find him.

The Vampire would kill them, only later to have new men following him. Now he returned to his homeland, tail tucked between his legs, not to go home and see his people but to hide in the lands where he knew the men could never track him.

During his journey he had seem some wonderful things. Beautiful temples framed by breathtaking surroundings. But, regardless of the sites, he was always on the run looking over his shoulder.

Now he was on the water, at the hands of his gods.

When he got to the port he signed on to work the ship, but he had no intention of working. The Captain, who was a weathered man would take no disobedience on his ship.

The Captain saw the Vampire swinging in his hammock, with no intention of working. He rushed the Vampire.

"You had better be dead or near death."

The Captain had spent most of his adult life on the sea. He lived a hard life and was a hard man. He demanded respect and enjoyed being feared. When he saw this Indian in the hammock, he knew he was going to kill him. Kill him and feed him to the fish, nobody would miss a goddamned Indian.

A soon as the Captain's hands touched the Vampire he spun out of the hammock with such speed and agility the Captain didn't know what was going on.

The Vampire pushed the Captain against the wall. The Captain, shocked with the strength of the Indian, still had strength in his voice.

"How dare you touch me! You will let me go right now, and beg for your life because right now you are a dead man. You do not commit mutiny on my ship!"

The Vampire moved his face closer to the Captain and smiled. His mouth widened into a sickening grin, and it was that moment when the Captain noticed sharp, long teeth coming down from behind the Vampire's lips. Soon there was a mouthful of teeth that should only be in the mouths of monsters or demons.

"If you want to value your life you will leave me alone, and the men on this ship will leave me alone. If I catch you or anyone else even looking at me queer, I will rip out the throat of every man on this vessel. Except for you. I will take my time with you. And that, I promise, is something you do not want to happen."

The Captain was only being held up by the strength of the Vampire. All the strength had left his legs. He struggled to keep himself conscious, because if he blacked out he knew he was dead.

"Y-y-you are the devil."

"Call me whatever you want, but believe me, you do not want to cross me."

The Vampire released the Captain and he collapsed to the ground. He crossed himself three times, and closed his eyes and said a small prayer. He was on a doomed ship with the devil himself. He prayed for his soul, and the souls for all on board. He would tell the men to leave the Indian alone.

No questions were to be asked, and the order was to be obeyed by all.

During the voyage the men would look at the Indian through the corner of their eyes. It didn't bother the Indian as long as he was left alone.

His focus was on the men hunting him. The Vampire noticed it was just not the white man who hunted him, and when he came across other vampires, they told him to trust no one, that their power was great.

A power so great that they webbed over the world. This worried the Vampire greatly, and he spent many evenings staring up at the stars contemplating what this meant and what he was going to do. All he knew was that he would not give up his fight, only regroup.

His mood matched the weather as the sky lit up bright with lightning and the ship was lifted and rocked by the waves. The men below prayed to their gods, but the Captain knew god would not hear his prayers because the devil was on board and had created this storm. He lowered his head and cried for the first time in years.

The Vampire made his way back to his room with unsteady legs. The rest of the crew had decided to sleep in another part of the ship. They had heard the Captain's warning of not talking to the man and leaving him alone. To the Captain's surprise they were still alive. Then when he saw the vast churning sea, he crossed himself. For a dreadful moment he thought maybe they were in Hell riding upon a sea of fire. The devil was just testing them, testing their faith. He called for all hands on deck, devil or not, there were repairs that needed to be done.

The Vampire came on deck to see the new day. Men were busy working, and busy avoiding his eyes. He looked over at the Captain and for a short moment their eyes met. The Captain, quickly lost the colour in his face, ran to the port side of the vessel and expelled the contents of his stomach into the sea. The men were shocked by what they saw, turned and saw the man they were warned about. They lowered their eyes and continued their work. Whatever power this Indian had on the Captain it was strong.

The following days were uneventful. One evening the Vampire came up to watch the sunset. He had seen thousands upon thousands of sunsets in his life, yet they still seemed to have a mystical power that appealed to him. He watched the colours dance into one another thinking of his journey.

He had met other vampires and learned of his enemy. They wanted to control the vampires. Vampires could live among other men as long as they stayed tame and did not strive for too much power. He was shocked when he found out some vampires helped the Organization by giving up news and rumours. The men who followed him were many in number but honourless. They would rather kill like assassins instead of killing like real men, eye to eye.

He watched the waves roll gently across the water, rocking the boat like a mother rocking her new born child, but behind him he heard the slight sound of footsteps.

The young man watched the Indian looking at the sea. The Indian had been the subject of rumour and curses since he had found his way on board on that day that seemed like a lifetime ago.

Gerald Horthan had been a member of this crew for only two years, and went by the name Squint. As the youngest and least experienced of the crew, he worked hard for the approval of the Captain and his mates. When he saw the fear of the crew, he was shocked. These were some of the toughest, hardest men he had ever met. The Captain, whom he feared *out of respect, was not himself anymore. There were rumours he was under a curse, and the cause of the curse was no secret—it was the man in front of him.*

Squint slowly unsheathed the knife from his waist. He had been told along with the rest of the crew to stay away from the man, but this was his chance. He would sneak behind the Indian and slit his bloody throat. Then at the sight of the dead Indian he would earn the respect of his mates, and more importantly the respect of his Captain.

He slowly raised the knife as the smile on his face widened. He could almost smell the blood that was about to be spilled. But the smile turned into a look of shock as the Indian quickly turned and charged him. He felt himself being pushed into the beam of the mast.

The Vampire grabbed his knife hand, pressing it above Squint's head and squeezing until the knife fell to the ground. The Vampire's other hand covered his assassin's mouth to hold in the scream. Squint's eyes widened as the Vampire smiled and a set of dangerous teeth appeared. His bladder released when the teeth entered his neck.

The Vampire took his time. He fed long and deep relishing the taste of his enemy. Since he had left his land, he had tasted the blood of many of his enemies, and he was willing to spill enough blood to stain the seas themselves.

When he was finished feeding, he dragged the young man to the edge of the ship and threw him overboard to be fed on again by the creatures under the surface.

The following day the crew searched for Squint, but the Captain knew what had happened. The devil had claimed a new soul, and now Squint was in Hell, floating on a sea of fire.

For the remainder of the voyage the men kept their distance from the Vampire, even more than before. No more blood was spilled by him, but that didn't mean the end of death on the ship.

A serious bout of sickness hit the crew resulting in three deaths. The Captain was sure it was because of the devil, and was surprised he didn't claim the entire crew. When they finally reached port, the Captain's hair was a solid white. When the voyage began there was only a few traces, now there was only a few traces of black.

Once on land the Captain drank heavily in the closest bar he could find. He sat alone, people whispering and glancing over at him. Men who had shared the sea with the Captain over many years were frightened when they saw the fear in his eyes. They didn't ask questions, they just knew something was very wrong.

He staggered out of the bar, and found the closest chapel. He stumbled in leaning on the pews to regain his balance.

The Captain was surprised when he awoke. First he was in a church. He had not been in church since he was a small boy. He also felt at peace. It was the first time in many, many days since he first met the devil that he felt at piece. A smile came to his face when he looked up.

There was a wooden carving of Jesus in front of him. The Captain crossed himself and with tears running down his face he ran the blade of the knife across his throat. He was found that afternoon laying in a pool of his own blood, with his vacant eyes looking upon the figure of Jesus.

The Vampire went into hiding.

36

Carl got home early from work. He and Frank agreed to do some soul searching and think about who would take the challenge. Dawn was pleased to see him home and he gave her an extra-long hug which she gladly accepted it.

He told her to get dressed because he wanted to go out for dinner and check out the town. Dawn immediately went upstairs, she knew this was strange behavior from Carl. They rarely went out for dinner through the week and if they did they would plan it at least a week in advance. She loved her man to death, but he was not the spontaneous type. Carl always liked things planned down to the minute, and would have a back-up plan ready just in case.

She went into the walk-in closet and took out her red dress, which was still wrapped in plastic from the dry cleaners. Dawn didn't feel like going out, she had a meatloaf ready in the fridge that only needed to be put in the oven. She wanted to watch a couple of her shows and go to bed early, but she was the wife of a detective. She was not sure how he could be surrounded by so much death and pain every day without it taking a toll on him. It took a toll on her. She rarely asked about his work because it got her down thinking there were monsters out there that would kill someone else.

Early in their relationship Dawn tried to get out of Carl what happened at work. He would just brush off the question saying she didn't want to hear the details. It was the details of his job that caused the sleepless nights.

She insisted on knowing so one day Carl sat down and told her. After dinner, Carl had told her of the case they were working on. A woman was charged in a double murder—the woman suspected her husband of four years of cheating on her. The couple had just had their first child, a seven-month-old boy, who was by all accounts up almost every night with colic. The wife was furious, believing the husband was not doing enough to help her with the baby, and destroying the sanctity of marriage by seeing another woman while she waited at home tired from lack of sleep with a child who wouldn't stop crying.

According to lab results and her confession, the woman drugged the husband's food and while he was unconscious she tied him securely to a chair. When he came to, he found himself tied and the baby's bathtub filled to the top. When the wife checked in on him and found him awake she came into the room with the baby in her arms. She looked at the husband and ignoring all his questions, placed the baby face down in the water.

The husband thrashed in his chair trying to free himself. The neighbours heard cries of help and called 911, but didn't investigate. The wife placed her hands on the back of the baby's head until it was dead. The wife then went into the kitchen, grabbed a steak knife and stabbed the husband 53 times in the chest.

When the police arrived she didn't resist and she even fell asleep in the back of the squad car. Her lawyer immediately started talking about temporary insanity, and postpartum depression.

It was later discovered that the husband, after a thorough check, was not having an affair. When the wife found out she went hysterical. For days she would sob and repeat the names of her husband and child. She was placed on suicide watch. Her cell was rid of any items that could harm her, including her blanket so she wouldn't try to hang herself.

She was found dead the next day. The woman had used her own teeth on her wrists to bleed to death.

It was the last time Dawn had ever asked Carl for details. If he wanted to talk, to get things off his chest, she would listen. For months she could not get the image of the father being tied up watching helplessly as his baby son was being drowned right in front of him.

She looked at herself in the mirror and went into the bathroom to touch herself up a bit. There was something wrong with Carl. She could tell. A wife learns to read her husband. When they are down, when they are hiding something or when they need some attention. She knew men were a lot like children, they needed to be kept in line without it appearing like they were.   When she walked down the stairs Carl was in the living room sitting on the love seat with a blank look on his face just staring at the wall. He was there but nobody was home. She hated his job. He loved it, but she thought it must kill a part of him each day. She was sure if there was a man inside him who had love and faith in society, it was long crushed by what he saw every day at work.

"Ready," she said as cheerfully as she could.

Carl looked up surprised that he hadn't heard her coming. "You look wonderful," he said taking her into his arms. He squeezed her tight and let out his own little sigh. It was a longer hug than usual. She looked at him and could see his mind working behind his eyes. She gave him a little kiss, wiped the lipstick she left on his face and told him she loved him.

There was something wrong, but she would not push him. If he wanted to talk she would be there to listen.

◊

Frank didn't go straight home from work. He walked the streets for a couple of hours hoping for an answer or a sign, yet no burning bush appeared for Frank Ryerson. He looked across the street and saw the building. He didn't walk there intentionally, but he was not surprised at where he ended up. The sky was starting to change colours and he worked his way across the road.

He made his way into the hospital and took the elevator to Alex Frey's floor. The nurse at the desk was going to tell him visiting hours were now ending, but Ryerson pulled out his badge and said he must ask Mr. Frey some questions regarding a police matter.

Ryerson pushed the door open and the blandness of the room struck him. He didn't notice this in all his prior visits. White all over the place. It seemed to envelop him when he walked into the room.

"Detective!" said Alex happily. "I would say I am surprised to see you, but after reading the paper today, I'm not."

"I take it you read the article." Ryerson pulled a chair up to the bed.

"Very smart. Did it work?"

"Yeah, we got the call early today from the vampire and the challenge will take place in a couple of nights."

Frey became very quiet. He was not a vampire expert right now, he was a minister. The detective didn't come here for advice, he came to cleanse his soul.

"Where is your partner?"

"Carl's at home. I think he planned on going out for dinner with his wife. He's just having a quiet night."

"I can see by the ring on your finger you're married too, but you want to spend a quiet night with a man covered in bandages instead of your wife. Too what do I owe the privilege?"

Frank looked at his ring finger and just nodded at it. He looked out at the window and saw the sun setting over the city. It really was a beautiful sight. It was funny how he never really noticed sunsets before.

"I just wanted to check up on you and see if you had any advice for us."

"You didn't come here for advice. I can see it in your eyes, I can see it in the way you are handling yourself right now."

Ryerson felt like getting up and leaving. If he wanted to talk, he would talk on his terms. He looked down at Alex with hate in his eyes. He was the detective. It was Frank Ryerson's job to read people's expressions, not this guy.

He closed his eyes and looked down to the floor. His mind flashed back to Shannon Chambers and the way he cried out. All the blood that flowed from his nose and mouth, with tears flowing in his eyes, begging the detective to stop. Frey was not trying to make him mad, he was trying to help. He could feel the burning in his nose and eyes as tears tried to form. He quickly put a stop to that. He may open up to this man but he wouldn't cry in front of him.

"I guess it is this challenge that is worrying me. If it was a physical challenge, I would rely on instinct and training. I would go right after his injury and just start pounding..."

"Injury? What injury?"

"He was shot."

"What! Why didn't you tell me this before?"

"Settle down, I was getting to it." *Do I have to tell you everything? Who does this little puke think he is raising his voice to me?* "Our vampire got involved with a street gang, they jumped him, he started vamping on them, and one of the kids pulled a gun and shot him."

Alex sat in bed with a very disturbed look on his face. A nurse started to come into the room and Ryerson rose and pulled out his badge and told her he was conducting a very important police statement. She didn't have much time to protest before Ryerson gently escorted her to the door.

"God damn it. I wish these hospital doors had locks on them." He returned to his seat and Alex was still chewing on this new piece of information.

"What? What is it? Do you think we should switch to a physical challenge?" Ryerson hoped.

"No! God no!" He chewed on his bottom lip thinking things over. His fingers and hands were starting to burn and itch. The itch was starting to drive him crazy, with the casts on his hands he had to try to ignore the sensation, but it was not working. He looked up and saw the detective slowly rocking back and forth waiting for him to talk. *God I hope the other detective is mentally stronger than this one.*

"If he is injured, he is going to be more dangerous," Frey started saying keeping his voice level and calm. "I was hoping before he would take you two lightly, underestimate you. But with him being injured, he will go into this with full concentration and focus because he knows he is vulnerable.

In a physical challenge with a vampire, even an injured one is still a bad idea. He will go in looking for a quick kill making him very dangerous."

Ryerson dropped into his seat. He was looking for help and encouragement at this visit, but Frey was only dropping more doubt onto him. It was a waste of time coming here.

"You know, I kind of wonder why I showed up here. Carl, I'm sure is feeling the same way I do, and he and Dawn went out for the night." Ryerson lowered his head. He had been beating around the bush for too long. He was wasting Alex's time and wasting his own. The last place he wanted to be was in a hospital room with a man who he had recently met. "Sometimes I look at my wife and think how lucky I am, then sometimes I look at her and wish I were single. I love my wife, but if she were to leave me I couldn't see myself falling apart like other men.

"For the challenge I was going to think about my love for Jill, and I don't know how I really feel about her. I don't know if I have ever felt true love for any woman. Even my mother..."

"Ryerson. Let Lethgate do the challenge. If you do it, you'll end up dead. You have too much doubt and you won't be able to hide that from the vampire."

Ryerson looked down at the weak, beaten man and realized this man had no power. How could a man like this help him, and what could this man know. Frank had dealt with hardships and dangers though his life and he never needed help. He certainly didn't need this man's help.

Alex Frey watched the detective pick up his coat and walk out of the room. It was not until he left did he realize he was holding his breath. He felt very tired, and let his head sink into the pillow. He looked up at the white ceiling wondering how many souls before him had spent time staring at it.

A pang of guilt lurched in his stomach. These detectives couldn't do this. Certainly not Ryerson. He was not sure of Lethgate, but if he was facing the same doubts as his partner they were both dead. The look of hate and pain in Ryerson's eyes raced through his mind haunting his thoughts.

He called a nurse and asked her to place a call for him. She came back when he was finished and hung up the phone. After the call he felt a little better. This was either going to make things worse or make things better, regardless, there was nothing more he could do for them. He closed his eyes and let the noises of the hospital lull him to sleep.

37

Ryerson and Lethgate stood outside the apartment door. The building was luxurious, marble shined to a wet, glimmering finish, solid wood polished to a mirror shine. To even get a ground floor apartment you had to be pulling in a solid, high six-figure income.

The detectives stood outside the penthouse suite's door. Neither knocked not knowing if they wanted to meet the person inside. Alex called them late last night saying he had a meeting set up, if they were interested. They said they were, but now standing at the door, both hesitated. They exchanged a quick glance at each other and Lethgate nodded. Ryerson nodded back and knocked on the vampire's door.

A voice told them to enter and both obeyed, reluctantly. The penthouse was gorgeous, something that would have been found in top designer magazines. The rich and famous would be envious. Everything in the suite whispered top of the line, and if you had to ask how much, don't bother, you would never be able to afford it.

Paintings on the wall that most museums would be jealous of. Historical artifacts that would be impossible to insure because the dollar amount would be unknown. Everything had its place, except for one thing—an old battered red La-Z-Boy recliner sat in the middle of the lavish surroundings with a man sitting comfortably in it.

The man—the vampire—was a balding old man, appearing to be in his early 60s. He wore gray track pants with a well-worn white t-shirt that didn't fully cover his large belly. The vampire had only one leg, the other just a stump above the knee. He carried a beautiful African Blackwood cane.

"Come closer detectives, I don't bite." The vampire gave a little laugh. "Actually I do bite, but I promise I will be on my best behaviour today."

They took a step forward and the vampire struck like a cobra after a mouse. He used the butt of the cane landing it directly into Lethgate's stomach sending him sprawling on the soft leather sofa beside him. The vampire quickly spun the cane and hooked the back of Ryerson's calf and pulled the detective towards him.

He wrapped his powerful arms around Ryerson pinning him tight. Lethgate started to reach for his gun. "Hold it, detective," the vampire said behind his dangerous looking teeth. His mouth was close to Ryerson's neck, and he could feel the vampire's hot breath.

"Look at you two. A poor old vampire with only one leg sitting in a beat up chair and he gets the drop on you. Imagine what that ancient vampire is going to do to you fellows." His hand worked his way down to Ryerson's thigh and the vampire gave a little squeeze and slowly moved it in the direction of the groin. Ryerson could feel the vampire getting hard underneath him. Ryerson struggled to break free.

"Shhh detective, settle down. I will let you go, but I just want you and your partner to sit quietly on the sofa. Don't reach for any weapons. We are just going to sit and talk."

And with that, the vampire released the detective. Ryerson moved quickly over to the sofa beside Lethgate, but remained standing. "Please sit detective. I will behave myself, I promise," he said with a smile. "Sit."

When both detectives finally were seated, the vampire looked around the room and flashed his cane over his head pointing it towards the priceless artifacts.

"It took me many years to acquire my fortune. Many of these artifacts were given directly to me from emperors and kings themselves. I know you have been told much about us from our mutual friend Alex, but I will go into further detail.

"Now, don't think I do this for any human. I am not doing it for you two, you are merely—a snack if you will. The reason I am talking to you is because of Alex. He is well received in the vampire circle, not because he has an interest in us, no, it is more of a respect. Did Alex ever talk to you about Australia?"

"What about it?" Lethgate asked.

The vampire closed his eyes and sighed. "If you continue to act this stupid I will take back my word about behaving myself. Now, did he mention Australia?"

"He just mentioned that the vampires there are really dangerous," said Lethgate hoping this was a suitable answer.

"Did he mention his time in Australia?"

"Briefly."

"So he didn't mention being hunted by vampires down there?" The detective's shook their heads no. "The reason we respect him is any man who can fight off Australian vampires has earned our respect.

"The Aussie vampires, for God knows what reason, are—well are just killing machines." He looked down and slowly spun his cane in his hands. "I have no idea why that is. I believe when all the continents were joined in one giant landmass, Australia was connected to India. Yet, if you go to India, you will not find one of these killing machines.

"I can tell you with all honestly, I would be terrified to he hunted down by a pack of them." The vampire slowly nodded his head. "Not just one, but six of them.

One mortal man survived being hunted down by six of the deadliest creatures to walk the earth since the dinosaur. He has the scars to prove it, but I guess he kept his shirt on, so you couldn't see them. I have walked this world for more years than I can count, yet if six of those vampires came after me, well, I'm not sure I could have survived.

"So it is out of respect that we talk to him, and let him study us. It is because of that respect that he is alive—and you detectives as well."

Ryerson hated this vampire. He had felt powerless against the vampire, and Frank hated feeling that way. He wanted to take the power back by placing a bullet in the vampire's brain. "If Alex can fight off six vampires, how is it one man put him in the hospital?"

The vampire slowly shook his head. "Obviously, you do not know fear well enough. I thought for sure you two men, in the jobs you have, must have experience. But maybe not. Mr. Frey merely got the shit beat out of him. Pain covered the fear. Being tracked down by vampires and having to fight them off—that is fear."

"Are you going to help us?" asked Ryerson.

The vampire gave out a loud laugh. "There is no help for you. You two will likely die if you try to challenge him."

The vampire could see the detectives starting to stir on the couch, he felt he was going to lose their attention and they'd leave. He made a promise he would help them. Personally he didn't care if they lived or died, but he would tell his story anyways.

"I am not an ancient vampire, but the one you are after is. We have been following him for quite a while. And when I say we, I mean the vampire community if you will.

"It is not only the Organization that watches him." The vampire gave a little chuckle to himself. "I will return to the subject of the Organization later.

"This vampire has been killing and causing terror for a long time. If you were to test his intelligence he would probably score a genius. I hear he can learn a language in days—quite extraordinary really. We watch him from afar, and sometimes we can get close to him. Most vampires can sense each other quite easily from across a room. Our friend seems to be a bit slower recognizing us.

"When he does catch on, he doesn't have much to say. He seems to be a loner. We have watched him kill from country to country and continent to continent. He will usually stroll into a city or town, and just leave behind a pile of corpses.

"Most of the time you would never know it. The Organization does a good job cleaning up his mess, but they have done a pretty piss poor job of stopping him."

The vampire leaned forward in his red recliner, looking closely at the detectives. "This isn't even his first time in this city." The detectives just looked at him with a puzzled expression, but remained silent.

"I think the last time he was here was about 30 years ago. If you think he has been a naughty boy this time," he laughed again and made a long whistling sound. "You would have really appreciated what he did back then. At least I did. He spilled a lot of blood and had a lot of people scared, but the media wasn't allowed to report it.

"Yeah, it was good times back then. We met briefly, I don't think I said more than a few words to him. But he more or less has the support of vampires because he kills you useless *humans*," spitting out the word as if it was poison, "and he also pisses off and kills a lot of hunters from the Organization.

"When I first talked to Alex, he seemed to have the impression that the Organization was our keeper and that they have us on a leash and smack us on the nose with a newspaper if we get out of line." He once again leaned back into his chair. "I let him keep that illusion. Some vampires are mainly watered down half-breeds, believe that.

"*We* with the richer vampire blood lines know the truth. Look around you detectives. I have more assets in this one condo than most of the Forbes' richest men have. If you were to put vampires on the Forbes list," he paused for dramatic purposes, "well, humans wouldn't even make the list.

"If the Organization wanted to kill us all, they would be dead before they even started. With money comes power, and we have a lot of power. We aren't the ones in government with all the power, we are the ones pulling their strings and writing their laws."

His eyes squinted into narrow slits. "The only reason you walking blood bags are still allowed to exist is because of our numbers. If we could produce like you, we would kill you all off in a matter of years."

Lethgate leaned forward not willing to show any fear. "If you vampires think you are untouchable, why are you using a cane? What happened to your leg? You must be more human than you think?"

The vampire only smiled and held back a warning of disrespect. "My blood line is as close to pure as you will get. But, unfortunately one of my ancestors went *slumming*, and fucked a human. We're not perfect." Twirling his finger in the air.

"As far as this," tapping the end of the leg stump with his cane. "Well, I lost this many years ago during the American Civil War. Me and my companion..." The vampire tilted his head up in the air trying to recall. "What was his name?

Patrick? Peter? Regardless. For shits and giggles let's call him Peter. Peter was a beautiful young man. A hairless piece of ass if there ever was one." He smiled at the memory.

"There was a battle starting early that morning and we decided to have a picnic on the hill side and watch the day's entertainment. I had *just* finished laying down the blanket when I heard a whistling noise and suddenly I was flat on my back. A cannon ball had gone astray and hit me just below my knee.

The vampire closed his eyes as if he could see it more clearly in his mind's eye. "Oh, beautiful Peter! That young man who I only thought was good at one thing, surprised me that morning. He immediately undid his belt and tied it tightly over my knee making a tourniquet stopping the blood. And there was a lot of blood. He kissed me on the forehead and told me to be strong and not to worry."

He looked at the detectives smiling at the retelling of the story. "My Peter was so brave, not a trace of panic in him. He squeezed my hand and told me he was going for help. I held his hand, and motioned for him to come closer to me. When he did, I pulled him down and tore his throat open and drank him dry."

The wicked smile returned to his face. "After all, I can always find another lover. I needed his blood to survive, and thanks to Peter, he saved me, *twice*."

"One thing that is true to both vampires and humans, detective, is that we are both mortal. Death will come for us all. I have aged and been reborn again time after time, but now—now I know the end is near. I will age and keep on aging until I die.

"I am at the end of my life cycle now and the knowledge I possess, and the history I have seen can fill catalogues and that brings us to where we started, detectives—the ancient vampire you want to challenge."

Neither Ryerson nor Lethgate wanted to hear the remainder of what the vampire had to say. Alex told them to meet him, so the vampire could help them. This crazy *thing* sitting in a crappy red recliner surrounded by millions, possibly billions in art work and collectables, was the furthest thing from helpful.

"You have a vampire who has been hurt badly. I talked to the doctor who took the bullets out of him." Ryerson was going to question *bullets*. The boy got one shot off, not more. The vampire continued talking and Ryerson let it go.

"He is extremely dangerous in a challenge of the fist. Being hurt, you would think that is your best chance at beating him physically. But when a vampire feels threatened to the point where he is fighting for his life, he can sometimes tap into a primal rage.

"I felt it only once and I can tell you that to vampires this feeling is like the best heroin high ever reached. I was no longer in control of my body. It felt as if someone was controlling me, making me move faster and feel stronger than I have ever felt in my life. Over the years I have tried to make myself feel that way again, but alas, I could not catch the dragon." The vampire snickered at this own joke.

"In a physical challenge we try not to reach for that feeling. We fight with honour even when humans do not. But with him being hurt, being sought by both you and the Organization, well, instinct may just automatically kick in for him.

"You have no chance of winning a fight. I could have killed you both when you entered here." The vampire pointed at Ryerson, "I definitely could have killed the cute one there. Couldn't I?" Ryerson looked away and tried to simmer the rage inside of him. He wanted to strike out against the vampire, but he knew if he tried, he would end up dead.

"Now a challenge of the mind? You have a better chance of fighting him. This is a vampire who has spent hundreds of years killing for revenge and hatred. His beliefs are set in stone for his crusade, and after living for hundreds, maybe a thousand years, I am pretty sure he has a stronger mental outlook on life than someone who has lived for 40 years give or take a few."

"We were told you can help us," said Lethgate raising his voice. "I'm not interested in all this talk about him being all powerful, I'm just interested in how we can beat him."

"You can't!" the vampire yelled, his voice echoing through the condo. "Have you not been listening to me? I am helping you! I am telling you to go back to your homes and continue with your meager little human lives. Go home and cut the grass and water your gardens and forget about all this talk about scary vampires and challenges.

"The vampire you want to face is filled with more hatred than anyone I have ever seen. He will kill you both, and will continue to kill, be it here, or another city or country. I am helping you by advising you to walk away.

"Unlike previous humans you were able to uncover the truth, part in luck and part Alex helping you. Why he would do such a stupid thing is beyond me, but where other humans knew when to look away, you wanted to see where the rabbit hole would lead you. Let me answer that for you now detectives." The vampire smiled, razor sharp teeth slowly exposing themselves. "It will lead you to your graves!"

38

The Vampire made his way into the small village. His pilgrimage to the south was nearly complete. He had ventured his way down through the south looking for answers, looking for reason. The world he knew had changed drastically, and with it his faith in humanity.

The white man had also spread his plague down in this fresh land. A new century was approaching, possibly his last, wished the Vampire. He was not used to seeing so much hate and pain. In previous years there were wars, but never on such a massive scale. The white man wanted to bring genocide to an entire race. If you were willing to lie in front of the white man, and be his slave you were spared. Anyone else was considered a threat and was eliminated.

Schools were set up to brainwash the young, and the Church ruled with an iron fist. The white man only believed in one god, and if you didn't share the same belief, it was beaten into you. The Vampire's beliefs were considered by white men as sacrilege and wrong, and on his voyage throughout the south he could see a broken people.

Their eyes were open, but any hope and fight had long since disappeared. He had met two other ancient vampires in his travels. He shared his pain with each and they responded in kind. Most of them rarely showed themselves. The white man had hunted down and killed many of the vampires. The Vampire was shocked when he discovered that some of the white men who killed them were vampires themselves. It mattered not that they shared the same blood inside, it was only the skin colour that mattered.

He had spent nearly eight years travelling, hopping from village to village for short times. These people, like his own, held vampires in high regard. They offered him much, even when they had little to offer. He helped in the development and care of each village.

He left the south with more questions than answers. A journey of self-discovery, which had lasted many years, and still had many years in front of it.

He made his way through Mexico and enjoyed the people. They were truly the salt of the earth. They knew how to enjoy life and they knew when to work. White men never understood this balance. They either ran around like a chicken with its head cut off, or they used their money to do nothing except bark orders and degrade people who had none.

He felt a kinship with the Mexican people and took pride in learning their language. If there was one place in the world he would settle down to die, it would be in Mexico. It was a land blessed by the gods.

He made his way into a village just before dusk. The village had no plaque or sign with its name, like many he encountered, but it had a familiar feeling to it.

The Vampire walked to the small tavern that was located in the middle of the village. The Vampire had planned on walking through the night, but wanted to stop off for a drink and something to eat.

He walked into the clay bricked building, which was dimly lit by lanterns. The people looked up at the visitor. They knew by the appearance of the stranger that he travelled from a far distance. Many had never seen an Indian from the north. They stared out of curiosity and continued on with their meals or drinks.

The Vampire walked to the bar and ordered his drink and meal. The bartender nodded and poured the stranger a shot of tequila. The Vampire didn't drink often. He saw the effects it had on many of his people. A once proud people were now beaten down by the power of the bottle. He only allowed himself a maximum of two drinks and only once a month. He would not allow himself to be taken by the power within the drink.

A party had been held there earlier in the day the Vampire could tell. There were many glasses sitting at now empty tables. One table was still in use with three men huddled around it. They had glanced up at the Vampire but had not given him a second look. The bartender served the drink and quickly scampered to the back room to see to the food.

In the dirty mirror behind the bar the Vampire saw a man enter through the door. He was walking kind of slouched with his feet dragging under him, he was obviously very drunk, but still in a mood to party by the looks of it. He walked to the men and stuttered a muffled greeting to them. One held his arm to balance him, but with also a touch of compassion.

His voice gradually rose and culminated in sobs. The Vampire couldn't help but feel sorry for the man. The man was in deep pain and he could hear that his friends were telling him to go home and get some sleep that tomorrow was a new start. The man lowered his head and said the pain would still be there, and he turned around to leave. On his way out the drunk glanced at the bar mirror and saw the Vampire watching him. The drunk squinted at the Vampire trying to see the reflection clearer through the mirror.

Not wanting a confrontation the Vampire looked away, hoping the drunken man would do the same. But he could tell by the shuffling of feet behind him that the drunk was coming in his direction.

"You bastard! You've got a lot of nerve to show your face here!"

"I think you have me confused with someone else, my friend," replied the Vampire in Spanish. "This is my first ever visit to your village."

"I had to bury my sister here today. She was 14, not even a woman and now she is dead." The man wiped his sleeve across his face to remove the spit, but there was a long line of drool, which hung off his chin slowly inching towards the floor.

"My deepest sympathy, my friend. I had no idea a funeral was held today. My prayers and thoughts are with you and your family. Please accept my..."

"It was a vampire that killed her." The Vampire stopped what he was saying and suddenly saw the recognition in the drunken man's eyes. "Yes, my friend," he spat out the word 'friend', "a vampire. Not you, but one like you."

From time to time the Vampire would meet a human who knew he was a vampire. Most people walked past him not giving him a second look, and yet others with a single glance knew he was a vampire. When he asked people how they knew, they said it was only a feeling they had. The same was true with this drunken man, but the problem was a vampire killed his sister, and this man was looking for a fight.

"She was at the river doing the wash when she was attacked. She was a beautiful, healthy girl who was full of life. Full of it! And some bastard vampire took her life!" The man sidestepped and grabbed a barstool and threw it at the Vampire. The Vampire easily ducked it, and it crashed on top of the bar sliding down its length breaking any dirty glasses on it.

The Vampire had only sympathy for the man. Another vampire had murdered his sister. He remembered his first home and he played an important role as a vampire, it was his job to release the elderly and terminally sick. He would be called to the bedside by the dying or by their family and they would ask him to release their pain.

The Vampire always considered this an honour and would quickly end the person's life. The family would also consider this a great honour, and all in the village hoped one day to be taken by the Vampire.

During his travels when he needed blood, he would go after the old or very sick. Blood was blood, be it young or old. He could never understand why some vampires would attack the young and strong. He had tasted young blood and found no difference. In front of him was a mad man who wanted revenge, but the man was no threat because of his drunken state. His friends at the table didn't want to get involved and the bartender was hiding in the back.

"I am sorry for your loss, my friend. I will leave you with my deepest sympathy."

"Don't you call me friend you goddamn vampire!." The gloss in his eyes seemed to clear. "I challenge you, vampire."

The words shocked the Vampire, but he couldn't help but grin, which enraged the grieving man. "Go home and sleep off your drinks. You don't know what you are doing."

"I CHALLENGE YOU VAMPIRE!" He yelled at the top of his voice. "A challenge! I want a challenge! A challenge of the mind! I may not be able to kill the bastard who took my sister's life, but I can take yours." The man's eyes squinted at the Vampire and his top lip turned to a snarl. "Maybe it was you who killed her."

The Vampire stood and looked up at the man who was three inches taller. "I never killed her, and don't ever think you can accuse me of such a heinous act. I will accept your challenge, and your friends will bury you next to your sister."

The drunk didn't reply but was stung by the words. He raised his wrist to the Vampire's mouth, and the Vampire did likewise. The Vampire bit into the wrist tasting the blood, which was tainted with alcohol. The Vampire was sad it was going to end this way. The drunk didn't stand a chance, and was only going to bring more pain to his family.

It was a challenge centuries old, and the Vampire had pity on this lost soul in front of him. He didn't want to end the man's life, his family had seen too much, having to dig one grave for the girl. His mind wandered a bit, and the pain came rushing in. The Vampire started to shudder. He looked at the drunk whose eyes were locked on his. The drunk was over-powering the Vampire. The man had very strong beliefs in God and his love for his sister. He was a man of conviction who was a strong figure in the community. The Vampire felt the man start to bite down harder into his wrist and the Vampire returned the gesture.

The Vampire started to control his thoughts and relaxed his mind, and blocked out any thoughts of doubt. For what seemed like hours he saw images of the man's life. He felt his pain, joy and faith—it was strong. A combination of the man's faith and the Vampire's sudden fear of the man's internal strength tipped the scales in the challenge. It felt as if the Vampire was falling down a deep hole, the sights and sounds around him quickly fading.

The Vampire realized he was near the brink of death, he felt very weak and scared. It was his will to live that helped the Vampire fight back. He tightened his eyes and focused.

The men at the table could only stare at the two men. They were too afraid to move, and from their vantage point they couldn't tell who was winning. Even the bartender stuck his head around the corner trying to see what was happening. He could get a better vantage point if he took a step out, but he dared not.

The Vampire didn't know how long the challenge had gone on. It felt like many hours and it was taking a toll physically. The drunk was starting to slip. He was not doubting his beliefs, but the alcohol was confusing his thoughts, making it harder for him to concentrate. The Vampire opened his eyes fully. He saw the drunken man in front of him starting to tremble. The man's eyes were looking glassy again from the alcohol. In the corner of the man's eye a tear dropped out. The Vampire lowered his eye with the tear and watched it roll down his face. He raised his eyes to the drunk and saw the blood in them. And that was it. The Vampires mind was released and the man's mouth relaxed from his wrist.

The drunken man dropped to the floor dead. The Vampire leaned against the bar unsure if he could move. His head throbbed and his mind felt dangerously numb. Fear surged through the Vampire. He didn't know if he would ever regain his mind fully again. When he released himself from the man, he wasn't sure he had won, because inside he felt dead.

He leaned over the bar and grabbed a rag and tied it around his bleeding wrist. He tried to focus his eyes but images blurred and seemed to shift in front of him. The men at the table still stood there. They made a slight move when their friend fell, but didn't want to get near the stranger who was a vampire. The Vampire knew if the men attacked him, there was no way he could defend himself.

The longer he stayed the more danger he was in. He started to walk to the door and fell over a table with a terrible crash. The wind was knocked out of him, and he had no idea where he was going. All he knew was he had to move. With only survival instincts to guide him, he started to crawl and after a short distance he realized he was luckily going in the right direction.

He continued to drag himself though the dirt and crawled away from the village into the brush of the wild. He expected his head to clear shortly but it did not. He started to cry softly and could feel the drool seeping out the corners of his mouth. After crawling for what seemed like many painful hours he felt his hand plunge into cold water.

The river. He crawled a little further and let his face enter the shallow water. He hoped the water would clear his head, but it seemed to do nothing. He let his body go limp, and all he could hear was the shallow echo of his breathing. He closed his eyes, just wanting to rest.

His eyes immediately opened when he heard a woman's scream. It came a distance behind him from the village. Everyone in the village must have heard about the challenge and now the death of their friend. The Vampire suddenly realized he was at the river where the drunken man's sister was found. Regardless of how weak he was he had to move. If they found him he was dead.

But he couldn't crawl any more. His body was so weak he wouldn't be able to go far. He didn't want to crawl into any brush, the villagers would know he was injured after crawling out, and they could probably follow his trail.

The only option was the river. The Vampire knew how to swim, and by the sound, the current was not strong at this point, but he was so weak he would surely drown. The Vampire didn't ponder for too long, slowly crawling into the river. It was his only chance for escape, and he had to move now. There was no telling if the villagers were already looking for him.

He crawled out further and the cold darkness of the water wrapped itself around him like a shawl. He felt his head drop under the surface and he felt so weak he was not sure if he could resurface. The Vampire let himself go limp and tried not to struggle. He surfaced and he rolled onto his back and let the current guide him.

Like a branch of a tree, he floated down the river letting the river be his guide trying to stay awake, praying the current would not get any stronger because he would surly die. He didn't remember much, he thought he was dead and was floating away, but his head hurt too much to be dead.

He awakened with a sharp pain in his side. He was stopped by a fallen tree and one of the branches was in the middle of his ribs. It was early morning and he had been floating down stream for a number of hours. He started to climb out of the river and his body felt weaker than it did earlier. The Vampire crawled onto shore and dropped in exhaustion. He slept long enough for his clothes to dry. With a white paste in his mouth he went back to the river and took a slow, long drink and made his way to some shrubs nearby. His head was still cloudy and his body felt as if he had been beaten.

Once again, the Vampire fell asleep in the shade and didn't wake until the next morning. When he awoke, his head was still sore but his body felt stronger, only stiff. He stretched and decided he better start moving out. He was unsure if anyone from the village was sending out a search party, but he decided it was better to leave now than find out.

He kept walking for six more days and avoided any contact with people. He came across a small town a couple days away from the border and stayed over night. It was nice to sleep indoors and get a hot meal. It would take another four months until the headaches stopped and he felt normal again.

He had learned a lot about others and himself through the challenge. The Vampire thought about the challenge and how stupid he was to take the man for granted. He figured the drunk was a weak-minded man who had no idea what he was in for. Never would he put himself in a situation were he took his opponent lightly. Like a mantra he repeated, "Never again."

39

The morning light crept over the city and Carl was awake to watch the unveiling. The bedroom glowed red before the burning of a fully exposed sun took it away. He had only managed to get a couple of hours sleep in the night. He looked down beside him and saw Dawn sleeping. Her eyelids moved back and forth, obviously in deep REM sleep, and Carl was wishing he could do the same.

He spent an hour watching her sleep, looking at the lines at the corner of her eyes. Laugh lines, women called them. He had never noticed them on her before. Dawn aged beautifully, looking to Carl, better every year. He gave her a gentle kiss on the forehead, and she made a face of being disturbed then continued on with her sleep.

He couldn't help but think if this was going to be his last night with her. Was the job really worth his life? He was paid to stop criminals, but vampires? Deep down he knew it was his job to finish this. If the vampire took any more lives with Carl not trying to stop him, he would never be able to get a good night's sleep ever again. His conscience would always be tapping him on the shoulder, taunting him. He couldn't live with blood on his hands. Death comes to everyone, and he would rather die with a clean conscience than live being haunted by ghosts of future victims.

He rose and went into the washroom and took a long shower. All of his police experience couldn't prepare him for tonight. There would be no back up, it would only be Frank and himself.

Eventually he got out of the shower and wiped the fog off the mirror and started to shave. It was a morning ritual, but this morning it felt different. He looked around the bathroom as if he would never see it again. The feeling of dread in him was strong. It was probably paranoia, but what if it were a six sense, preparing him. He wiped the mirror again and finished his shave.

Lethgate was in no mood for breakfast, the thought of food stirred the butterflies in his stomach. Again, his thoughts went to tonight. He and Frank against a vampire.

Frank. He was the best partner Lethgate had ever had. He walked into the living room and sat down in his leather recliner. On the arm he saw the repair patch that covered an old hole. Regardless of the quality of the repair Lethgate could always see the patch. Nobody else could see it, but at times to him it stuck out like a sore thumb.

What was he going to do about Frank? Yes, he was the best partner he ever had, but there was a darker side to Ryerson. He was not afraid to take matters into his own hands even if they were against the law he was supposed to uphold. Lethgate thought back to Shannon Chambers. He knew Frank had put him in the hospital, and Frank knew Carl knew. He wouldn't come clean about it though and brushed it off as if it were a simple traffic ticket.

They had never talked about the challenge and who was going to do it. He traced the repair in the leather with the tip of his finger. Did Frank have a strong enough mind to take on the challenge? Did he? He believed that he himself had the stronger mind for the challenge, but how could he tell Frank? Frank would take it as an attack. *What are you saying? I'm weak minded? Too weak in the head to do it? What you don't believe I can do it?*

He rubbed his face with the palms of his hands and sighed deeply into them. What was he going to do with Frank?

◊

Frank finally made his way into the house. Jill was already at the table sipping her morning coffee.

"Where have you been? Have you been out all night?"

"Oh *great*. Here we go with the questions." Ryerson thought.

He pulled his mug out of the top drawer above the fridge and poured himself a cup. He explained to Jill they'd had a call last night, and it shook him up some. He said he went for a walk and just needed to clear his head.

She reached for his hand asking if he was alright. He pulled his hand back at her touch and said he was fine, he was just worn out. Reluctantly, she pulled her hand back and wrapped it around the coffee mug. It seemed at times to her the only warmth she ever received was from the coffee cup.

Frank looked around the kitchen and saw the flower stencils on the walls. "I'll be glad to never see those again." The thought startled him. He had every intention of returning tonight, but on a subconscious level he was expecting to never come home again.

The coffee no longer tasted refreshing. He poured it into the sink and told Jill he was going to bed. Climbing the stairs he wondered if this would be the last time he ever climbed the stairs in his own house. He shut the bedroom door behind him.

Jill softly started to cry in the kitchen. She couldn't live like this anymore. She had to talk to Frank. She was part of his life and she wanted to be let in. She wanted to know his secrets, his fears and his dreams. She wiped the tears off her cheeks and started to clean up, she wasn't going to let herself cry any more today. She was going to talk to Frank, she decided. As she washed out her cup she promised herself she would talk to him. He was tired today, but she would confront him with her feelings tomorrow.

◊

Patrick arrived at the location early in the morning. Later that evening the vampire and the two detectives would meet. He was in a building a block away from the assigned meeting area. It was a wide-open lot below the old water tower.

He wanted time to familiarize himself with the area. He was going to make his move tonight and he wanted everything well planned so it would all go flawlessly. He briefly thought about scaling the water tower and waiting there, but Patrick knew the vampire would also scout the area out. The vampire was hurt and wouldn't be taking any chances.

He looked up at the old green water tower. He experienced a strange feeling of déjà vu. It was an olive green tower with rust spreading out across its seams like vines did across ancient cities. Spreading out until there was nothing to see. At the middle where there was a walkway Patrick could see all the graffiti. The ladder climbing to the walkway was nearly 12 feet off the ground yet teenagers still managed to find a way to climb and spray paint their messages for the world to see.

There were messages of love. He could make out 'Danny luvs Jodie'. Patrick figured Jodie was probably banging some other guy or she was a lesbian. Danny was probably somewhere else spray-painting his love in hopes of getting some. There were a few 'fuck offs', but the one that kept catching Patrick's eye was 'Fear not the Coming'. *Fear not the coming.* He had seen that message before. Déjà vu. Goose bumps ran down both his arms and joined at the small of his back and raced up his spine to the base of his neck. He gave a shudder.

"Someone must have walked over my grave," he thought. It was an old saying he picked up from his grandmother. *Fear not the coming.* He could not take his eyes off the message written in bright orange letters.

What was coming? Death? The death of the vampire and the detectives he told himself. *Someone must have walked over my grave.* He turned away from the window and took out his handgun to clean. It was cleaned and oiled the night before but he wanted to get his mind off the water tower. *Fear not the coming.*

Death was coming, and it gave him goose bumps again.

Someone must have walked over my grave.

◊

Ryerson and Lethgate spent the day tidying up some loose ends and working on another case. It had been one they had been working on for three months that was unrelated to the vampire cases. It was supposed to be a murder/suicide.

A young man, 23, went to his girlfriend's house after they broke up over the phone. No one was home beside the girlfriend. The boyfriend forced his way into the house and neighbours reported hearing yelling. There was no history of violence on the boyfriend's end so that is why the girlfriend didn't call the police when he forced his way in.

Neighbours said the fighting lasted for nearly 10-15 minutes before they heard two gunshots, followed by a third. When police arrived they found the girlfriend dead on the living room floor with two gun shot wounds. One to the chest and one to the abdomen. In the kitchen the police discovered a second person down. After a quick inspection they noticed he was still alive and they rushed him to the hospital.

After shooting his girlfriend, the boyfriend went into the kitchen, got a beer out of the fridge, drank half of it then put the gun to his own head.

The boyfriend was in a coma and doctors said if he ever came out, he would be in a hospital or institution for the remainder of his life. He wasn't brain dead, but the damage he had done could never be repaired. If he ever woke up he would likely have no idea who he was, where he was and would not be able to recognize or talk to anyone in his family again.

That afternoon Lethgate received a call the boyfriend had died during the night. There was no urgency to the case. After inspecting the scene, they wrote up the report and waited on it. Today they filled out a report on his death, attached it to the original report and both signed the case closed.

The day moved like a turtle but the time to meet the vampire finally arrived. They left their desks and went to the car.

Outside the night had fully arrived. While sitting at the same desk earlier Lethgate watched out the window and couldn't remember a more beautiful sunset. He wished he'd taken more time in his life to enjoy the simple pleasures of life such as this. The orange and red of the horizon and how there were many different shades of blue in the sky each getting darker to create the on-coming darkness.

In the car Lethgate glanced up to the heavens but could not see any stars on the clear night. The city always killed that spectacular sight with all its lights. The city was busy trying to keep an evening sun. Always keeping busy, always something to do. If there was a flaw in Lethgate's life it was he didn't give himself the chance to kick back and take it easy. He was the type of person who always had to do something. Now he promised himself after tonight he would take more time for himself.

It was okay to be bored, and to stop and smell the roses. Humans were not put on this planet to work from day to day with constant pressure and stress with the hopes of being able to relax when they retire. Of course he had to work, but he could reduce the pressure and stress he put on himself. Things would be different after tonight he told himself. Tomorrow he would be a new man—if there was a tomorrow.

Lethgate was drifting in his own thoughts when Ryerson spoke. It made him jump.

"I think you should do the challenge," he said looking straight ahead. It was hard for him to say and impossible to say looking at Lethgate's face.

"Why? What's wrong?"

Ryerson clinched his teeth. He didn't want to say why. He wanted Lethgate to just agree and that would be the end of it. He also knew Lethgate was not going to accept an answer of "because."

"I don't think I can do it," he hated saying this. It made him feel weak. "I just mean I don't think I could do it as well as you. I know you have some strong beliefs and you have always led your life by them. Me? Well I guess I am more of a spur of the moment, sometimes quick to fly off the handle kind of guy. It works for me in most situations, but I don't think it will work here.

"I'll back you up full, you know that. I just think of the two of us you are the stronger one."

Lethgate couldn't believe what he'd just heard. Frank rarely spoke openly, and never about himself. He wanted to tell Ryerson that it took a lot of guts to say it, but that would only make things worse on him.

"Alright." And that was it.

No more words were spoken in the car and they slowly crept up to the warehouse district. Ryerson saw the green water tower and felt the butterflies in his stomach. He wished he had arranged for back up. They could have had a SWAT team set up to take out the vampire at first sight.

But this was between them. Only one would take part, the other was there for support. If Carl died Frank didn't know what he was going to do. Would he try to arrest the vampire or fight it? This was a matter of honour. Could he let the vampire walk away?

In his vision the water tower grew. Looking like a big green alien space ship with graffiti on it. 'Fear not the Coming' he read. "Here we come," he thought.

They parked a block away and made their way on foot. The two had been spotted coming by a pair of eyes, which hid in one of the offices in the adjacent building. Both men looked around but the eyes were well out of their sight. "Two down, one to go," Patrick whispered to himself.

He was not concerned he had not seen the vampire yet. He knew he would arrive last, and he also knew the vampire had no idea he was there. He was a hunter, he knew his prey and he knew how to be invisible. He just waited.

Lethgate and Ryerson waited under the water tower for the vampire. The water tower felt heavy above them, as if the air was thicker and the gravity more intense in this one area. Lethgate sat down. Ryerson looked at him and joined him. The vampire would not attack them unexpectedly, this was a challenge. It would be face to face. Man to beast.

◊

The Vampire was making his way to the water tower. He would have been there hours earlier to scout the area and to make sure there was no one who shouldn't be there, but he had spent most of the day sleeping. The gunshot wound was throbbing in his shoulder, sending shards of pain across the top of his back and up his neck.

He still felt a bit drowsy but the air was slowly waking him up. He needed to be alert, and ready. It was not only the detectives he had to worry about, but also the hunters. The Vampire needed all his senses, he had to be ready for anything.

He looked up into the night and could only make out a few stars. "They destroy the land, and they are now destroying the heavens."

As he walked he reflected back on his life. He had seen many lands and met countless people. He had seen his people and his land taken away from him. At times he wished death would have taken him to ease the pain. Living the number of years he had, was a curse. The things he had seen, the greed, hate and the disregard to the great spirits.

While he walked he felt himself walking in the past. Walking towards the beginning. Not the beginning of his life, but the death of it. The death of his old life and beginning of a new one. A new century had dawned, and in the Vampire's mind it was only the beginning of the end. His mind raced back, not to the beginning of the 21st century but to that of the 20th century.

40

He was an older man at the turn of the century. His hair was grey and his face lined with wrinkles. The Vampire prayed he would just continue to age until he passed, but he felt his body changing—he felt his body slowly starting to rejuvenate. He was not as quick as when he'd had a younger body, but the strength never seemed to diminish.

He had left his lands for many years. He would travel trying to understand the world, and come home for a couple of years before moving out again. Now he returned to stay. The land was no longer his, but now belonged to the white man. His people were scattered and broken, living on reservations. A once huge land they lived on was now assigned land—defeated land.

Walking through the villages of his people the young walked with their heads low, and the old would meet his eyes, but the fire behind them was long extinguished. The young didn't look like the youth he had once known. Their skin showed they were native but the clothes they wore were the white man's. In the distance he could see a church. The white man could not give his people land without leaving them alone. The white man had to completely change the Indian. The Indians were starting to forget their past, and once valued beliefs. The white man had the Indian down, and kept his foot on their throats.

The Vampire watched a youngster walk by and stopped him. "Son, where are the rest of the children here?"

"At the school nearly 40 miles away."

"Why so far, could they have not built one closer?"

The young boy had a suit on. It was wrinkled with small holes in it, an obvious attempt to bring the white man's culture to the Indians. "Sure, but being far away the children have to stay. The children live there."

"What about you? Why are you not there?"

The boy looked at the Vampire in the eyes. There was fire in his eyes, but his shoulders were slumped. His spirit was broken. The Vampire knew, sadly, his people would never rise again. "I ran away. I always run away. They just got tired of bringing me back. The rest of the children here are ones their parents refuse to send. But they will be sent off soon. The white man's law says so."

"Why did you run away?" The vampire saw something in his eyes.

"No one listens. Goodbye." And the boy walked away.

The Vampire watched the youngster stroll down the street kicking at the dirt, head down, not caring where his feet took him.

The Vampire decided to go to the school.

The school was located outside of a white man's town. There was a church connected to the school. It was two stories, covered in drab white brick. The white man never made anything natural. They never blended with their environment, they had to stand out.

The Vampire walked into the school. There was a small room with filing cabinets and worn out wooden desk. A woman saw the old man at the entranceway. "Yes? What do you want?"

There was harshness in her voice. Impatience and anger. This woman worked with children? "Can you speak English old-timer?"

"Yes I can."

"Good for you. What do you want?" The woman was stocky, with fat arms and a pudgy face. Tiny glasses seemed to be stretched over her fat face. She wore a flowery dress, but a flower she was not. Just a weed in an expanding garden of weeds.

"My grandson..." the Vampire started.

"What? Speak up old-timer. What about your grandson?" She had a whiney voice. Already the Vampire wished he could speak to someone else. This woman was rude and had no intentions of being nice to an old Indian.

He ignored the rude woman's remarks and continued speaking.

"My grandson will possibly be starting here next spring. I just wanted to look around and ask a few questions." He had no grandson, he just remembered the little boy he met. The boy seemed to have a broken spirit and the Vampire wanted to know why.

"Possibly coming here? Old man, it is the law. Too many of you don't want your children in school. You would rather teach them your backward ways. Here we try to open their eyes to the world and make them useful to society." Her eyes narrowed the more she spoke. She was used to a feeling of power, and in this building she was the queen. Everyone answered to her, and she loved the feeling.

"Now I would like you to leave. You can look around when you return with your grandson next year and we will answer any questions then. Now please leave, I am very busy."

The woman returned to her wooden desk and sat down in her chair. The chair creaked in protest to the weight and the Vampire waited for the chair to buckle under the load, but it was strong wood and held.

The Vampire turned around and headed towards the doors. To his left was the front door and to the right a flight of stairs heading up. Using his natural speed the Vampire darted towards the stairs before the nasty woman looked up. When she lifted her head she couldn't see the old man. "Fast little bastard," she thought. "Must have scared him more than I thought."

The Vampire continued up the stairs and noticed the only thing on the walls was a single crucifix. The place was very drab and cold. He felt depressed just looking around. At *the top of the stairs was the hallway with three doors on each side. It must have been the bedrooms for the children. He walked and heard voices coming from the second door on the left. He slowly knocked on the door and the voices of children immediately hushed. He pushed the door open slowly and looked in. There were two boys, both appearing to be about 13 years of age sitting at attention of the edge of their beds.*

They looked up at the old man, and still didn't move or ask who he was. The Vampire could see the fear in their eyes, and this deeply troubled him.

"Hi there," the Vampire said looking at the boys. They said nothing, and the Vampire shut the door so no one could see him talking to them. When the door shut the boys both stiffened and looked terrified.

"What's wrong boys?" The Vampire asked concerned with the boys' expression.

"Nothing." Was the only thing, which was peeped. In the room, there was nothing on the wall except another crucifix. The lone window was so dirty you could hardly see through it. There were two bunk beds cramped into the room with hardly any room for anything else. The boy on the left had a small scar above his left eyebrow. Sitting down, it was hard to judge the kid's height but the boy was a tall, lanky youngster. "A lot of speed in those limbs," the Vampire thought.

The second youngster was much shorter, seemed as timid as a mouse. The boy's nose looked crooked, as if when he was younger it had been broken. Both boys had hard eyes. Hard, meaning that they had seen a lot in their young lives. The boys were scared, but the eyes told the Vampire, they wanted to know who he was and what he wanted.

"I'm not here to hurt you boys. You are not in trouble. I just want to ask you boys some questions." He looked at each boy, and they both looked as if they were preparing themselves for the firing squad.

"Why are you scared? I'm not going to hurt you. I'm your elder, you can talk to me. We share the same history though our blood. You can trust me."

"We can't trust anyone around here," said the timid boy. He wouldn't keep eye contact. He would look up at the old man and then stare back at his feet.

"What happens in here, boys?"

The boy with the crooked nose pleaded with the Vampire. "Listen mister, if they catch you in here with us, they are going to punish us. Please, please leave. We don't want any trouble."

The Vampire could see tears welling up behind the crooked boy's eyes. He looked over and saw the timid boy quickly wipe at a tear, which escaped down his cheek. The Vampire could all but smell the fear emulating from the boys.

"Boys, I promise you no harm will come to you."

"What are you going to do?" said the timid boy still staring at his feet. "You are an old man, and there is nothing you or anyone else can do." The pitch in his voice rose as he finished speaking.

"Look at me!" The Vampire ordered the boys. Both slowly raised their heads and looked up at him. He locked eyes with each of them, refusing to look away. He slowly started speaking not taking his eyes off of them. "I promise you. Nothing is going to happen to you. I will make sure of it."

The boys felt a shiver go down their spines. The old man didn't look as old to them anymore. Behind the wrinkles they saw energy and power seeping through. His body didn't look weak like many of the elders they had seen. He looked powerful and dangerous. The timid boy saw truth in the old man's eyes. He was not going to hurt them.

The Vampire gestured for the timid boy to sit on the other bed. He slowly sat down on the edge of the bed and looked at the two boys in front of him.

"Do they hurt you here?"

The Vampire could see the boys were afraid of answering, but the timid boy just answered with a simple nod of the head. The Vampire could see the boys starting to shrink in front of him.

"What do they do to you?"

The boy with the crooked nose looked at the Vampire. A tear streaked down his cheek and he didn't try to wipe it, he started his story from the beginning. The lanky boy was called Michael and he was named Peter. The Vampire cringed at hearing white man's names attached to the Indian boys.

They began to tell the old stranger their story.

Michael was very excited about attending the school. When he was a very young boy his mother had died and his father the next day just walked away and never came back. It was his grandmother on his mother's side who raised him. She told him of the school at a young age. All of the boys on the reservation were expected to go to the white man's school.

The white men would come onto the reservations with soldiers to make sure all the youngsters were sent. Some of the children would be sent to school hundreds of miles away with their family having no means to visit them. For many children, their families grew into strangers.

Michael's grandmother always said to him it would be a new start for him. "You will learn to live like a white man. You will learn how to live in his world and not be confined to an area of land. Learn the way of the white man Michael and you can see the world and be an equal."

Michael's eyes would grow and a smile would spread across his face, excited at the adventure before him. "You will never be equal with the white man in your heart, Michael.

Our people are pure of soul and heart. The white man's heart is stained. Remember who you are, and where you come from and you will never stray."

When Michael left for school there were no tears. He gave his grandmother a kiss and left with the white men. Some boys would cry, their families begging the white man to leave them—sometimes blood would spill from the soldier's guns. This was a new beginning for Michael, he would learn the white mans world.

He didn't remember much of the ride. Hardly a word was said to him, but that was okay. He was going to learn to be a better person like his grandmother always promised and maybe some day he would be rich and have his grandmother stay with him and she would be so proud.

When they arrived, Michael was disappointed in the size of the school. The school had only about 40 students and looked dirty and not kept up. It didn't matter though, this was his new home, and the building would look beautiful in no time.

He was led up to a room that he shared with three other boys. When he opened the door two older boys looked up at him. They looked him up and down and turned back to what they were doing not greeting their new roommate. The other boy, younger than the other two, just lay on his bed with his back to everyone.

Michael was shocked by the appearance of the room. It was a tiny little room for four boys with two sets of bunk beds. He noticed under the beds neat piles of clothes were stored, not having room for any furniture. He carried his clothes in a sack so he took the clothes out, folded them and place them under one of the beds.

The two older boys each lay on a bottom bunk. The younger boy was on the top leaving the other top bunk for him. As quickly as he could, he climbed the bunk and stayed silent. He later found out the older boys names were Jericho and Hidden Sparrow. During his time there neither boy spoke to him, keeping a pact only among themselves.

The two older boys later left leaving the two younger boys alone. Michael rolled over on his side propping himself up on his elbow.

"My name is Michael." Daring to speak out loud.

The other boy stayed on his side refusing to speak. Michael rolled onto his back and just stared at the ceiling. He always kept his grandmother's voice in the back of his mind, telling him he would be better off.

That night he went to sleep with no one in his room willing to talk to him. A tear ran down his cheek but he just reminded himself that tomorrow would be a new day, and his roommates will talk to him, once they got to know him.

In the morning he just followed the others and stuck to their routine. The school wanted the boys to bath every morning because they said most of the boys had horrible hygiene. For nearly 40 boys they only had four tubs, and they would use the same water, never changing it even when it got dirty.

The older boys would go first and the young ones would go last. By the time is was Michael's turn the water was brown. Later he found out some of the boys would pee in the water before they got out. Needless to say, Michael would be in and out in a hurry.

His first breakfast was a worry. Things had started off badly to say the least and he was worried what they would be fed. The tables were set in three rows of three with two large tables at each end. A plump, short woman rose and immediately the room hushed. It was the same woman who would later be rude to the Vampire. She was not a nun, there were a couple of priests who sat at her table, and she was only referred to as the Head Missus.

She lowered her head and started the Lord's Prayer. Michael dared to peek around the room. He didn't know the prayer and didn't want to get in trouble. He noticed Jericho a couple of tables over just stared at his plate. Michael just decided to move his mouth and he would pick it up after a couple of days.

The Head Missus ordered each table to get in line for breakfast one at a time. When it was his time, Michael joined the line and grabbed a metal tray like the rest of the boys. Silence in the line was strictly enforced. He wanted to ask questions of the boys around him and introduce himself but he didn't want to start any trouble.

When it came time for the food his stomach was churning. He lifted his tray for the men who were dishing out the food. He gave them a weak smile and no smile was returned. A generous portion of porridge was slopped on his tray. He also received two slices of bread and a drink of milk.

He sat back at his table and looked at the food. It certainly didn't look good. He had never had porridge before and was worried about eating it. The other children around him were eating it with no signs of distress. At the head tables the staff had theirs brought to the table and they were eating it and seemed to enjoy it. Michael took a small portion of it on the end of his fork and placed it timidly in his mouth.

It didn't taste bad, didn't really have a taste at all but it was very filling. The bread was fresh, made that day and the milk was delicious. He had images of lumpy milk and stale, hard bread. After breakfast it was time to start classes. Some of the older boys went to the church for different lessons.

While walking to class, Michael could hear the thunder booming outside and the rain beating down on the roof. He had always loved the rain.

The classrooms were simple rows of student desks with a large teachers desk facing them. Behind the teacher's desk was a partial black wall. Michael was amazed when he saw the teacher writing on the black wall using a small white stick. He had never heard of a slate-board or chalk before. There was a small pail and an old rag, which was used to clean the board allowing it to be re-used. He had no idea what was on the board because he couldn't read, but it didn't matter it still captured his attention.

The teacher was one of the priests at the school, his name was Father Mathews. He was a tall lanky man with a hawk-like face. His eyes seemed to be too close together, with a long, slim nose, which hooked out over a small mouth that almost seemed lipless. When Father Mathews got discouraged with the children his lips would pucker and nearly disappear off his face.

The lesson was regarding an explorer and his journey. Michael tried to pay attention but his eyes always returned to the storm outside. The rain was pounding against the window and the lightening was so bright he would have to squint at times and he could almost feel his seat vibrate when the thunder clapped. The lesson Father Mathews taught was completely out of his mind. He could not keep his eyes off the light show Mother Nature was producing.

Michael soon noticed as he stared out at the dark sky, father Mathews was no longer speaking. When he turned his head he had no time to react to the stick. It caught him flush on the side of his forehead and there was a sickening 'thwap' sound. He fell out of his chair and hit his head on the edge of the desk beside him. It took time to get his thoughts straight when he was lying on the floor. His head was spinning with black dots dancing in front of his eyes.

Michael noticed there was shouting going on and soon realized it was Father Mathews yelling at him. "...up! You better learn to pay attention! God will never be with lazy people..."

Michael just pushed himself up and sat in the chair. He didn't look at Father Mathews, he just looked at the front of the room and tried to focus on the board. The words seemed to dance over the slate-board and the room was spinning slightly. He grabbed both sides of his desk to stop himself from falling over. Michael was sure if he fell over, Father Mathews would hit him again or start yelling at him.

293

The class started over and Michael could feel the blood running down each side of his head. The other boys around him would give him a quick peek but would not stare for fear of the wrath of Father Mathews. He could feel the blood running down under his shirt and running down his smooth chest and arms. The blood also dripped onto his desk. Michael was worried he would get in trouble for messing up the desk but he refused to let go of the corners of the desk and clean the mess because he was sure he would still fall out of his seat.

Father Mathews soon looked over at him. "You're making a bloody mess over there. Go see the Head Missus and get yourself cleaned up, you savage!"

Michael carefully got up, with his head spinning and managed to make his way slowly out of the classroom. He was certain he was going to get struck again for taking too long but he made it out of the class without receiving another blow.

He made it out into the hall and walked down leaning on wall trying to figure out what happened. Did Father Mathews snap? He would surely be released, maybe even lose his priesthood. When they contact his grandmother and told her of what happened, she would be angry. Angry at the treatment he received, but she would also be heartbroken. She had so many dreams for him, and she was sure the white man's school would be the answer to those dreams.

He worked his way down to the Head Missus' office and stepped in. His head was still spinning slightly, and he tried his best to stay steady on his face. "Um, excuse me..."

The Head Missus raised her head and had a look of annoyance to be disturbed by a student. The look of annoyance soon left her face when she saw the blood trickling down the side of his face. "What happened to you? Speak!"

"I was just sitting," his voice echoing in his head, not sure if it was coming out clearly or not. "Father Mathews, I don't know why, but..."

The Head Missus stood up, her bulky frame seeming to expand in front of him. It was her face though that alerted Michael. She had a look of anger on her face, just the same as Father Mathews had.

"You were not paying attention were you? Fooling off, not wanting to learn! How can we do our jobs when you people don't want to learn? Do you want to be bloody savages like your ancestors?"

What was happening? Why was she yelling? He could still hear the storm outside, but the storm inside was getting worse. He did nothing wrong, all he did was look out the window.

"Go down to the room at the end of the hall, last one on the left. Do you know left from right?" Michael's head was spinning and his head was throbbing. He wanted to cry but part of him told him to hold it in. He knew he would be in real trouble if he started to cry. The Head Missus reach out and grabbed him by his left wrist. Her grip was like a hawk's talon and she twisted lifting his arm. "This is your left! Got it! I'm warning you, you give us a hard time and you will not enjoy your stay."

Michael just kept nodding his head yes. He clenched his eyes shut. The look on the Head Missus face was worse than the pain, and he thought she was going to break his arm. When she let go he just kept nodding his head. She yelled at him to get out and he walked down the hall towards the room, which was on the side of his aching arm. He got into the room and there was a small cot in the room. He sat down on the edge and tried not to close his eyes, just starring at his feet. He wanted to lie down, but he didn't want to get yelled at. He would have stood, but he felt as if he was going to collapse. When he closed his eyes, the room would spin quicker. He just starred at his feet wishing he would wake up from this dream.

Michael didn't remember much about what happened next. While waiting he had passed out, and the person treating him tried to keep him alert, but he just kept on passing out. He woke up in his room and his hand went to his head where he felt a bandage wrapped around it. His head was pounding and he felt very sick to his stomach. He noticed the other boys in the room—Jericho and Hidden Sparrow were each reading, and across from him the other young boy with the funny shaped nose was also holding a book but was looking at Michael. It looked as if he was going to say something but decided against it and returned to his book.

Michael lay in his bed not believing the events that had unfolded. He felt his head again, just to make sure he hadn't just had a nightmare instead. The older boys in the room ignored him, but the other young boy would steal a glance every once in a while. The two older boys kept to themselves. He was also getting very hungry, but a feeling inside of him told him dinner was probably already over, and it was unlikely he would get anything tonight. He sank his head gingerly into the pillow and closed his eyes, hoping he would just sleep until morning when a knock came to the door.

The three other boys immediately closed their books and Michael could feel the tension in the room. He looked up and noticed Father Mathews entering the room. He looked at the three other boys, making eye contact with each before looking down at Michael.

"Come with me," said Father Mathews. "I think we should talk."

"Just take a seat," Father Mathews said as he opened the door to his room.

The room was small like the other dorm rooms. The room was located at the one end of the school that housed most of the staff. In his room was a small bed in the corner with a crucifix over the headboard. There was a small round table in the corner with four chairs around it, nothing on top. The room had a very antiseptic feel to it. The small dresser by the bed had a hairbrush and a washbasin on top, nothing else. Michael found it strange later when he thought back to the room, that there was no mirror above the wall. Maybe the Father had a small one in one of his drawers that he used.

"Sit down at the table, Michael." The priest pulled out a chair and sat down looking at Michael. He had a hard glare, but Michael kept eye contact. He didn't want to appear weak but he felt his hands shaking slightly and his knees were relieved of his weight as he sat.

"We got off to a shaky start today didn't we? You must understand that I was only doing my job. I have nothing against you Michael, I'm sure you are a nice boy and I like you. I like all the boys in this school, and I'm sure you will too, as you get to know them better.

"The thing is, discipline is very important to young men. You will learn three things here Michael. You will learn to be a good Christian, learn to be a man, and learn discipline."

Father Mathews got up and walked over to his dresser. "Would you like a drink?"

He pulled out a bottle of wine and two glasses. Michael watched the priest pour two glasses of wine. He had never had wine, and his grandmother had always warned him of alcohol. It was the one true evil that the white man had brought with him. The drink would steal your soul and devour your life.

The priest put the glass on the table in front of Michael and he just starred at the red liquid, which looked like blood. The priest sat down and took a drink and looked at Michael and smiled. "Go ahead. It is one of the few luxuries the church allows us to indulge in."

The boy looked down at the drink afraid to touch it. Afraid he would loose his soul and his grandmother's love. He whispered, "No thanks, I'm not thirsty."

"For Christ sake just drink it. Most of you damned savages are alcoholics anyways. Might as well drink something as respectable as wine instead of the whisky you barbarians usually drink. Now drink!"

Michael slowly lifted the glass to his lips while the smile on Father Mathews face grew larger the closer the glass the drink got to the boy's lips. Michael had a little sip and it burned going down his throat. He tried to stifle a cough as the priest laughed. "Trust me Michael, the taste grows on you." The priest leaned over the table and gave the boy a rough pat on his shoulder then he leaned back in chair laughed, and had another drink.

The priest started talking about his own childhood and said he understood the fears, that go along with growing up. Michael just nodded, wondering when he could leave. Father Mathews kept telling him to drink and his stomach was feeling very sick. The priest got up and went over to his dresser and took out the bottle again and brought it back to the table, refilled both their glasses and placed the bottle in the middle of the table.

Michael noticed something strange when the priest got up to get the bottle. He noticed how dark and gloomy the room seemed, and quiet. The candles threw an eerie glow and made the corners look very dark. He looked beside the bed and for the first time noticed the planks covering the wall. He realized they were covering what was a window. Instead of shutters covering the windows, he had nailed planks over the wall. A chill ran down his back.

The priest noticed the boy looking at the covered window. "Ah, you've noticed my handiwork, huh? Or lack of. This window faces east," the priest pointed in its direction as he took a long drink from his glass. "I like a dark room, and I couldn't find any fabric thick enough to keep the light out. It doesn't look pleasing, but it does its job. Drink up, boy!"

As time passed the priest kept making Michael drink. The boy's head was spinning and he just wanted to sleep, but part of him forced himself to stay awake. The priest got up and stood behind the boy. Michael didn't move and swallowed hard, suddenly very scared. The priest placed his hands on the boy's shoulder and started to massage them. "You've had a tough first day my son. I'll make it feel better."

The priest's hands grinded the boy's shoulder. A tear streaked down the boy's face, too afraid to talk. Father Mathews hands were very rough and they moved from the shoulders to Michael's chest. "Please don't." Michael said and the priest threw him roughly to the floor, the chair bouncing and coming to rest against the wall.

The boy didn't know what to do. He looked at the door and the priest stepped in front of it, as if he understood what was going through the boy's mind. The priest walked over to Michael and picked him up by his hair and threw him onto the bed. The priest fumbled with the boy's pants and when Michael put up a struggle the priest punched him in the back of his head.

Michael's head was swimming in pain. He wanted to stop the priest but his arms felt very heavy, too tired to move. A part of him wanted the priest to just get it over with. With the pain inside his head, he didn't have the strength to fight.

He didn't know how long the attack lasted, he just remembered praying for death, asking both his gods and the white man's. When Father Mathews got off of him he told the boy to leave, and if he mentioned this to anybody he would cut the boy's throat.

Michael finally found his dorm room and made his way through the dark room and crawled into bed with his clothes on—it made him feel less dirty. He looked over across the room and with the moonlight coming in through the window could see they boy with the crooked nose looking over at him. Michael rolled over and prayed for death to take him in his sleep.

The following week was hell for Michael. Every evening Father Mathews would come and get him, take him back to the priest's room and he would rape the little boy. Father Mathews would forgo the wine, and would just throw the boy onto the bed.

Michael would walk to class in a daze and any lessons would quickly leave his head. He didn't care what was being taught, and he hated hearing about the white man's god because it didn't exist. How could a god allow that to happen?

Michael found himself at the office door of the Head Missus. He wasn't sure what he was going to say, but he had to say something. He was scared of the woman. She was looming and domineering, but something needed to be done.

"Excuse me miss?"

"What is it?" The Head Missus barked.

And all of a sudden Michael started to cry and couldn't get a hold of himself. All of the pain and waves of emotion released in her office. She got out of her seat closed the door and led Michael to a chair and made the boy sit down. It took her many minutes until she calmed the boy down.

She asked him what was wrong and Michael poured the whole story out between giant sobs. His throat felt raw, and his words would sometimes get stuck, but he forced them out, exorcising the demons inside. When he was done, the Head Missus eyes looked very strong—trying to see through the boy as if looking for any lies in the story.

"Come with me Michael." She placed a surprisingly gentle hand on his shoulder and gave a soft squeeze. "Let's get this taken care of."

She led the boy up the hallway and eventually made it to Father Mathew's room. Michael flinched at the sight of the door, but the Head Missus gently guided him to the door. She knocked.

Father Mathews opened the door looked at the Head Missus and then at Michael. A look of shock was on his face. "This boy has told me an interesting story Father," she said.

"Has he?" Was all he could say not taking his eyes off of Michael.

"As you know, Father, we can't have this sort of thing going on at this school."

Father Mathews continued to stare at Michael. The boy could feel the hate searing into him. He looked up and saw the Head Mistress staring down at the boy.

"Lies will not be tolerated," she said staring deep into the boy's eyes.

It took a moment for him to understand what just happened. "No," he yelled. "No!"

She grabbed the boy with an iron grip by his shoulder, letting her nails sink in and break his skin. "Father, can you please take Michael here and teach him what happens to little boys who lie?"

He pulled the boy inside the room and shut the door. Michael could hear the Head Missus's footsteps leaving down the hall. He looked up to the priest and was immediately floored with a punch to the stomach. He desperately tried to get air into his lungs, but no matter how much he tried he couldn't. With a sudden rush, he managed to gasp down some air in his burning lungs.

"Goddamn little savage!" Father Mathews said as he kicked the boy in the face. "You ever, ever!" Another kick. "If you ever tell anyone again you will be dead." Another kick. "And I will make sure you whole fucking family is dead too!" Stomp. "Understand me?" Kick. "Do you understand me?"

But Michael couldn't answer.   His jaw was dislocated and he was knocked unconscious. Michael woke up three days later and would spend four weeks in bed recovering from his injuries.

Lying in his room he pretended like the other boys to be reading. He held the Bible in his hands but refused to read its words. He rejected the white man's god, and his way of life. He would go through the motions until he was old enough to leave—or die.

Peter—the boy with the crooked nose—had visited him on a couple of occasions. Michael would peak through the slits of his eyes and watch Peter sitting by his side. If he gave any indication of waking up, Peter would get up and leave the room. They never talked, but Michael noticed Peter looking over at him more frequently.

The boys jumped when the door opened. Father Mathews stood at the door. Michael just closed his eyes and waited for the priest to call him. "Peter come with me." Michael lay there stunned. He was sure he was going to go through it all again, but this time Peter was called. He was partly relieved, but felt terrible guilt because what if the same thing happened to Peter that had happened to him?

He lay on his bed and waited. Time seemed to go so slowly, and the remaining light, outside stepped aside for the cold darkness of night. Jericho and Hidden Sparrow didn't seem concerned about Peter being missing, they weren't concerned when he finally arrived back. They never asked where he was or what happened. They just never cared.

The door slowly opened and Michael propped himself up on his shoulders and watched Peter come in. Peter didn't look over, but Michael didn't care, he was not going to stay quiet any longer. "You okay?"

"Goodnight," Peter answered with a sniffle to subdue his tears.

On Sunday after the church service Michael kept close to Peter. The service was long and drawn out, with hymn after hymn. Michael sang with the rest of the boys because if he didn't know the words or refused to sing there would be trouble from the priests.

After the service was free time. Most of the boys would play or go for a walk—they just tried to keep out of the priest's way. When they made their way outside Michael came up to Peter and said, "We have to talk."

Michael grabbed the fabric on Peter's shirt to steer him in the direction of the shed, but Peter didn't resist and walked along not making a fuss or asking any questions. They got behind the shed, gave a glance for any priests—the coast was clear.

Michael sat down and Peter followed suit, leaning against the shed.

"I know what happened to you," Michael said to Peter. "I want to try to help you."

"How can you help me, huh?" He said with a tone without hope. "You have no idea what happens in this place."

"I think I have an idea," Michael said back rhetorically.

"Yeah I guess you do." Peter's face lightened up and he looked handsome for a boy his age. "Michael that was not the first time one of the priests did that to me." Michael was stunned. "It has been going since I arrived here two years ago."

"I had no idea."

"Just keep your head down and do what you are told in class, just try to blend in. And be wary of all the priests. Father Mathews seems to have a bigger appetite for young boys than the rest, but at one time or another all of them has—you know—to one of us."

Michael sat just staring at Peter. He seemed so calm about it.

"Sorry you learned the hard way about the Head Missus. If I had known you were going to her I could've told you. I saw her do the exact same thing to some kid when I first arrived here. Good thing too, I guess, because I was planning on going to see her. She is just as evil as the rest of them."

"Why wouldn't you talk to me," Michael felt close to tears. "Why wouldn't you tell me this and be my friend."

"I guess I got used to not having friends. Living with Jericho and Hidden Sparrow is not the most pleasant thing, as I'm sure you'll agree. They keep to themselves. I guess I got used to keeping quiet, and not having a friend."

"Do the priest's go after those two?"

"They used to," admitted Peter. "But as they got older and bigger they started fighting back. The priests leave them alone now. I wouldn't be surprised though if one day both go missing and are never seen again."

The two boys continued talking until they had to go in for dinner. They talked about the abuse for a short time, and their hate for the school and priests, but they mainly talked about their homes and family.

Over the following weeks the two became as thick as thieves, never sharing their world with anyone but themselves. Their friendship was very personal. They shared a pain that made them stronger, but now they sat on their beds as a strange old man with powerful eyes listened to them.

"All the adults here do this to you?" the old man asked.

Peter nodded. "The Head Missus doesn't. She'll just hit us, but she knows what is going on. Even the caretaker here will hurt the boys in the same way as the priests."

"I want you boys to do me a favour. I want you to stay in this room no matter what. No matter what you hear, you stay in your room." The boys nodded suddenly very aware of the power residing in the old man. "When it gets dark I want you two to leave. No one will follow you. Do you know how to get back home?" Peter shook his head yes. "Take your friend with you, and you can help him get home too. Now stay here."

The old man stood up, some how looking taller and younger than when he entered. He left the room and the boys looked at one another. They made sure the door was shut tight and huddled together on the bed, heeding the old mans warning.

The Vampire walked down the hall towards the stairs when a man in a black robe turned the corner.

"What are you doing up here? Only students and staff…" No more words would ever leave the priest's voice as the old man grabbed his throat and tore it open. The only sound was a gurgling then silence.

The Vampire made his way downstairs to the office where the fat woman sat behind her desk. "Sir, I asked you to leave, you cannot…" The Vampire threw the chair out of the way and walked around and grabbed a handful of the fat woman's hair.

"You knew what was happening here! You knew what these priests were doing and you allowed it! You knew!"

The Head Missus tried to free her hair but the old man's grip was like a vice. There was no give, and his eyes seemed to burn fire. She tried to yell out and when she did the Vampire gave her a slap hard across the face and grabbed her hair again and tilted her head back so she could see his face clearly.

She could feel the hairs being torn out by the roots, and tears started to roll down her pudgy face as she started sobbing.

"How many children have you made cry!" He pulled her hair harder, and she cried out. "How many children came to you for help and you turned your back on them and gave them back to those monsters? I will send you to your god, and let him judge you."

He pulled her head back and bit into her throat. He tore a big chunk of flesh out of her neck and the blood started to flow. He held her hair and spit the mouth full of flesh and blood into her face. She was not worth tasting, he walked out of the office leaving her to die.

The Vampire hunted down all the priests and killed them all. The rage built up in his body and he could not control the hatred. The hatred of the white man, and what they had done to his people and what they were doing to the young. The white man took his people's land, they took the fight out of his people, now they tried to break the spirit of the young.

He came to the door of the priest the boys told him about. Father Mathews. He kicked open the door and the priest jumped out of the chair he was working at. He had not heard any of the deaths beyond his door.

"Man of God," said the Vampire. "I will send you to hell where you belong." Father Mathews dropped to his knees. He didn't try to fight, he didn't demand an explanation or beg for forgiveness. He just started to cry. He looked at the old man's clothes and saw the blood, freshly stained all over them. The blood on his face and hands—surely this was his day of judgment. He knew he had failed in his life, and what the old man said was true, he was going to hell.

The Vampire made sure before he died and went to hell, he would feel hell on earth. He gagged the priest with a pair of discarded socks on the floor and slowly started biting of pieces of him. Fingers, ears, nose. Whatever he could tear off with his bare teeth without killing him.

He started to rain his fists down onto the priest. Every strike making a sickening wet, crunching sound. He stopped the barrage of punches and reached for the priest's holy book. This book meant nothing to him, and if it meant something to God, then let God strike him down right then and there.

He removed the bloody socks from the priest's mouth and started to stuff pages of the bible in it. When he could get no more in, and the priest face was turning purple and his eyes started to roll back into his head he started to jam the entire bible into his mouth. The corners of his mouth spit open making a hideous trail of blood and flesh across his entire face.

The Vampire looked down at the monster and spit on his remains. No amount of suffering was good enough for this man.

Blood dripped from his chin and from his hands as he made his way through the school. Any of the youngsters who saw him quickly went to their rooms and shut the door. He walked into the chapel and saw the caretaker cleaning the pews. The man had his back to the Vampire and the Vampire walked to the man to tear out his throat and dispose of all the evil living here.

The man turned around and the Vampire stopped in his tracks.

The caretaker was Indian. This man in front of him saw what was happening to the young—which were his kin. He let the white man do this to his own people and he even participated. Tears rolled down the old man's face, he stood looking at the scared caretaker.

The caretaker knew what the old man was. He had never seen a Vampire before, but had heard their legend. He saw the old man with blood on his face and hands and could tell by the tears in the Vampire's eyes that he knew the caretaker's sins. He crossed himself.

The Vampire let out a scream when he saw the Indian caretaker cross himself. He ripped at his throat and pounded on the man. The Vampire cried out loud while continuing the beating long after the man stopped moving.

He rolled off the caretaker who was a bloody pulp. The Vampire wanted to torch the building but was afraid one of the boys would still be hiding somewhere and would get trapped. He walked out of the building and started to walk. He didn't know what direction, nor did he care. This land was no longer his—or his people.

He walked, not looking back, promising to himself, his ancestors and his gods that the white man would pay. Pay in blood.

Ryerson and Lethgate sat under the water tower not speaking but with an understanding between them.   The sense of danger churned in their stomachs. Lethgate tried to steady his breathing, attempting to keep his mind clear before he stepped forward and completed the challenge.   The anxiety was worse for Ryerson. He was going to be a spectator in the challenge, helpless and uninvolved.   What if something happened to Carl?   Would he draw his gun and shoot the vampire?   It was supposed to be an honoured tradition with the winner walking away, but it wasn't his tradition. He remembered the warning of the other vampire—he dishonoured the tradition, he and his family would be hunted down and killed. His stomach rolled and cramped bringing waves of nausea.

He felt as if he had to vomit when he saw a man walking towards them. The nausea swelled and sank in his stomach.   There was no time to get sick.   He nudged Lethgate and both men rose to meet the vampire walking towards them.   He was only a small man, but he walked with determination.   Ryerson had never been so scared in his life.

◊

Patrick was in position.   The two police detectives rose to meet the vampire. Patrick gripped his gun by his side and started to make his way to their location.

◊

The Vampire spotted the two men and walked towards them. His shoulder hurt and he felt slightly weak, but he would show no pain. He would not give his opponents an advantage by showing weakness.

The men were standing for the Vampire waiting for him. They both looked strong, fear showed in both men, but that was not necessarily an advantage for the Vampire. A man who faced fear head on, driven by the fear could accomplish anything.

The white skinned detective showed the most fear, but attempted to cover it more. The black skinned detective looked scared, but seemed more comfortable in showing it. This man worried the Vampire—there was something about him.

The three men just stood facing one another not saying anything until Ryerson broke the silence.

"We've never done this before so we don't know what is supposed to be said or done," he said shrugging.

"Which of you will do the challenge?"

"I will," Lethgate replied. A lurch turned in the Vampire's stomach. He knew something was wrong, and tried to block it out of his mind. If he worried about it, it could taint his thoughts and cost him his life.

"Which challenge?"

"Mind." Lethgate kept direct eye contact with the Vampire. He hoped the Vampire couldn't hear his heart, which seemed to be drumming in his ears. He was sure if he looked down he could see it pounding through his shirt.

The Vampire locked eyes with Lethgate and the feeling of something wrong increased.

"We don't have to do this. You can give yourself up." Ryerson knew the Vampire would not give up, but the steel in the Vampire's eyes made his knees feel weak. A gentle breeze caught Ryerson and he closed his eyes for a brief second. In a single second he tried to enjoy the breeze and cool feeling over his face. He felt this might be the last breeze he would experience.

"It's too late to give up. This is part of my destiny here. I cannot walk away—and you could not let me."

"Why?" asked Lethgate. He wanted to say more, but he was afraid his voice would betray him.

"I have seen much in my years. Too much. People I loved stolen from me. I have seen my people tortured and killed for pleasure. I have seen my land taken away to see it levelled and replaced with ugly gray buildings. The water I once knew as pure is now tainted with poison. I have travelled much of the world and have seen the worse in mankind.

"I declared war a long time ago. I don't expect you to understand, why should you? It's a war I will never win, but it's a war I will not stop. I may never get my revenge, and I will never spill as much blood as was spilled against my people, but I will try while there is air in my lungs."

"Very noble, very touching." The voice made the Vampire, Lethgate and Ryerson turn, and they saw the hunter. He had his gun aimed at the Vampire, with a slight grin on his face.

The Vampire's jaw clinched. He knew something was wrong, sensed the danger, yet was focused only on the detectives, and let this dangerous predator sneak up on him.

"Declared war a long time ago did you?" he spat out. The hunter's face looked at the Vampire revoltingly. "So goddamned righteous are you? You make me sick. I am going to enjoy killing you."

"You are a tough man with a gun, let's see how tough you are in a challenge?" The Vampire said.

Ryerson looked over to his partner. Lethgate was looking down at Ryerson's ankle, letting him know and gave a slight nod that he knew of the gun. Lethgate started to plant his feet and Ryerson wanted to shout out and tell him to stop, but he had to act fast.

"There will not be a challenge with me, or..." the hunter was distracted by seeing the black detective diving to his left reaching for his belt. With pure instinct Patrick shot landing a shot that hit the detective in the arm. He was going to pull the trigger again when something felt wrong. The black detective didn't have a gun and focused his attention on the other detective who was crouched low pulling up his pant leg reaching for the hidden weapon.

Alarms seemed to be blaring in his head as he lined up the shot, but this was not the danger. It only took a few seconds to take his attention off the Vampire, and when he turned to look he felt a hand grab his shoulders and searing pain in his throat. He squeezed off two shots that went blindly into the air.

He felt the gun slip from his hands and felt himself falling to the ground. Everything seemed to be in slow motion. He heard the metallic clink of the gun bouncing of the cement three times before is settled. His body was falling, but it felt as if strings were lowering him, as if he was a marionette, being put gently down after the performance.

But time came back to speed when his body slammed into the concrete. He felt the blood spurting out of his neck but he felt too weak to raise his hands to stop the flow. He looked up and saw the water tower, and from that angle, was still able to read the graffiti, 'Fear not the coming'. Death came quick with no feeling of what was coming afterwards.

The Vampire spit the flesh and blood in his mouth onto the hunter and continued to spit, as if the blood was battery acid. He lifted his head and the white detective had his gun pointed at the Vampire.

The Vampire let out a small laugh, "There is no honour in your people. Never have, never will be. You'll have to kill me because I will not be captured alive."

Ryerson, keeping the gun on the Vampire, looked down and at Lethgate, and could see his partner was still alive. Lethgate moaned in pain, lying on the concrete but he would live. Ryerson looked back at the Vampire who looked at him with disgust. Ryerson lowered his gun and tossed it aside. The Vampire continued to stare, his face not changing expression, but his eyes could not hide the shock.

"Let's get this over with. One condition though," Ryerson said as he slowly approached the Vampire. "You let him go," he said nodding towards his partner.

"Of course." The Vampire said walking towards the detective.

"How?" Ryerson asked feeling his knees getting weaker, the closer he got to the Vampire.

The Vampire held out his left arm to the detective. "Bite the wrist and draw blood in your mouth. Swallow the blood and keep drawing on it."

Ryerson hesitantly grabbed the wrist. He thought of turning back and getting the gun, but there would be no turning back. He looked over at Lethgate who was watching. Ryerson saw Lethgate mouth the word '*no*' but he thought of his love for his injured partner and bit the Vampire's wrist.

"Harder," the Vampire said with clenched teeth. The coppery taste filled Ryerson's mouth and he swallowed the blood. He kept his eyes shut and just pictured his injured partner, and he bit down harder on the wrist.

The Vampire grabbed Ryerson's wrist and bit down. The pain seared through Ryerson's arm. He could not believe the strength of the Vampire's bite; he could feel the blood pumping out of his wrist into the Vampire's mouth. His knees felt like they were going to collapse, until he opened his eyes.

The Vampire was starring right back at him. Their eyes locked. Ryerson could not feel any pain in his wrist. He started to see pictures in his mind. He saw beautiful land with blue rivers and crystal clear lakes. He saw an Indian woman, she wasn't attractive, but there was love and life in her eyes, pride in the way she carried her shoulders. Images went though his mind of people and places Ryerson had never seen. Beliefs whispered in his mind, repeating like a mantra.

Ryerson realized the challenge had begun. Time seemed to stand still. The Vampire's life filled his mind, he felt the Vampire's pain. Images and feelings slowly unveiled themselves. At the same time he was able to experience his own life and memories. Memories he had long forgotten.

He pictured Carl lying on the ground, lying in blood. The feeling of love for his partner filled his heart and he felt the Vampire jolt. The face of the Indian woman covered in blood, tears in her eyes, appeared in his mind again, and pain seared though the detective's mind.

He thought of his grandmother, and sitting in the living room talking with her. Both sharing a cup of tea, both laughing. His grandmother had been dead for many years but she lived in his mind, and he felt the power in his mind build again.

The Vampire thought of his god, and his deep beliefs in his faith and his spirit. The detective was strong, but he refused to let the thought enter his mind. He thought about the pain the white man had inflicted on his people, and the revenge, which was owed. He thought about the two women he loved and his unborn child. The pictures and images seemed to rifle through his mind, as if flipping through a photo album.

The two men starred into each other's eyes, the Vampire looking up into the detective's face, but locked in the mind—seeing and hearing each other's beliefs and emotions.

◊

Everything happened fast. Lethgate remembered dropping in his stance, faking for a gun hoping the diversion would give Ryerson enough time to shoot the man from the Organization. He felt the pain in his right arm just before he landed.

He wanted to roll out of the dive, but when the bullet hit, he landed hard with his head bouncing off the pavement.

Lights exploded in his head and he felt nothing. He was not sure how long he was out, he didn't feel it was long but when he regained focus he saw the hunter on the ground dead in a growing pool of blood with the Vampire standing over him. He quickly turned his head and felt a bolt of pain shoot through it, followed by a steady throbbing in his right arm. He closed his eyes and focused on staying conscious. He was shot, he remembered, but hopefully nothing to worry about. His head was still swimming and he slowly opened his eyes, not wanting to bring on a head rush or further pain.

When he finally focused on his partner he saw he was standing in front of the Vampire. Ryerson looked over and Lethgate tried to yell no, but his voice refused to cooperate, just emitting a small croaking sound.

He saw Ryerson bite into the Vampire's wrist, and the Vampire followed suit. Both men stood very still starring at each other. After a short moment both men started to twitch. Lethgate started to get up. It was his challenge not Frank's. Frank was not ready for this, he wasn't going to win.

He noticed Ryerson starting to shake a bit more violently and his shoulders started to round and his body seemed to be going limp. Frank was losing. He was close to death.

◊

It was a strange sensation being able to see and feel the Vampire's thoughts while seeing his own. The images seemed to swirl in front of him and cloud over when another belief came in.

He thought about his parents and how much he loved them. His childhood as a little boy and running down the stairs to open his presents on Christmas and a big breakfast being cooked in the kitchen. The thought made him smile, and he felt the Vampire flinch.

Again he turned his mind back to his partner. He would do anything for Carl, and he knew his partner would do the same. Suddenly a strange image flashed in his mind—the bloody and beaten face of Shannon Chambers. The Vampire's teeth seemed to tighten on his wrist. Chambers was a piece of shit and he did what he felt was right, but doubt crept in the back of his mind. He remembered how he brushed off Carl when Carl tried to talk about it, and he remembered the look of disappointment on his partner's face. He felt his knees buckling.

He knew he was losing and with that thought he felt weaker. He immediately thought of his wife to stop the negative thinking. He pictured her on their wedding day and how beautiful she was, but Ryerson found it strange it took him so long to think of her. The Vampire kept thinking between two women he knew long ago and their faces flashed before his eyes numerous times in the challenge, yet this was the first time he thought of Jill. He loved Jill, but they had their moments as well.

He loved her, but he didn't worship her like some men do to their wives. He loved living with her, but a lot of times he needed to get away. Did that mean he didn't love her? Sometimes when they had little fights he would be seething with anger, something very strong and deep inside of him, which just had to get out. He would never hurt her, he was not that type of person. Another bloody image of Shannon Chambers flashed in front of him. His mind seemed to be expanding like a balloon with too much air, a thin membrane ready to burst.

He tried to change thoughts but couldn't. All he could picture in his mind was a balloon getting bigger and bigger, getting ready to pop. Until he felt a hand on his shoulder.

◊

Lethgate got to the two men and grabbed them both. He wasn't sure what would happen, but he had no choice—his partner was dying. He started to push the two away and tore at the wrists that were being bitten. With one powerful pull, Ryerson was thrown to the ground gasping as if he just broke the water's surface, struggling for breath.

Lethgate looked at the Vampire and his eyes were wide open and a stunned look on his face. His bloody mouth was gasping like Ryerson's. The Vampire's eyes met Lethgate's but they appeared to be glassed over. Lethgate raised his wrist to the Vampire's mouth, but the Vampire didn't react. Lethgate placed his wrist right against the Vampire's mouth and the Vampire opened his mouth slowly and bit down on the wrist.

It was only a small bite at first—the Vampire's lips were still twitching around the detective's wrist, then the Vampire bit down with full force. Lethgate let out a small gasp, surprised by the Vampire's jaw strength. He grabbed the bloody wrist of the Vampire and put it in his mouth and bit down.

The challenge of the mind continued.

◊

The Vampire didn't know what happened. He felt the white detective going limp, close to death, but something happened. His mind screamed inside his head and was silent. His eyes were open and he could see but he couldn't register what it was. He seemed to have had an out of body experience, totally detached from both body and mind.

He saw the black detective in front of him. "Danger," his mind suddenly screamed. After all it was the detective and not the hunter that was the danger he kept feeling. His mind was racing with warnings but he could not pick any of them up. His mind seemed to be bleeding out his ears, and he had no control of his body. He felt the wrist of the detective in his mouth.

He wanted to end it. He couldn't continue, this was not right. The detectives broke the rules, but he couldn't speak and he felt his jaw tighten over the detective's wrist. He wanted to spit it out. DANGER. His mind screamed again.

He felt his wrist rise towards the detective's mouth. He tried to focus his eyes on the man, but they were hazed, and his body was too weak to resist.

He felt the detective bite into his arm. He could feel the teeth breaking his flesh. Then it happened.

He felt the detective's teeth sink in even deeper, like a cat exposing it's claws. The teeth seemed to be growing in his wrist and suddenly the minds mixed.

The Vampire's eyes opened wide, completely clear and stared into the eyes of the black detective whose eyes were also open wide. DANGER!! He suddenly understood. Their minds mixed but he couldn't control the thoughts, it didn't matter if he could. He now understood the warnings all along, but now it was too late.

Both men's faces clenched in a silent scream. The black man's eyes filled with blood and he suddenly dropped. The Vampire could feel his wrist tearing free of the man's jaw, blood spewing on the ground.

The detective was dead, and the Vampire had one last chance to look around. He should have known better. His knees buckled and he started to fall. He should have known, why was he so blind? He hit the ground but could feel no pain.

His eyes were open but he could not see. Life was leaving his body, he had lost his final challenge. But it was a challenge he could not win. Throughout his life he could never recognize another. Two vampires cannot compete in a challenge of the mind.

The detective didn't even know until the last seconds of his life. Somewhere down his bloodline was a vampire. It was hidden deep inside of him, finally coming out. The Vampire's eyes rolled in the back of his head. His final thought, "I should have known."

Epilogue

Sandy, the hospital volunteer, who he was starting to appreciate every day of his stay, wheeled Alex Frey off of the elevator. He was used to living alone and having people in his line of study shun him, but here was a sweet woman who volunteered her time to help people get back on their feet, or to just offer company. Alex promised himself when he got out of the hospital he would go shopping until he found the perfect gift for Sandy, to thank her for the much needed companionship.

"Why did you want to get off on his floor?" she asked as they wheeled onto the sixth floor recovery wing.

"I heard someone I know was brought in here last week I just want to drop in on them."

"A friend of yours?" Sandy asked.

"I guess he is. Someone who came to me asking for some help and advice."

He knew Sandy wanted to know more, but she was the type of person who waited for someone to open up, instead of asking questions. She was a very patient woman.

They rolled down the hall until they came outside of room 6103. Alex glanced in and saw Frank Ryerson lying on the bed with an IV in his arm, and one of his wrists bandaged. Alex knew where that wound came from.

The detective had the room to himself, and Alex turned to Sandy. "I want to talk to my friend for a couple of moments. Alone if you don't mind."

Sandy smiled and put a soft hand on his shoulder. "Aren't you sweet. Wanting to be alone with your friend and not wanting to hurt my feelings. You go on, and don't be so silly."

He smiled at her. Could he possibly start something with her when he got better? He kept thinking she was probably like this with all the patients she helped. But you never know. He smiled at her and she wheeled him into the room and left him alone with the detective.

Ryerson was lying propped up in his bed staring straight ahead of him. He didn't seem to notice Alex by his bedside.

"Detective can you hear me? Detective? Frank?"

Ryerson finally looked over, but no sign of recognition showed up on the detective's face.

"How are you?"

Ryerson just looked at him with a blank face.

"What happened Frank? What happened at the challenge?" Ryerson's eyes lit up slightly but nothing came out of his mouth.

"What happened with the vampire?" This time a tear ran down the detectives face.

"Lost." Ryerson managed to say.

"You lost Frank?" But he couldn't have. If Ryerson had lost, he should be dead.

"C-c-carl stopped him."

"What do you mean, Frank? Did you or detective Lethgate challenge the vampire?" Ryerson only starred blankly at him.

"Did you challenge him Frank?" Ryerson only nodded slightly. A thought came to Alex. "Did Lethgate break up the challenge, Frank?" He shook Ryerson. "Did Lethgate break it up?"

Yes, his head nodded.

"Where is he now Frank? Where is Carl?" Only another tear went down his face.

"Can I help you?" another voice at the door made Alex jump. He wheeled around and saw a man standing there. "I'm just visiting" said Alex. "He's... he's a friend."

Thomas only nodded his head slightly and came into the room. He looked down at Ryerson and said hi. Ryerson stared ahead with wet eyes appearing as if he didn't even hear him.

"How do you know him," Thomas asked.

"I helped on a case." Alex admitted.

"This last case?" Thomas asked.

"Who are you?"

"I worked with Frank and we grew up together. Both he and Carl were good friends of mine."

"What happened? To Carl I mean."

Thomas looked down at Alex and took a seat on the other side of Ryerson. He patted the detective's hand and looked across at the man in the wheelchair.

"No one knows. He is officially reported missing, I don't think anyone will ever find him." Thomas added sadly.

"What do you mean? How do you...?" He could not finish the sentence.

"I came in here the night they brought in Frank. I stayed by his side along with his wife Jill. The only injury was his wrist that seemed to be... well bitten was what the doctor who first examined him said. Now there is a new doctor handling him, and he says they are defensive wounds from a knife attack. I took a look at the wounds, I opened up the bandages and took a look, and the first doctor was right.

There was no way any knife could have made those wounds. The strange thing was, his wrist was bandaged when he was found. Otherwise, he surely would have bled to death.

"Anyway, that night Jill went down to get a couple of coffees for us, and I decided to stay behind with Frank. He looked physically fine, other than his wrist and a couple of small bumps and cuts. But when he would open his eyes he just looked right through me. The odd time he looks fine, and mutters one or two words, but most of the time he seems to be on another planet.

"The doctors, both of them, say he is suffering from extreme shock. When Jill left I whispered to Frank asking what happened. Everyone has been talking to him trying to make him talk, but for some reason he answered me. He was asleep when he answered me. I mean his eyes were closed, and he was thrashing in his bed, but he appeared to be talking in his sleep.

"He talked about a fight or something he was involved in, and how Carl stopped it and fought the guy instead. I remember him saying, 'Fear not the coming,' whatever that means. He kept saying 'dead.' I asked him if he meant Carl. He said both of them. When I tried to ask who else was there he only said 'both of them.'

"He was only whispering and sweat was running down his face, but he said men took them away. He stopped talking and went back to sleep. The good news is that he seems to be coming around a bit. He smiled at Jill yesterday before his eyes seemed to glaze over. Today he even squeezed her hand when she held it."

Alex looked down at the detective who was now looking in the direction of the other man, but when he looked closely he could tell Ryerson was not looking at the man—just the wall behind him.

"I should really go," said Alex. "I truly hope the detective gets better soon." He could tell the man wanted to ask some questions, but he appeared aware that asking questions would not help the situation and it would be best to let it go.

With the help of Thomas, Alex wheeled out of the room slowly where Sandy was still patiently waiting. Her face lit up with a smile, "home James?" She asked in a hokey English accent. Alex smiled at her and just nodded his head yes. He would definitely buy her something nice, maybe even ask her if she wanted to go out for dinner.

As they rose in the elevator Alex Frey knew the detective would never recover fully. He was in the middle of the challenge of the mind when for some reason Lethgate stopped it. He probably saw Ryerson losing and interrupted it. But why did Ryerson take part in the challenge? It should have been Detective Lethgate, unless they changed their minds just beforehand. Ryerson's mind would not be able to recover from the broken challenge. It was lost when the challenge was severed.

As for the Vampire, he knew he was dead or in the same state as Ryerson. When Ryerson mumbled to his friend about men taking them away, he knew the men were from the Organization. They had known about the challenge and took the Vampire and Lethgate away. They taped up Ryerson's wrist, cleaned up the scene and probably called 911 for an ambulance to pick him up.

But why didn't they take Ryerson? They probably figured Ryerson's mind was now mush, and they could hire their own doctors to take care of him and report any change in his condition to them.

"Here we are," she said rolling him back into his room, "Back where we started."

It was impossible to go back to where he started. He didn't even know if this was the end, but maybe he could try to make this a new beginning.

"Thank you Sandy." A good gift, and definitely dinner he thought and smiled.

The end.

Acknowledgements

Thank you to Tracey Haggert who edited this book when it was a warm mess, and just in its beginning stages. Thank you to my wife, Christine, whom I can never say enough about. This book would probably never have happened without your help and support. Thank you to Jenny Groat for your talent on the cover design and your willingness to do whatever it took to make it right. Thank you to many dear friends who shared words of encouragement throughout this process, and finally to you the reader, thank you for taking a chance on a new, self-published writer.